Nowhere

Shane Christopher

BERKLEY BOOKS, NEW YORK

THE BERKLEY PUBLISHING GROUP
Published by the Penguin Group
Penguin Group (USA) Inc.
375 Hudson Street, New York, New York 10014, USA
Penguin Group (Canada), 90 Eglinton Avenue East, Suite 700, Toronto, Ontario M4P 2Y3, Canada
(a division of Pearson Penguin Canada Inc.)
Penguin Books Ltd., 80 Strand, London WC2R 0RL, England
Penguin Group Ireland, 25 St. Stephen's Green, Dublin 2, Ireland (a division of Penguin Books Ltd.)
Penguin Group (Australia), 250 Camberwell Road, Camberwell, Victoria 3124, Australia
(a division of Pearson Australia Group Pty. Ltd.)
Penguin Books India Pvt. Ltd., 11 Community Centre, Panchsheel Park, New Delhi—110 017, India
Penguin Group (NZ), 67 Apollo Drive, Rosedale, North Shore 0745, Auckland, New Zealand
(a division of Pearson New Zealand Ltd.)
Penguin Books (South Africa) (Pty.) Ltd., 24 Sturdee Avenue, Rosebank, Johannesburg 2196,
South Africa

Penguin Books Ltd., Registered Offices: 80 Strand, London WC2R 0RL, England

This is a work of fiction. Names, characters, places, and incidents either are the product of the author's imagination or are used fictitiously, and any resemblance to actual persons, living or dead, business establishments, events, or locales is entirely coincidental.

NOWHERE

A Berkley Book / published by arrangement with the author

PRINTING HISTORY
Berkley edition / May 2007

Copyright © 2007 by Matthew J. Costello.
Cover design and illustration by Tony Greco.
Interior text design by Kristin del Rosario.

ISBN: 978-0-425-21588-3

BERKLEY®
Berkley Books are published by The Berkley Publishing Group,
a division of Penguin Group (USA) Inc.,
375 Hudson Street, New York, New York 10014.
BERKLEY is a registered trademark of Penguin Group (USA) Inc.
The "B" design is a trademark belonging to Penguin Group (USA) Inc.

PRINTED IN THE UNITED STATES OF AMERICA

10 9 8 7 6 5 4 3 2 1

To Graeme Devine and Rob Landeros—
the original two guests, when *way* more than seven
were soon to arrive . . .

PROLOGUE

The
Future

THE man sits on a simple wooden chair. The curved wood curls behind him, like jumbled musical notes, making the chair's back a neatly tied wooden bow.

His appearance . . . nothing initially remarkable at all.

Though, like any of us, it could change over time, the hair longer, the hair shorter, now with a beard, then replaced with a mustache, till finally replaced with nothing. But now his hair is short, sandy-brown, with a few stray strands curving over his forehead.

Looking closely, you can see that the hair has been receding for some time.

The eyes, though.

A different story, the eyes. An eerily brilliant blue. Piercing, powerful. Hard not to stare at those eyes if you were chatting with the man.

He wears black jeans. A cream-colored short-sleeved shirt. A few dark hairs on his arms catching the candlelight.

He sits, legs squarely planted, facing a woman.

You may know the woman; you may not.

But whether you know her or not, her position, her situation would immediately make your heart go out to her. Only certain people could look, observe, and not be horrified.

In the true sense of the word, in all its mammoth meaning.
Horrified.

Before taking that heartbreaking look, though—one more
detail that you would not know. And it's this:

This is *new* for the man; this particular arrangement is different. Circumstances have made him alter his particular way
of doing things. That may be important to know, to understand what happens.

And the woman?

We first see the hair. Dark, flowing, lustrous waves of black
hair. And then the eyes too, almond-brown and so intensely
focused, staring straight ahead as her wrists and legs struggle
against the circles of tape that wrap around so tightly holding
her prisoner.

Because that's what she is—a prisoner.

And did she ever imagine that this is what would happen to
her, that she would find herself in such a situation, so hopeless, trapped, with only worse to come?

Worse to come.

A key question.

Did she ever imagine this?

The rest of the image: her legs bare, a denim skirt, a pale
blue blouse, all of it marked by the circles of heavy gray tape,
such an incredibly strong tape around her wrists.

Her lips, mouth—also covered by the tape, looking like
some medieval mask, a punishment for an ancient transgres-
sion now lost in the mists of history.

The man reaches out and pats her knee.

His hand *rests* on her knee, but not in any lascivious way.
No, it's nearly reassuring the way the hand touches her. Reassuring her that everything will be fine.

When anyone could see that it would never be fine again.

His monologue with her stopped for the moment.

A faint rumble in the distance, the slow deep bellow of a
thunderstorm still in the distance, still miles away. But coming
closer, bearing down.

The man's accent—

Hard to place. A hint of something European perhaps, but quickly melting into other untraceable sounds, laced with a fierce attempt for the generic sound of mid-America,

"I've never done this before," he says. "I mean, never took the time to talk to someone. But you deserve that. I think—" His hand squeezes her knee. "After all, you did some remarkable work, you found out so much." He laughs. "Too much. I'll want to understand how you did that. The clues you found, the mistakes I may have made. In return—I will explain, as much as I can, as much as any person can, how this happens. How it's been happening."

He takes a deep breath.

"Do you understand what I am saying?"

Looking at the woman, mummified in gray tape. Nodding, shaking her head . . . *yes*.

"Good. I knew you would. Part of you will appreciate this. Appreciate what I am telling you. Think of it as a journey and—"

Another rumble of thunder, less distant this time. The booming sound closer, rolling toward this room.

"A big storm coming. Maybe a nor'easter, hmm? I imagine . . . it will be best to finish before it gets here. All that thunder, lightning, rain—the noise."

Now the man nods.

"Yes, definitely will want to be done before then. So—let's begin." He smiles, his blue eyes warm, filled with an appearance of compassion. "Let me start by correcting a few misconceptions. You have only very small pieces of the puzzle you grappled with. Very small. But don't feel bad, you have so much more than anyone else who tried. Their efforts . . . pathetic. You did quite well—"

The man stands up and walks to the window. He pulls open a wooden shutter.

No light; just blackness beyond.

"Of course you had help. Still, rather amazing. Too close, as I said before."

The man closes the wooden shutter.

He turns and walks back to the woman. He reaches out a hand and caresses her cheek. He strokes her hair. The woman makes muffled mewling sounds, squelched screeches, a scream that can't escape the lockjaw of the tape.

"One error . . . where I might have come from. I am afraid you had that all wrong. Very romantic. All those ideas about my history."

He sits.

"But history is in the past. History is stuff that has happened." He shakes his head as if explaining a very difficult concept to a little child. "This—right now—is not history. Did you know that?"

He reaches out and grabs her chin, roughly now, holding it tight. "Maybe you had that all . . . wrong too." He squeezes, and tiny tears form in the woman's eyes.

We know those eyes . . . .

We have seen those eyes before!

He releases her.

"But not to worry. We still have some time and I will, as they say, set you straight."

The man stands up again just as another low boom rolls in from outside. He walks to a table and picks up a shiny piece of metal; a blade, simple, broad enough to be something used by a butcher or perhaps a knight when his sword gets slapped away in a duel.

The knife catches the scant light, glows.

More sounds from the woman, struggling against the tape, eyes wide.

The man sits down calmly.

Rests the blade right on his knees.

"I may want to confirm some things with you. How you learned certain things, how you figured them out." A smile. "But I'll start first, okay? And tell you about a time . . . a place . . . a world you can only imagine . . ."

BOOK ONE

The Present

1

"SO, what is this?"

David Rodriguez held up a thin wooden skewer.

Mari grinned. She imagined he knew quite well what all the items on the small stick were.

"You weren't listening, were you?" she said.

"Um, not really."

She leaned forward. "This here is—of course—an anchovy. And here, pimento, and this—"

She tilted her head.

"Not sure what that is. Looks like an olive."

"Guess you weren't listening either."

She laughed and took a sip of the dry red wine. She watched David turn and look around, scanning the restaurant.

"Getting crowded," he said. "How ever did you find this place?"

"My friend Will. He dated a gallery owner from Little West Twelfth Street. I met them here once for too much sangria and tapas."

He turned back to her. "Cool place."

And Mari could sense that he had something to say, that hanging over their dinner conversation was something unsaid. Waiting. She didn't like it. After all, she had assumed that after what they had been through together, after what her newspaper ended up calling—rather mundanely—the "Warehouse Murders" . . . that they would move in together.

That didn't happen.

Instead, some nights she stayed at his place. Some nights he came to her place. Either way it always felt good. But there were also nights when they stayed in their respective apartments, and that—as they say—gave her pause.

Imagine . . . a New York man with commitment issues.

Though she knew that what they had been through had left them changed. *We'll forget what happened,* David had said. *It will all fade.*

But that was wrong. You didn't see what they had seen. And have it just vanish like a bad . . .

(Dream)

"David?"

"Yes."

"You have something to say?"

"I always have something to say."

She didn't respond. David turned and looked around at the room. "What's this place called? I didn't see a sign out front."

Always the detective, she thought.

"Tia Pol. So . . ."

"Okay. I saw Johanna the other night."

Mari looked away. She thought David's ex was out of the picture. Completely.

Did she have that wrong?

"And?"

"She didn't file the papers. So, well—we're still in legal limbo."

"But you signed them, and then she—"

He held up a hand. "I know. I *know.* But after that night—"

That's how they referred to it . . . *that night.*

As if those two words were sufficient to somehow encapsulate what had happened to them. That night, that bad night, that nightmarish night, that . . . unbelievable night.

For that's in fact what it was—unbelievable.

"So what are you saying?" Mari suddenly felt as if it was hard to breathe in the room.

"All I'm saying is, she hasn't done anything *legal* yet."

There was more.

"And?"

"But she wants to do something about our Block Island place."

"You said it's just a cottage."

"Yeah, but either one of us has to take it over, or we have to sell it. And there's stuff there—"

Mari felt like standing up and walking out. She had heard similar tales before, but never did she expect to hear crap like this from David.

You tend to trust the man who saved your life.

But nothing like the whiff of another woman to make all that trust slip away.

"And there's more?"

He nodded.

The waitress, a broomstick-thin waif with jet-black hair and silver rings clipped through every visible part of her, came over.

"Some more small plates?" she asked. "More wine?"

Mari shook her head. The evening had turned sour. She felt threatened and exposed.

A good old New York romance, she thought.

There's a sucker born every minute.

"So—we're going there this weekend. Make kind of an inventory, see what the real estate people say, figure things out."

Enough, Mari thought. *Enough for now.*

"Sure. Makes perfect sense. Nice little trip to . . ." She hesitated, then: ". . . fucking Block Island."

She stood up.

"Mari. Come on. I'm just trying to—"

She grabbed her bag, but rushing now, and she nearly pulled a chair down with the strap, sending it tumbling to the floor. Other patrons circled the soon-to-be-free tiny table, a premium item in the crowded place.

David grabbed her wrist, and then stood up.

She saw him wince.

The cane was gone, had been gone for a week. But still—if he rushed and put weight on his leg, it could send a jolt of pain up his side.

Good, she thought. A little pain for him now felt like just the right thing.

"Mari, it's only to figure out—"

"Good. You go." She leaned close, aware that people were so close they could easily hear every word. "You go and *figure out* things. On goddamn Block Island. I'll keep busy. I never had a problem doing that before."

She turned and started squeezing her way out through the jumble of people.

David moved to keep up.

But Mari was smaller, better suited to navigate the sea of people, racing ahead of David, out to the night, still warm though summer was nearly over. Catching a break, she spotted a cab pulling alongside the restaurant.

She held out her hand, waved.

In moments she was cloistered in the darkness of the cab.

"Eighty-fifth and Second," she said. It was a good two blocks from her apartment.

There was no way she could head right home now, to the empty apartment.

Mocking in how silent and empty it could be without David.

Fuck, she thought.

Then, *Fuck him.*

The cab roared uptown.

2

DAVID pushed open the door, bulldozing a stack of menus that had been slipped under it. He now had a collection of a half-dozen menus from the same Chinese takeout around the corner.

Might make good wallpaper, he thought.

He turned on the light. He had picked up around the apartment, thinking that Mari might come back.

Think again . . .

That went well, he thought. Just blundered right into it hitting all of the wrong buttons. He took off his sport coat, digging out his new cell phone. The phone did everything but bake bread. Video clips, music, Internet.

Half the things it did still had David stymied.

Welcome to the future.

Should he call Mari?

No. He'd only get a few more curt words about his ex-wife, commitment, and New York City men. Better to let her wait a bit.

His landline rang. He walked over to the small couch and grabbed the cordless phone from a crack in the chair where it nestled.

Maybe Mari had second thoughts?

"Hello?"

"Home early? Quiet night?"

"Hi, Johanna—"

Not Mari, but who he thought would soon be his ex-wife.

That is, if she filed the papers David signed months ago. What was the problem?

"Just checking you're all set for tomorrow. Pick you up at ten. I have a reservation on the two-fifteen ferry out of Westerly."

"Right. I know that. You told me."

He sat down, and though he no longer needed a cane to get around, any time he tried to bend his knee, the metal still scattered around his kneecap quickly shot nice little spikes of pain racing to his brain.

"Yes, David, I *know* I told you. But I'm going over it again. You have a history of forgetting things."

"Yeah. You told me that. A lot."

Christ, he couldn't handle this trip—even a simple overnight—if they started in on each other. It would be twenty-four hours plus of torture.

And maybe he had already jeopardized his relationship with Mari.

But they had to do this. Decide what to do about the stuff in the cottage, talk to the real estate people . . . decide whether to rent, sell—and somehow get back to the mainland not having ripped each other's throats out.

He took a breath. "I'm all set."

A pause at her end. "Good. And David—thanks for, well, doing this. That place meant a lot to us."

He pictured the cottage, sitting so close to a cliff, facing east, isolated from the touristy center of Block Island. Great sweeping views of the Atlantic. Gorgeous when the sun made the sea seem alive with blues and grays and greens. Terrifying when storms rolled in as if they would gobble the island whole.

"It did."

Suddenly he felt so tired, as if all he had to do was lean back in the chair and drift away to an incredibly deep sleep. "See you in the A.M., Jo."

"Good night, David."

He put down the phone and then forced himself to get up, and actually make it to his bed.

And with each step thinking, *Will I ever be a hundred percent?*

MARI should have gone straight home. But she knew if she did that she'd only get angrier.

Better to do her venting out in public, slowly and quietly simmering.

She ducked into Vespa on Second, the Italian restaurant bustling and the small bar packed. But one stool looked free at the far end.

She hurried to it.

Carlo, one of the regular bartenders, with lady-killing jet-black hair and eyes like black pearls, appeared instantly, a magic drink genie.

"Alone tonight, signorina?"

"Yes, Carlo. Very observant."

He smiled. His flirting never teetered to the lecherous; he just was warm, engaging, and as comfortable as the guy who manned the coffee cart outside the *Daily News* building.

Though if she had to sleep with one or the other . . .

"The usual?"

She shook her head. Any serious spirits, such as that to be found in a cosmo or appletini, would kick her head into someplace she *definitely* didn't need to go.

"No, Carlo. Maybe some dry white wine? A little seltzer on the side."

He smiled as if her choice gladdened his night. Is there anything better than a great bartender? Maybe an extraordinary masseur. Or a really good nail person.

Or perhaps—a lover.

The cloud came back as if it had been waiting . . . just over her shoulder.

"Sounds perfect," Carlo said. "And . . . hungry?"

She shook her head.

Carlo nodded and walked away to get the chilled wine.

"Guess you come here a lot."

Mari turned to look at the man who had just said those words.

"Um, yes."

The man, older with the sides of his head flecked with gray, nodded. "Seems like a nice place. Never been here before. Maybe I should eat here sometime."

She nodded. A half smile. Mari didn't want any random chitchat. She wanted some quiet bar time to think . . . about David, their relationship, her fears.

Every single woman's fear in Manhattan.

The fear of the good one, maybe the great one, getting away.

"Name's Jack. New to the neighborhood. You . . . live around here?"

Another nod, a close-lipped smile. At some point a nonresponse would get impossible and her imagined time with a cold glass of wine would vaporize.

"Yup, I just moved here." Jack killed his drink, which Mari could see, out of the corner of her eye, was something golden brown, coating a tumbler full of cubes. Bourbon, scotch?

Serious drinking stuff.

"After the divorce—" he added.

Thank you for that info, she thought . . .

"—decided I did not want to stay in the 'burbs. So dull, no nightlife. Kids were older. So got a small place down on York. Right near that little park—what the hell is it called?"

"Carl Schurz Park."

"Right. Jeez, a lot of dog owners there." He laughed. "Hope they bring their baggies. You know, for the droppings!"

Scintillating, she thought.

Can I kill this "Jack" now?

Carlo returned with her wine and seltzer.

Her eyes did a small roll, and she hoped Carlo saw that she was looking for a rescue from this land shark hitting on her as though she was a big chunk of fresh female chum thrown into the sea.

Carlo leaned close—elbows on the bar. Almost close enough so that the man—old divorced Jacko—might think that they were an item.

"So Mari . . . how's things?"

She could feel her stool companion looking at this, deciding whether to end his foray.

Mari took a sip of wine first. Then:

"Hm, nice. The wine, I mean. Other stuff, currently sucky."

Carlo grinned. "Currently . . . sucky. And why's that?"

As if feeling invisible tentacles peeling off, peeling away from her, she felt Jack's attention start to fade.

That's it, she thought, *return to your morose self-pitying state.*

And as soon as she thought that, she felt guilty. The guy just wanted to talk. And as for self-pitying, isn't that exactly what she had in mind?

"Men problems." Another sip.

"Men?" Carlo said, grinning.

"Okay. A man. You know, the guy I come in here with."

"Seems nice. What happened?"

"Guess—I got a bit jealous. There's an ex-wife floating around, some unfinished business, and—"

Carlo was nodding. "I get the picture. Has you worried, eh?"

"No. Not at—"

But his eyes were trained on her like dark lasers.

She smiled. "Maybe a little."

"It's the way things go, eh, signorina? Sometimes the man is worried, sometimes the woman, sometimes both. Part of the game. I say . . . just be glad you feel that, that you care, and you know—"

He uncorked the bottle of wine and topped Mari off.

"—he'd be crazy to lose you, crazy. Beautiful, smart—"

She laughed. "Okay, enough. You earned your tip for tonight, *capiche?*"

A big grin from the handsome bartender in this small restaurant, candles flickering . . . where everything suddenly seemed a lot better.

"Good. You enjoy your wine. And if you want some antipasto, you let me know."

She nodded, thinking, *Sometimes the right decision is . . . to not go home.*

3

MONICA Klein teetered out of the Spice Market in her Jimmy Choo heels. She flipped open her Razr and checked her messages.

She scrolled through the list of new messages, a few from her other girlfriends also out on the prowl, one from the dweeb she met from Match.com for the fastest mojito ever consumed, and one from Mom and Dad.

All eminently ignorable.

She thought: *Is* ignorable *even a* word? Something to be ignored? She looked over at Soho House. A private club, but she had batted her lashes and shown enough cleavage one evening that they had let her in. Nice pool, great bar, and lots of sexy Brits.

But she saw a line gathered outside, and the doorman obviously delivering the news that sorry, the club is closed to non-members.

She could call up her single girlfriends for a rendezvous.

But—and she hated to accept this—she'd like to hook up tonight. Hell, even some heavy make-out time would be good. And clustering together with a gaggle of her girlfriends was *not* the way to go for that.

Too late for the lions' cage that was 5757. That scene

chilled by nine. Pegu Club? She had been there for a drink, but how was it for men, *straight* men? She didn't have a clue.

She allowed her wobbly steps to carry her down a block, past the Gansevoort Hotel, then down a street where the Meat-packing District suddenly turned all businesses and ware-houses again.

The block looked quiet, empty.

She thought of hesitating, but for some reason she seemed to have narrowed it down . . . to the Lower East Side. Her eyes flashed.

She suddenly *knew* where to go.

THOR.

The Hotel on Rivington. She ate there last week, and the bar was four feet deep in what looked like unattached males.

She smiled. Yes, definitely the place to go.

She heard a cough, and suddenly turned.

Some . . . creature huddled in the shadows under a loading platform. Another cough.

Maybe this wasn't the safest block to be walking down. Monica picked up her step and then, in true good-and-wise– New Yorker fashion, fired a glance over her shoulder.

The figure, probably some homeless guy, settled in for the night.

She took a deep breath.

A balmy night. Warm, but not humid. The last sweet eve-nings of summer. In a flash, the cold would roll in, and then the snow, the ice, and the city would become a fortress of gray stone and frozen water.

Ninth Avenue lay ahead. She even spotted the occasional cab heading downtown. It hadn't turned tricky to get a cab yet—but after midnight, this part of Manhattan could turn into a cab-less ghost town.

She reached the corner, and within moments a cab flew across three lanes of traffic to pick her up.

"Rivington, off Ludlow."

The driver said nothing, but she imagined he was none too pleased. Like salmon spawning this time of night, they preferred to stream upriver, to Grand Central, to the midtown bridges and tunnel, heading out of the nighttime city . . . back to some home in the far-flung boroughs.

MONICA finally forced her way to the bar.

"A Merlot," she gasped. Though something far stronger would hit the spot, with the bar this off the hook, this crazy and buzzy, she knew she needed to pace herself.

Another martini would have her looking for a friendly wall to lean against.

The bartender, an automaton operating at high speed, sloppily poured the red wine and gently slid the glass to her.

"Eleven dollars," he said over the din.

Eleven dollars. Christ, the whole bottle probably cost less than that. Nightlife took its toll on a working girl's budget. Not for the first time she had to wonder if this—the great Big Apple—was where she really belonged.

She handed him a ten and a single, and scooped up the wine.

The room was alive with a sea of people, all chattering at the same time, the words jumbled together until everyone might as well have been speaking some yet-undiscovered language.

She looked around for a target.

Late twenties, tall, fit, well dressed.

Bingo!

And she found one.

MONICA laughed and, trying to be casual, leaned over and patted Mark's forearm.

Mark was good company, and since they had scored a booth off to the side, she could actually hear what he had to say. He looked at her when she spoke, and even asked a question or two to keep their conversation going.

She decided to be bold.

She put down her wineglass—how many was that now?

three? four?—and dug a pen out of her clutch purse. She wrote down her cell number.

She pushed the napkin to Mark.

"There you go. My number."

He picked up the napkin.

"Thanks."

She waited for him to offer his number, standard operating procedure these days.

But he pocketed the napkin and drained his vodka on the rocks.

When a voice boomed from the throng still gathered at the bar.

"Marco? Kemosabe!"

Monica turned to see the guy addressing Mark. A beefy guy, tie open, suit coat off, waved.

"We gotta catcha train, buddy!"

Monica turned to look at Mark. Train? He doesn't live in the city? Shit. Where does he live, Merrick, Patchogue, or—God—Westchester?

He turned to her.

The smile evaporated from his face, fun over, game over, and Monica *knew*. Not only did this attractive and intelligent guy live somewhere you had to take a train that had a schedule . . .

The prick was probably married.

Good one, she thought to herself.

And it also explained why he didn't slide his number to her.

She was tempted to ask for the goddamn napkin back.

But what for? He would probably crumple the napkin into a tight little wad to destroy the incriminating evidence, and then toss it into a corner trash bin as he sailed home, his male ego once again propped up by a "could-have-had-her" conquest.

She stood up.

"Yeah, I got to go too. It's late."

Mark stood up. "Hey, I really—"

But Monica had been there too many times before. "Save it.

Have fun mowing the lawn tomorrow. Or whatever it is you suburban husbands do to keep sane."

She grabbed her shiny silver clutch, and—looking at the still-heaving crowd one more time, debating whether staying might also be an option—Monica Klein walked out the door of the bar/restaurant, to the lobby, and out to the now chilly night air.

MONICA realized that she should have stayed by the hotel to get a cab. That would have been the intelligent thing to do.

But then she'd bump into . . . *Marco* again, with his chunky wingman. She couldn't stomach that, so she headed down Rivington, then made a right on Norfolk.

And the noise, the glances, the alcohol cloud . . . faded as gooseflesh sprouted on her bare shoulders.

4

NOW Monica could only hear the steady click-clack of her Jimmy Choo shoes.

She thought . . . *Jimmy Choo shoes, Jimmy Choo shoes* . . .

And on the lonely street it made her laugh. But then another thought—where the hell was she heading? Maybe Kush, where you could still smoke due to some bizarre hookah loophole? Or Arlene's Grocery for a cheap beer, some loud thrashing band—?

She stopped and looked at the tiny face of her watch.

11:10. Too early for a real night out. But then, if she did call it a night, there was always tomorrow. Though the city could become deserted on a late summer's Friday night, the last siren call of the Hamptons all but irresistible to the hordes of New York singles.

Thursday night was the night to hook up.

She stayed there a second, waiting, thinking—

"Hey—"

She spun around, her heart rate jumping by factors of ten. She hadn't heard anyone; she hadn't sensed anyone—which on the streets of New York was far more important. A real New Yorker had that incredible ability to sense that something wasn't quite right, that you weren't quite alone, that—why, yes—you might even being followed.

Monica had heard nothing at all.

And she thought, *I haven't had that much to drink, have I?*

The "have-I" question, when the gaggle of drinks blurs into some unknown and unknowable number.

She was sure that she wasn't drunk. Steady on her heels, relatively clear in her plans—or lack of plans.

But when she spun around, she didn't see anyone. Though she had heard a voice.

Then: a laugh.

And from the shadows of a building—with a brooding stone entrance that sheltered the door from light—someone slipped into the milky white streetlight. Into the glare of an anticrime light, tungsten-white like those annoying headlights on all the German luxury cars, those headlights that said, *I got a fucking car that cost 50K and you don't.*

The lights here catching . . . a man . . . a pin-striped suit, a shirt . . . blue. Maybe not blue. This light played tricks with the color. Wavy hair, light brown, maybe even blond. He smiled.

A British accent, she thought. Or some kind of accent. Slight. So slight it might be affected.

"Sorry. Did not mean to startle you. Just stepped into this little alcove here—"

He gestured at the brooding entrance that had hid him.

"—to use my last match for a smoke. We Brits haven't gotten the word yet. About—the dangers of smoking!"

He waved an unlit cigarette in the air.

Instinctively, Monica did two things: First, she took a few steps back, farther to the curb, even more into the pool of light. Then, subtly, a glance up, then down the street to see if anyone else was near.

And though she saw a car heading uptown one way, and another downtown, there were no people on this block.

She turned back to the man.

This *surprise* man, who'd popped out at her. Her heart still racing but now his words—educated, smart, crisp—giving her some reason to relax a bit.

"Last match and, well, it didn't take."

She was facing him squarely now and she could see his face better. Rugged good looks . . . could be midthirties, maybe older. His eyes, though—so blue, even in the whitewashing effect of the streetlight.

"You wouldn't happen to have a light for a visitor from another land, would you?"

He smiled.

And—important to Monica—he didn't move a step closer.

"I don't—"

"Ah, another sensible American. Getting harder to find beautiful women to beg lights from." Another smile.

And Monica smiled back.

"No, I mean I never smoked. Just never—"

"Wise decision. Maybe I'll just have to go back to my hotel and get some matches from the bartender. Still legal to do that here, eh? Carry matches?"

And that made Monica laugh. "Yeah. That's still legal. And a lot of other things."

God, what made her say that? Flirting with someone on the street just because they're a Brit and, from all appearances, really good-looking.

"That's good to hear. Grew up dreaming about New York. Fun City and all that."

"There's a lot of fun to be had here. You just can't—oh, wait."

She opened her clutch purse. Whenever she went someplace new, she grabbed matches if they had any. And even with a shoot-on-sight order for all smokers, a lot of upscale hotel and restaurant bars still provided delicate little boxes of matches.

"I think—"

And that's all it took.

That brief *look* down.

Her guard being lowered for just a second.

That's all it took, for everything to change, and the nightmare to begin.

Monica didn't notice the man look left and right, checking the street much the same as she had done.

Only he checked it for a different purpose. Her guard had gone down by then, reassured by so many comfortable things—his look, his voice, his clothes.

She didn't know, of course, how fast things could happen.

Because, well, this had never happened to her before.

And if she had been able to slow down time, she could have seen how cleverly it was mapped out, how this was enacted by someone with experience.

She looked through her small clutch, pushing away a small box of mints, a tiny wallet with credit cards, some folded bills at the ready, looking for the matchbox that she thought might be there.

A match, a light for the elegant man with the unlit cigarette.

That cigarette now tossed to the sidewalk.

Then an arm around her throat.

The air immediately cut off. Yanked backward, off her . . .

Jimmy Choo shoes, Jimmy Choo shoes, Jimmy—

Back to the horribly dark hole that was the building, thinking that she would be dragged into the building, already thinking how stupid, how impossibly *stupid* to have let down her guard, for even a second.

She would have yelled, screamed, begged. All three, careening over each other, tumbling, pleading.

But his arm around her throat closed her windpipe, crushed her larynx tight.

She could feel her eyes bug out, whether from that intense pressure or fear—there was no way for her to tell.

Monica now felt the stone pavement under her now bare feet. Bits of grit that her feet rolled over as he dragged her back. In mere moments, Monica was in that darkness, the milky white light and the sidewalk an eternity away.

She felt the man's face close to her ears.

"Now that wasn't so bad, was it? Lickety-split, and here we are."

She wanted to tell him: Do anything, take anything. Just don't hurt me. She didn't want to be hurt; she didn't want any pain. But there was no way for her to tell him any of that, not with his arm locked tight around her throat.

Then a crazy thought.

Something she learned in a one-night class at the Learning Annex. *Self-Defense for the Single Woman.*

Her legs were free. She could move them. And there was something she remembered from the class—if you couldn't use your hands, if you couldn't claw at an attacker's face, at his eyes, *use your legs.*

"Bet you are thinking it wasn't a good idea to walk down here, um? Probably not the first bad idea you ever had. But don't worry—"

She gulped, the only noise she could make. He said . . . *don't worry.* And she grabbed at those words as if at a life preserver. Maybe this would be okay.

Maybe—she shouldn't do anything.

But no. The thing they hammered home that night. Don't think—don't *assume*—that things are going to get better. Act to protect yourself before it's too late.

She tried to imagine where his body was in relation to her legs, and where her target was. His crooked elbow kept the pressure constant. Not enough to cut off the supply of air, but enough that all she could do was open her mouth and gulp a pathetic bubble of air while he whispered, his voice in her ear, almost in her head.

Deep, soothing, gentle—

"Shhhh," he whispered. "Don't worry. Right . . . okay?"

Again she considered not acting. Maybe he'd take her small shiny clutch purse and move on.

She felt something hard pressing against her side. A sickening thought; she knew what it was.

It was time.

She tightened the muscles in her left leg, readying it. Straight back, fast. To strike below the hardness. Fast, hard, then run.

The instructor had said . . . that there didn't exist a man on the planet who couldn't be brought to his knees by a good kick there.

That night it made everyone laugh.

They laughed as if any possible use of the maneuver was an absurd possibility. And yet—here she was about to use it.

Perhaps—

(A small voice in her head whispered . . .)

—To save her life.

She brought the leg up and back, fast, bending at the knee, sending the calf, the foot up, heading hard toward the man's crotch.

Except—

Such a foolish plan . . .

The man's other hand caught her leg at the calf, just above the ankle, and she could feel how strong it was. Such a big man's hand, catching her gym-toned calf in his hand, then squeezing it as if he wanted to press all the juice out of it.

Worse than any pulled hamstring. An electric pain shot right to her skull. Silent tears poured out of her eyes.

Not crying because of what happened, but crying from the sheer agonizing pain.

The voice again, as the man released the leg and it fell back into place, the foot hitting the pavement like a marionette doll.

"Now didn't I tell you not to worry? You should believe me, trust me."

She heard something then, a sound, unrecognizable at this point. A noise, while a dozen horrific images danced through her head.

Then: a car!

Speeding down the street, but going so fast, ignoring any speed limit, streaming past their secret dark alcove.

"Easy now," the man whispered.

And then she felt it. The man teased her with it. She felt it just outside her skirt, the sharp metal point pushing in oh so gently, just enough so she would know.

Know what it was.

She began to struggle crazily, every part of her body moving. But her life-or-death struggle, that ancient dance of survival when one creature intends another's death . . . came too late.

Because as it began—

As soon as she knew what was happening . . .

The blade slid in.

More electric bolts to her brain. The agony an intense explosion, but then masked with something else.

She didn't know what her body was doing. She didn't know what goes on when an assault, a deadly attack, occurs like this. The sensations overwhelming, then finally all but blocked.

Save the streetlight.

And the sound of liquid dripping, dropping from the hole in her midsection.

The sick squishing noise as the blade *turned*.

The man said words but none of them registered.

Until she felt him release her throat, and she could scream. *She could scream.*

But as she fell forward onto her knees, then her head smacking to pavement, her last thought was that—no, there would be no screaming. There was nothing more than this.

And then—there wasn't even that.

5

DAVID walked up to the closed gate that led to the ferry's covered area for cars.

Two of the crew stood to the side, smoking cigarettes, laughing, oblivious to the line of cars waiting to get on the boat from Westerly to Block Island.

"Excuse me," he said.

The two men turned, but just barely.

"Aren't you supposed to load now. Ten minutes ago, even?"

David's question provoked big grins from the men. One of them scratched his head as if pondering a massive math problem. "Supposed to? Guess the ferry is *supposed* to do a lot of things." A big grin. "But the boat pretty much does what Cap wants."

Cap. The ferry captain. For all the years that he and Johanna had been coming to their Block Island cottage, they'd had to put up with the whims of the ferryboat captain. Actually *captains*—two of them that David knew—but each using the same playbook, leaving whenever the hell they wanted to.

And God forbid if someone should show up and want to get onto the ferry at the last minute.

David had seen that priceless act too many times.

"Cap"—no matter which one—would raise his hat off his

brow, his little sea captain's cap, as if that would let him get a better look at whatever had just strolled up to his mighty ship.

Then with a nod and a disgusted grimace, he'd say: "You want to take the ferry and you didn't advance-book?"

The words *advance-book* made it sound as though the most ignorant ten-year-old would have known to do that.

All that juicy scorn, pouring out of Cap, the crew reacting with undisguised glee. The people on the boat so glad that they weren't the targets for the captain.

David knew better than to argue with the crew. He turned and walked back to his Accord.

"Let me guess," Johanna said. "It will sail when it sails."

David smiled. "Exactly. And it will load when it loads."

He looked over at small ticket booth that also advertised coffee and food.

"What some coffee?"

She shook her head.

The ride up had been mostly quiet. The start, with David driving, had his ex-wife sleeping, leaning against the door.

Every now and then he'd sneak a look at her, the long brown hair flecked with blond catching morning sun. Curled up almost like a kid. Beautiful, to be sure. And for a few minutes he'd forget what had pulled them apart.

But he didn't have to think too long to recall that.

To summon the arguments.

The fights.

About his job, about the danger, until both of them realized that horrible moment. Both of them hit that same terrible wall.

That dull, gray thud of a moment when you realize . . . *this is not working.*

Followed by that other awareness, a simple and clean thought like a surgical knife slicing into skin.

It's over.

"Yeah, guess I had enough caffeine too."

He walked over to the driver's door. Everyone in the long line of waiting cars stood outside, looking at the ship as if that might possibly speed the process. And it seemed like there was a lot of people waiting too . . . even though the season was ending.

Or maybe it was to gulp those last few precious sea breezes. Hear the chattering of the herring gulls, or catch the occasional black-backed gull darting between them one more time.

"Knee acting up?" she said.

"Hmm?"

"Just now. You seemed to favor your left leg. Bit of a hobble."

David smiled. "A hobble? Yeah, well, it's not perfect. I'm off the cane. And usually the leg's pretty good. But all that sitting. Gets a little cramped."

"You could probably use a massage."

Her words came quickly.

A massage. Something any spouse could offer another. To ease some pain. Or a prelude. The words came too fast, though, before Johanna could check them, stop them . . . realizing what they both knew.

What they both accepted.

They weren't spouses, and the days of massages were over.

At least, that's what David assumed they both knew.

"I could use a shot of Makers' Mark."

"We'll pick some up," Johanna said quickly.

David nodded, the odd moment passing.

Then the clank of the folding iron gate cut through the sound of people talking and gulls screeching overhead.

One might almost expect cheers, David thought. But none of these long-experienced Block Island visitors would dare tempt the wrath of Cap by doing anything to mock this ritual.

The goddamned gates were open and soon the ferry would begin its sleepy haul out to the island so far off the Rhode Island coast.

DAVID drove up the winding dirt road carefully.

Not many cars had been through here. They had rented it out a few weeks this summer, but they had hit the season late and for most of August their cottage sat empty.

With the mailbox at the far end, the road was little used.

He drove over a big chunk of rock embedded in the dirt road, and the groceries in the back—milk, cereal, some fruit, bottled water—bounced up in the seat.

The narrow dirt road led up at a steep angle—one of the reasons they liked this place. It sat alone, on a rocky outcrop that faced east, right out to the fierce Atlantic.

The downside was that the small cottage caught the full brunt of all the major storms. It was a scary place in a nor'easter, as David knew.

But the small cottage was built like a wooden fortress. And though the windows rattled, and wind shrieked through slits in the wood frame, it stood bravely facing whatever nature threw at it.

And, on a gorgeous morning, the *view*—

Well, David could never find the words to describe that view. Too many colors, pastels, swirls and wisps of clouds, the way the dew-wet grass and bushes glowed as if someone had just turned their lights on.

Indescribable.

I'm going to miss this place, David thought.

He stopped the car by the front door. All looked secure, shades drawn. Door tight. The brown paint—perhaps not the best color for the brave little cottage—was flecked, peeling. Might be something they'd have to do. A new paint job.

More money out . . . before they got their money back.

Johanna got out first.

David popped open his door, and—as if he hadn't really gotten any better at all—he slid his leg out. All this damn sitting in the car, the constant pressure on his knee—the pain kept growing.

But he hurried out and stood beside Johanna, who had already dug out her key.

She looked at him and smiled. "It's going to smell," she said.

"We'll open the windows."

She put the key in and unlocked—perhaps for the last time, David thought—what had been a shared dream.

But now was simply a reminder of just how badly things had fallen apart.

6

MARI knocked on the open hospital door. A man lay sleeping on the nearest bed, outside the covers, looking like a beached whale, his great stomach a massive curved island.

In the other bed, near the window, she saw that Will was also sleeping.

For a moment she debated leaving.

Let him sleep. Get his rest.

That's what she told herself. Part of her knew that she wouldn't mind being let off the hook . . . to pass on this idle bedside chitchat.

Then Will's eyes opened and she saw him slowly turn to the door.

"Mari," he said in a sleepy voice.

She smiled and hurried to his side.

He smiled, his blond hair making him look boyish—though his boyish days were decades behind him.

"Hey, kiddo," she said.

"*Hey* to you. What's the matter? Nothing better to do on a Saturday? Quiet Friday night?"

Mari smiled back as she busied herself grabbing a chair. A heavy-looking blue chair with wooden arms and a cushiony seat sat in the corner, a pile of towels on the cushion.

Mari dragged the chair close. She piled the towels on the foot of the bed.

Will leaned up and looked at the towels. "I must be getting a bed bath today." Then to Mari: "Ever have a bed bath? Seems like the most useless thing."

"Nope. Never did."

"A real treat. Must be a blast to administer too."

"Maybe you'll get lucky and have some hunky attendant tend to you."

Will shook his head. "Last time I had a Large Marge who seemed more repelled by the process than even I was."

"I bet you're—"

But she stopped, seeing Will look around the room.

"Need something?"

"Yeah. See my water cup? It has a straw so I don't drool all over myself."

Mari turned, and then saw the pale orange cup with a spout near the stolidly old-fashioned desk phone.

"Got it," she said. She walked over and grabbed the cup, then brought it to Will's lips. Like a little kid, he took a deep sip. Then another.

"Thanks. I needed that. Though a bit of vodka would be better."

"When you get out."

"When? *If . . .*"

Mari sat down. "What are they saying?"

"Who knows? Got so many doctors looking at me. Some say it's just a little flare-up, some mild skin carcinoma that they can deal with, no heavy drugs, no radiation. For now. Other guys aren't sure."

"You told them you've been on your regimen?"

Will nodded. "Yes, ma'am. Told them that I've been a good Boy Scout, taking my fistful of pills three times a day. Even when I get smashed, I never forget that. So—" he looked around, then reached out to the small table with the phone— "knock on wood, and all will turn out okay."

Mari reached out and grabbed his hand and squeezed. She

wondered if he was telling her the truth, the whole truth—or just an edited version. Had his HIV kicked into high gear? Was he one of the current generation of patients who was going to slip through the cracks, despite all the new drugs that seemingly postponed the Grim Reaper forever?

"I miss my running partner," she said.

Will pointed a finger at her. "As long as *you're* still running. Your body will go to hell so fast once you lay off running. Not to be vain, but a girl's body is everything."

"A woman's body."

A small laugh. "Okay, a *woman's* body." He took a breath. "Another sip?"

She brought the straw to his lips and he took a big suck of water.

"Cold enough? Need ice?"

"It's perfect. So, how are things with your man? All cool there?"

Mari looked away. Will knew how long she had endured the eternal Manhattan hunt for a man. He seemed to take vicarious pleasure in her finally finding someone.

Though *finding* wasn't . . . quite the right word.

"He's away this weekend. With the ex."

"Ouch."

"They own this cottage, so they need to meet with real estate people, decide what they're going to, divide stuff up, and—"

"You're pissed. Majorly pissed."

"Is it that obvious?"

"Well, the temperature in the room jumped a shitload of degrees."

In answer, the man in the next bed snorted, a hippolike sound from the sleeping patient.

Will laughed again. It was so good to see him laugh. Even if they had stumbled on a subject that she didn't particularly want to talk about.

"I mean, did he have to go with her? I don't think so."

"But they're split, Mari. Over. What are you worried—"

She leaned close. "You're telling me—same situation—your

current hottie going on an overnight to Fire Island with an ex,
and you'd be fine?"

"Okay, I get your point. But you got to have faith it will all
be cool."

"Maybe not after the send-off I gave him."

"Oooh—gave him some shit?"

"A bit."

"Hmmmm . . . well, when he gets back, don't even mention
it. Tart yourself up for him. Make him forget the weekend."

"I'll try."

Now Will squeezed her hand.

"And the other stuff? Your dreams?"

"Here and there. Sometimes I sleep like a baby."

"And other nights—?"

She nodded. "I'm back in that warehouse. I can feel the
wire around me, smell the place, see the others . . . dead . . .
close to dying."

"And you see David? Dream of him too?"

"Yeah. The man that saved me."

"Your knight."

"Precisely. My knight. Off with his beautiful ex-wife for
the weekend."

Will laughed.

The overhead light came on.

"Good morning, Mr. Meyer."

Will leaned close to Mari as best he could. "Here she
comes. Bath time."

But the words were loud enough to be heard by the nurse.

"Yes, it's bath time and I am afraid, miss"—the short black
woman looked up at Mari—"I'm afraid you will have to go."

Mari turned to Will. "I'd love to stay."

"You're going to miss some show."

"Yeah. I bet. See you tomorrow."

"No. Go out and get crazy tonight. If I'm still here
Monday . . . come then. Got it? Get out and party, damn it.
It's . . . Saturday night!"

"Right. Orders received. I'll do my best."

The nurse came out of the bathroom with a basin of soapy water, and scooped up the towels. She shot Mari a glance.

"Okay. My cue, Will. Enjoy bath time."

The nurse had already begun getting her sponge ready for the attack. Will mouthed, *Help me*, then grinned. "Remember, Saturday night, baby girl."

"Don't worry. I'll carry the weekend torch for both of us. See you soon."

He nodded, and Mari turned and left the bedside, walking out into the corridor.

7

THE real-estate agent, a woman with wavy long hair and dangling gold hoop earrings, leaned across the table.

"Look, I will be honest with you folks—"

And David thought . . . *Your ears have to perk up when a real-estate agent says that they are about to be honest.*

"Please do," Johanna said.

"The season's just about over. Half the places around here are empty. Some even shuttered. In another month, after the leaves change, this island becomes a ghost town. I head back to Providence myself."

"And your point?" David said.

"This is—" She looked around at the cottage, at the small dining area off an almost-kitchen, then back. "Cozy living room, but not a place to have a big party. And the queen bed? Just about fits in your bedroom. This place of yours, it's cute and all, but you're going to need the right buyer."

"Or renter?" Johanna said.

"Same thing. Either way, now may not be the time to do anything with it."

"You mean we should just let it sit here?"

"Yes. I could have done something with it this summer but, well, I understand you folks were having some difficulties."

David thought if the agent called him and Johanna "folks" one more time, he'd be tempted to grab her two giant hoop earrings and see if he could swing her around the cozy living room.

Johanna looked over and—in a move that took him back to their early days, the good days—she reached out and touched the back of his hand. A signal, as in, *Don't say or do anything, we need this lady.*

"So you're saying, wait?"

The woman beamed as if Johanna had just cracked the Da Vinci Code. "Precisely. Come early spring, maybe even late winter, people start sniffing around, looking for their summer places. Then this cottage will go in a snap. By then, maybe you'll know whether you want to rent it, sell it. Either way, Ed and I will be there for you."

How comforting, thought David.

"I mean—if anyone comes by looking for this kind of place—of course we will show it."

When the woman's Cheshire grin shifted from Johanna to him, David forced himself to smile back. After all, they would need this woman and her partner to sell the cottage, to move past this leftover bit of business from their marriage.

"Great," Johanna said, standing up. "So we'll just sit tight till spring." She fired another look at David. "Then see what we want to do."

"Exactly." The woman stood up, bracelets jangling on her wrist. She stuck out her hand. "In the meantime, make sure you close the place up good and tight before the bad weather. We'll want it to show as good as it can."

"Will do," David said.

Johanna escorted the woman out to her Lexus SUV, a vehicle that announced that *Hey . . . I'm a good goddamned agent.*

And standing alone in the room, David wished that they had been able to close this chapter.

Now, it remained open.

* * *

THEY had decided to head into town for dinner, to the Harbor Inn.

It occurred to David that they probably could have headed back to New York. Would have meant taking a late ferry, and an even later return to New York on I-95. But they could have done that.

Instead, they'd be spending the night here.

Sleeping arrangements had been discussed with a quick, *You can take the couch?*

When they parked his Accord opposite the general store, Johanna turned around.

"Maybe grab a bottle of wine? For later. I'm not much of a bourbon drinker. Might as well enjoy our last evening on the island."

David smiled. "Told you we should have gotten cable. I'll get you a Pinot, then—the Harbor Inn? Seafood?"

"Works for me."

David popped open the door. As he slid out of the seat, he was aware of doing so in one smooth move, trying hard to hide that his leg still sent stray spikes of pain to his brain.

And why is that? he wondered.

Could it be that the leg, his wounds there . . . went to the heart of why they'd broken up? How she couldn't live with the danger, the fear, until it turned into a marriage with three things in it . . . Johanna, David, and the job. And there was no way they could all live together.

He walked over to Fine Wines and Spirits, which in this case was completely accurate since the owner's name was Fine.

David hoped that the owner wasn't there, that Gerry Fine had turned the place over to some twenty-one-year-old townie behind the counter. That would be easier.

But no such luck.

"David, hell . . . where have you been all summer? Rent your joint out or something?"

David smiled.

"Things got busy back in the city—"

"The *Big* Apple, hmm?" Fine said, saying "Big" with just a

hint of barely hidden scorn. The year-round Block Islanders like to think that they lived on a paradise, and anyone who'd choose pavement and streetlights over this rocky jewel in the Atlantic had to be crazy.

And who knows, David thought, maybe they were right.

"I'll take"—he reached out and grabbed a bottle of Merlot—"this. And . . . do you have a cold Pinot Grigio?"

"You bet!" The owner hobbled to the small wine refrigerator in the back. David assumed that the man had some kind of hip problem . . . probably something he could fix on the mainland.

But the mainland?

Old Mr. Fine would sooner put up with his pain.

Island people, David thought. *Strange birds.*

"GOT some wine?"

"One white, one red—"

"As always," Johanna said.

David nodded. They sat on the side porch of the Inn, looking westward, out to the harbor, the fishing boats, now all back for the night, the sun low, already close to touching the water.

"We never could drink the same wine."

"Red gives you headaches," David said.

So much history, he thought. They knew so much about each other. And where did all that go, that knowledge, those connections, that understanding?

Just . . . vanished . . .

He looked up, and saw that Johanna, backlit by the now burnished red sun, was looking at him.

"So what do you think?" she said.

"About?"

"The cottage. Waiting. Selling, renting it later?"

"We have no choice. What else can we do? Not like either of us needs the money. We can wait."

She smiled. "Yes, we can."

Then, with the sun halfway below the water, their shore

dinners arrived, glistening with the fried glow of flounder and fries, little cups of cole slaw barely able to fit.

And like so many times before, they ate by the sea as a perfect sunset played out behind them.

DAVID thought: Did they both feel the tension? Or was it just in his head, this . . . tension?

Something in the air.

With Johanna, and himself.

He put the wine down, and searched in a drawer filled with everything from an oyster knife and screwdrivers to fondue forks and—he hoped—the corkscrew.

Finding it, he opened the red first, then the white. Johanna brought over two glasses.

David filled one, then the other—and then they raised their glasses.

"To what . . . moving on?" she said.

David nodded. That's what this was supposed to be about. *Moving on.*

Then why didn't it feel that way? he thought.

They sipped, and then—

Not at all unexpected, Johanna came close.

"You know, David . . . I guess . . . it's funny—"

She was inches away, so close that if he took a deep breath he could inhale, smelling her perfume, the slight trace of scent that almost wasn't there. Her scent mixing with the salty smell from the day, from their sitting outside the restaurant as the heat and humidity gave way to a slight chilling breeze off the sea.

But he didn't move.

Didn't step back.

"Being here, it's, well—kind of hard. We had good times," she said.

He nodded.

That they did.

"Maybe it went all wrong . . . being in the city. A crazy

place. The streets of New York. Here, it always seemed right. Didn't it?"

"Usually."

Another thought flickered in his head. This is a woman he loved . . . and, and—

Maybe she had this . . . *moment* in mind all along.

She tilted her head up, her lips close. David remembered what it was like to kiss her. Never bad. Always good.

Sometimes—way better than good.

She leaned close. Her lips touched his. Dry, just glancing off his. The slightest pressure and—

Then more pressure, and she leaned into him and kissed hard.

And for a moment it was as if the kiss might be magical, a fairy-tale kiss. He remembered all the good kisses, the delicious moments in the bed here, in New York—those moments when everything else vanished. But also how all that changed. How there were suddenly guilt, bitterness, anger, until he didn't want to go home.

Couldn't go home, and they both knew—

They knew, he reminded himself.

That it was all over.

And then—Johanna must have felt it.

Because she broke off the kiss.

Pulled back, and looked him in the eye.

She raised her glass of red wine, saying nothing for those few seconds that, to each of them, spoke volumes.

The magic of the kiss failing.

"To the good times," she said, taking a sip. She stepped back.

It was over.

8

MARI turned to Julie Fein, whose appletini was already in need of a refill.

"Not much happening here?"

Julie turned, a gusty breeze from the roof of Soho House catching her wavy hair.

"It's early, babe. Just eleven. Give it a chance."

Mari had let Julie talk her into going out—and hitting the streets of Manhattan in search of fun and men . . . reminding her of how much she was glad she was past all that.

Or *thought* that she was past all that.

"I'm out of practice," Mari said.

The Soho House—a private club—was crowded, the rooftop pool girded by a crowd in summery clothes, while a few people actually swam in the pool, looking like sexy props provided by the management.

Still, through the steamy mist of the humid late-summer night, the city glowed with the foggy look of an impressionist painting.

There are worse places to be, Mari thought.

Julie touched her arm. "Hey, see that guy?"

Julie nodded to a corner of the outdoor patio.

Mari turned and saw someone—tall, tight T-shirt and black jeans, holding a beer, flanked by two other men. He definitely was looking in their direction. She turned away.

"God, I feel like I'm under surveillance."

"You're just out of practice, babe. He's just checking you out."

"Or you. Either way, he's making me squirm."

Julie leaned close and gave her a little hip-bump. "And sometimes . . . squirming is good, hmm?"

Mari smiled. "Sometimes."

And once again she thought of David—how many miles away, out in the goddamn Atlantic, on an island with his ex.

Great.

Perfect.

Why the fuck wasn't he here? Why did he leave her stranded in this sea of pool-based sharks?

"Uh-h—heads up, kiddo . . . he's walking this way."

"Fantastic. I think I better go."

Julie's hand went to her wrist. "Hang on."

And then the man in the T-shirt was there. A gym rat, from the looks of things; puffed-out chest, solid biceps. Someone with too much free time. A good-looking guy—but was she in the market for a guy?

She had thought no.

But maybe that was all wrong.

"You ladies look like you need refills."

Ladies. That's what men called women when they were trying to get laid. In private, at their all-male watering holes, they had other words, she was sure. Chicks, cunts, bitches.

"I'm okay, I—"

But Julie took her glass from her and handed it to the man.

"Two more of the same would be great."

Mari rolled her eyes, but the man kept his grin plastered on his face as he sailed away.

"Look, Julie. I don't want to rain on your parade, or your aging beefcake. But I have a guy, and—"

Julie shifted her stance, so she was right in front of Mari.

"Oh, really? You do? How interesting. Then where the *hell* is he? Saturday night, and—"

Mari looked away.

"Hey, sorry. Went too far there. But you're my bud. Someone's gotta watch your back. And I don't like seeing you played."

Mari said the next words tightly, mad that her friend might be right. "I am *not* being played."

She had never told Julie the whole story of what happened that night . . . the night she went to the warehouse, the night when all those people were killed and David—

David . . .

—saved her.

Christ. Mari had been bound by what—fucking razor wire—by someone who had already butchered a half-dozen people, and, and—

But she didn't tell Julie, or the others.

David took care of telling the cops.

Because . . . well, would anyone believe what had happened? That they had been drawn there, lured there by a killer who could do a whole lot more than cut them to pieces?

A killer who could enter their very dreams.

And—Christ—David killed him; he saved her.

And after that, they were together, joined by that, and by their secret.

"Hey, you going somewhere? Blanking out on me?"

Mari looked back to her friend.

"Hey, Julie. I gotta go. I'm no fun tonight, I guess."

"No, stay. Have another drink, I'm sorry that I—"

Now Mari reached out and touched her friend's wrist. "No. It's me. I'm a bit edgy. And things with David, well, who knows how the hell they are? But you stay. Enjoy the night, and Mr. Designer T-shirt. I'll see you at the paper Monday. And"—a slight squeeze—"I promise to be more fun. Just not . . . tonight."

Julie nodded. Mari caught their refreshed drinks sailing back. She quickly gave her friend a hug and kiss on the cheek, and then did an end run, to the far side of the pool . . . and out to the elevator to the ground floor and West Thirteenth Street.

MARI didn't think about the streets and safety.

Like most New Yorkers, she believed in the mantra of the new safe New York. Crime's way down, killing *way* down, and places like this—once the domain of ambi-sexual hookers and drug dealers of every kind—were just part of the new safe wonderland that was the new New York City.

Except—after that night she found herself reacting oddly to things.

Not exactly paranoid. But every now and then she could feel the hairs on her arms stand up, as if someone waved a statically charged comb only inches from her skin.

She'd step into an elevator and openly scan every face, searching for secrets, perhaps searching for danger.

Then there was something that she hadn't even told David.

Part of those moments, those looks, that feeling of danger, seemed like some new *sense* she had.

As if—

As if . . .

She had been changed that night. *I'm not the same,* she thought. *I'm changed.*

And she wasn't sure it was a good thing.

She heard a cough just as she nearly reached the corner of Washington Street.

She assumed that the best way to hail a cab at this time of night was to hit Eleventh Avenue. But it meant moving away from the bustling part of the Meatpacking District, down a few quiet blocks before reaching the broad avenue, lit by lights that made it as bright as a baseball field or—with the speed of the cars racing to Brooklyn and Jersey—a NASCAR track.

But here, a block away, she was still in the dark.

The cough again—just ahead.

She slowed. Took a breath.

Something about shadows. What they hide, what can stay hidden.

Some primal, so primitive.

Mari turned and looked at the shadows, her eyes not quite adjusted to the darkness, now that the street lamps were ahead.

Until—

She could make out two figures.

Two people, men, women, one of each? She couldn't tell.

One smoked, the other crouched down, doing something to the smoking one.

Mari kept moving, thinking . . . let's grant the romantic lovers some privacy.

As she passed, she heard wet sounds. *Wet,* she thought. The sound of sex, no matter of what variety.

She did fire a glance over her shoulder as she passed. Just to make sure. But she also noted . . . no hairs standing upright on her arms now.

No electric sparks firing behind her eyeballs as she scanned the shadowy scene of the couple, then turned to continue up to the corner of Eleventh Avenue.

It's safe, she thought.

And amazingly enough, she *knew* that.

At the corner, a small bodega was still open. A tall brown-skinned man stood at the counter smoking, while a short lady next to him listened to him talk.

By this time of night, Bloomberg's smoking regulations started to go out the window.

The store had a rack of papers outside.

El Diario, the *New York Post,* and then, inside on the counter . . . the first early edition of the *Daily News.*

Mari stopped.

The owner hadn't yet covered the main section with the comics.

She could scan the front page, the headline, a photo—

The photo showed a tarp on the pavement and shuttered buildings in the background. Lower East Side, she guessed.

The headline was simple, straightforward as only her paper could do it . . . NYC SLAUGHTER.

She picked up the paper. She read the caption below what she guessed must be a body covered by a tarp. Slaughter in the Lower East Side. LES, as the hipsters called it. Even from a distance, the cover photo caught the massive spread of blood that bloomed from whatever was under the tarp.

Whoever, Mari reminded herself.

Who.

The paper had beaten the police to the scene.

It was the only explanation for the eerie photo.

Then—in the corner, an elegant strappy high-heeled shoe.

And the reporter must have had a look at the person under the tarp, the dead person—

No, not just dead. Not just killed.

But slaughtered.

And then, slowly, like a sick wave washing over her . . . the hairs on her arms began to rise, accompanied by an icy chill that turned her bare skin into a sea of gooseflesh.

Except there was no icy chill, no wind from the river—just a terrible fear.

The owner and his wife stared at her as if she was crazy.

Mari put down a dollar and walked out with the paper.

JUST outside, Mari held her cell phone close, standing in the light, in the safety of the bodega window, with the just-bought paper under her arm.

Then she heard the mechanical instructions to . . . *leave a message, please.*

"Joann, it's Mari. Sorry for calling your cell. But I just saw tomorrow's front page, the story on the killing. I'd like—"

How could she put it . . . without sounding ghoulish?

"—I think it would be a good story for me to track." She

hesitated for a second, thinking what she might add to make the city editor inclined to give her the assignment. Then: "I—I think after everything, it would be a good fit."

Christ, *good fit*. Like buying a business suit. Well-tailored, hangs well. Sounded so stupid.

"I'd like to hit it tomorrow—if you give me the green light."

Mari waited, as if the blank message space could respond. But then Mari ended . . .

"I'll leave my phone on. Thanks."

She hit the red button, killing the call.

Would the city editor, Joann Gully, give it to her? Ever since the Warehouse Murders, the woman, a pro from the days of typewriters and linotype, seemed to step warily around Mari, as if she might be disabled.

Maybe I am, Mari thought.

And maybe this is the thing to cure me.

She rubbed her arms, the gooseflesh barely subsiding. At least now there was a cool breeze blowing off the nearby river.

She walked to the corner, and scanned the avenue for a cab with the telltale white light on showing the cab's number. The street was filled with them, hungry late-night sharks hoping to squeeze a few more bucks out of the Saturday night.

Within seconds, one stopped—and Mari got in.

9

THE man, nearly soaked through to his skin from sweat, turned down one corner, then immediately froze. He reached into his back pocket and pulled out a map stuck to the inside of his pocket.

Father Brian Henning opened his sodden map of Singapore.

He knew he was in the right part of Singapore, the ancient, inner city that was the "Chinatown" of the exploding island state.

But suddenly the signs, which had been in a helpful English, had turned to Chinese. He stood at the corner of a small alley, and didn't have a clue where he was on the map.

He scanned the lattice of main avenues that gave way to smaller streets and squares, finally ending in a squirrelly maze of near alleys.

Even with his glasses on, Henning couldn't really see the map that well. He pushed his glasses up to his bushy white hair. He tried to mentally backtrack, finding a spot he recognized until—

There. Upper Cross Street! Yes, he passed that a few minutes ago. But walking in what direction? He searched the colorful map for some hints on how to orient it. He could see the harbor, and there Hong Lim Park, China Square, and—

Damn. He turned the map. At least now he was looking at it correctly.

Then someone stood beside him.

"Excuse me," the young girl with flowing jet-black hair said, "you perhaps need some assistance?"

The man smiled. "Yes, assistance. That would be . . . wonderful. I'm afraid I've gotten myself totally lost and"— he looked up—"the signs here, bit hard for me to read."

The girl nodded, gamine, almost boyish, and smiled. "You know the name of the street you wish?"

"Yes. Yung-tao."

The girl's face clouded over for a second as if she expected to immediately know the name of the street but was now embarrassingly stumped.

"I am sorry. You say Yung-tao?"

Henning nodded. He thought he had been rescued, but now . . . well, it wasn't the first time that he had thought he had been rescued and had been wrong.

A quick ripple of remembrance shot through him.

Sometimes, something from your past pops up, a reminder of who you really are, what and who are really under your skin, behind the forced smile, the wise words, the appearances . . .

Our real humanity.

Like Our Lord said . . . let him who is without sin . . .

Great line that. A killer line.

Nobody volunteering to be that first stone thrower.

The girl extended a hand. "Maybe—if you please—I could see your map?"

Henning handed the wet map to her.

"I'm sorry. It's so humid, so hot, I'm afraid."

The girl looked up with a smile. "Not to worry, I can see quite clearly. The street must be small. I live near here. I should know it. That is, if it's—oh, wait."

She turned the map.

"There it is." She giggled. *Delightful,* thought the man. The laugh, the joy. So foreign to him. "I have found it."

He took a step closer. Her narrow index finger pointed to the tiniest of squiggles. "Here. You see. There it is—so hard to see. You need a bigger map."

"Next time," Henning said.

The girl looked up, and around. "Not sure the best way for you to get there. I think . . . I think . . . yes. Stay on the main road here. Go"—another glance down—"three more streets. Then go down Boon Tat Street. Stay on that, and yes—it will take you to your side street . . . to Yung-Tao."

"Thank you so much. But if the sign is in Chinese?"

Another smile followed by yet another apology. "Oh, yes. It will be. I will write it for you."

She opened a purse, and dug out a pen. Then—

"May I?" she asked, pointing to the map.

"Certainly."

She wrote the characters on the map.

"That way you will know for sure."

She handed the map back, and their transaction was ended.

"Thank you so much. You've been . . . an immense help."

And he wanted to add . . . *and the most delightful thing I've experienced in weeks.*

Delight . . .

Not much of that in my life. The very word sounded foreign.

"So glad to help," she said. "And good luck, Father."

Henning took the map from the girl, and then, as she moved briskly away, he froze.

Father.

How did she know he was a priest? No collar, no regulation suit. A bright striped shirt that any tourist might wear.

Or did she mean it merely as a sign of respect?

He turned the map so he could use it to guide himself to the small alleyway, and started walking back to the main road.

*   *   *

HE looked down an alleyway clogged with kids, chickens, and even a small goat tied to a doorknob. The kids raced back and forth, making the squawking chickens fly up in the air, screech, then land before beginning the whole thing again.

As he started walking toward them, the kids stopped to look up at the tall gray-haired man, and then resumed their playful torturing of the chickens.

Henning could see that there were numbers on the doorways, often more than one.

He was looking for number 26.

He passed one door with a 17, 18, and a 22. The other numbers must be . . . somewhere else. A little past it, he came to a single door, with a 26.

Good, he thought, *that should make things easier.*

He looked for a doorbell button but there was none. And no knocker. He rapped on the door, and again the nearby kids looked at him as if his behavior was extremely odd.

Henning smiled at the kids; then he rapped again.

Finally he reached out and turned the doorknob, and it opened.

Of course. No locked doors on this lane, not with the guardian kids and their attack chickens outside.

He walked in.

HE took the stairs slowly.

Strange how stairs had gotten for him, how they had changed. He could remember the day when he took stairs two at a time.

Now a single step seemed to take on Everest proportions. And while he hadn't told his doctor in Rome this, every step brought its own bit of pain with it.

Stupid not to tell him. He's there to help me, Henning thought.

But he had suffered enough tests, enough procedures. And he took so much medicine already to keep his blood pressure down and his cholesterol in check.

It was all probably okay, this small pain.
He reached the top step, and another door.
He knocked again.
And this time, the door opened.

10

THE priest walked into a smoke-filled apartment, a single room with an unmade bed, a small desk, and the tiniest of kitchen areas.

A woman—cigarette in her mouth—hit the keys of a laptop.

"Have a seat, Padre. I'll be right with you. Got an e-mail that has to fucki—um, sorry. *Needs* to go out."

"Yes, I—" Henning looked around for a place to sit. But there appeared to be only one chair, presently occupied. He walked over to the bed, and sat down on the twisted pile of sheets and comforter.

"Almost done," the woman said.

Her fingers moved with lightning speed on the keyboard. Then she closed the top of her laptop, and turned the chair around.

"I'm surprised you have an Internet connection here."

She laughed. "A connection here? Dubious. Though I bet there are some illegal wi-fi signals floating around if I want my files stolen. You know how much identify theft goes on over here? This place is the Wild West."

"Then how do you—"

She picked up a thin phone. "GSM satellite phone, world-wide service. Hooks right up to my computer. Could use it in

Antarctica. In fact, have used it in Tierra del Fuego, which is pretty fu—God, sorry again, Padre, have to . . ." And here she put on a Southern accent—*"watch my mouth."*

"It doesn't matter."

She nodded, as though what Henning had said was more than just a polite comment. "Yes, it doesn't matter, does it? Doesn't matter at all."

That weighty question resolved, the woman stood up. "Hey, you want to take the chair? No reason you have to sit on the bed. Never got into the habit of making beds. I mean, why make it? Just going to mess it up again."

Henning smiled at that. Despite the woman's language— worthy of any portside bar—and her smoking, she was charismatic, beautiful in a careless way. But she must be mighty intimidating for most men.

He guessed she was lonely.

And that was without factoring in the brilliance.

Because this woman, Dr. Lisa Griffino, was one of the most brilliant physicists on the planet. Brilliant, controversial—and obviously an eccentric.

"I'm fine here, Dr. Griffino."

The woman pushed her red-brown hair back. Though she probably didn't spend much time taming it, the hair flowed around her face, waves that reminded Henning of some old movie star.

Ava Gardner? No. More . . . Maureen O'Hara in *The Quiet Man*.

"Make you a deal, Padre. You don't call me Doctor, and I won't call you Father. I'm 'Lisa,' and you can be 'Brian.' "

Henning smiled. "Deal."

"Okay. We best cut to the chase. I had to wonder after your e-mails to me. Figure . . . you must have had a good reason to come all the way here, to Singapore, to my rathole in the backstreets."

Henning nodded. He thought about what he was about to say, how it would all sound. How much to tell—and how much, if anything, to leave out.

But he imagined she would quickly sense any holes in the story, any details omitted.

So no omissions. At least not any conscious ones.

"Oh, I have a very good reason, Lisa. Maybe you have a glass of water, before I start? It might take some time."

The woman got up, and went to the tiny sink. Henning watched her rinse out the smallest of water glasses. Then she filled it and brought it to him.

"Water's okay here," she said. "At least it hasn't killed me."

Henning took the glass. He became aware of how he was still sweating, the air so close, no air-conditioning here—his shirt sticking to him.

The physicist's eyes were locked on him.

"First—you are perhaps the only person to hear what I am going to tell you. Things that go back thousands of years."

She tapped out another cigarette.

"To the time of Christ?"

"Even before that." A breath. "Way before."

The woman reached for a yellow pad. "Interesting. Mind if I take notes?"

Henning hesitated. Was it safe for her to take notes? It could provide evidence of what she knew, what she was doing. Could having these notes hurt her?

It was the reason he always traveled with nothing.

Just what he knew.

The things that he knew.

"Yes. Go on. You m-may need them. But please. No one else must see them, know of them. For your protection."

Another laugh. "For my protection?"

Henning did not laugh in kind. "Yes. Absolutely."

Another sip of water.

It was just past midday.

And he began.

11

FATHER Henning stepped out to the alleyway, out to the twilight of the setting sun.

The time he spent with Dr. Griffino . . . Lisa . . . flew by. First he told her everything, asking her—at first—to not interrupt.

Let me just get through this, he thought.

But that plan soon fell apart, and every time he told her one ever more incredible and fantastic detail, it led to a whole series of questions.

He realized pretty quickly that she was an atheist. Nothing against atheists. Quite a natural position for a scientist to take. But it colored how Henning told her the tale.

That's what he thought of it as . . . *the tale.*

As in . . . *once upon a time.*

But there was no way he could completely keep God out of it. God, the universe, belief—all that supernatural stuff.

No way. So he didn't. Even if Dr. Griffino's atheistic sensibilities had been offended.

Sensibilities were the least they had to worry about.

And on through the afternoon, until the light left the window blinds as the tiny apartment grew more somber. After a half dozen cups of tea and some crumbly cookies that he passed on, but soon ate as hunger took over. He had suggested getting some dinner, but he saw that he had, in fact, lit a fire under the circumspect Dr. Griffino.

Good. Precisely what he'd hoped to do.

A fire, so that she might help. She could think on what he said. And they could talk again.

Because there wasn't much the Church could do. Not with a mystery so enormous, so gigantic, so deadly.

He turned down a narrow alley that led to Cecil Street, back to the bright lights and a stream of cars and all the bustling hurry that was Singapore.

He was tired. He was hungry.

But he didn't sense any danger.

After all, why should he?

LISA Griffino looked down at her yellow pads. For once she hoped that her hopeless scrawl would prove readable to her hours after writing down what she had just heard.

A glance told her that she'd best start looking at the notes, rewriting them, as soon as possible.

But she also knew that she had an excellent memory. It was—for now—almost as if she could replay the afternoon, the near-confessionlike meeting with the priest.

And what did she think of all this?

Think. Yes, perhaps the key question. She knew what she *thought* of a lot of things, from the nature of quarks, to what really happens when a star collides with a black hole. All based on a mix of theories and fact.

But this?

What were the facts, what were the theories, and—

She thought of a William Blake poem.

Blake, the mystic poet, artist, someone from the eighteenth century who spoke of the divine as if he had been there, seen it.

Tyger! Tyger! Burning bright
In the forests of the night

What immortal hand or eye
Could frame thy fearful symmetry?

Not about tigers at all.

Blake talking about the divine, and such chilling words. Fearful symmetry.

Lisa stood up, suddenly aware of her feeling of being thrown into a weird stew of facts and theories. And religion!

She hated religion.

And then, she knew she felt something else—fear.

I'm afraid, she thought.

Afraid. Never really ever been afraid of anything, not since she became an adult, not since the closet monsters hiding under the bed had all retired.

She turned.

Something glinted in the corner of the ratty bed that came with this furnished rental.

A cell phone.

She walked over to the bed and picked up the phone, Henning's phone.

She could still catch him. Only gone a few minutes, and she knew how she had told him to wind his way out of here.

She grabbed her small bag with all her essentials. Passport, wallet, BlackBerry. Not something she'd ever leave in the apartment, not in this neighborhood. Besides, she might get some food while out, sit somewhere, and think about everything before meeting Henning again tomorrow.

Lisa ran to the door, and raced down the stairs.

HENNING looked down at his standard-issue black shoes. Priest shoes if the Good Lord ever made a pair. And on one shoe, the black laces had somehow become untied.

He knelt down to tie them, the broad avenue still many twists and turns away.

The shadows had lengthened here so that in this narrow

alleyway, dotted with shops with signs in Chinese giving no clue to what they sold, the shops were closed, shuttered tight.

Siesta, he thought, or closed for the night?

Or—

He pulled the errant laces tight, and then began looping them, tying them. His knees ached. He was so tired, drained; he just wanted to get back to the hotel.

Then, while he kneeled as if genuflecting . . . a voice.

"Good evening, Father."

Henning looked up.

The man was before him, his body outlined by the glow of the sky above, but with enough light that Henning could in those seconds see—

Blue eyes, sandy-blond cropped hair, a bit spiky in the style that so many young executives seemed to like. He wore a beige suit, but with an open shirt . . . looking out of place in this alley probably never seen by tourists.

Henning finished tying his bow, then struggled to stand, his knees so unreliable, so wobbly—as if the hard bone was turning into jelly.

In a wriggling twist, Henning stood, taking a deep breath as he did.

"Excuse me," he said, "but do I—"

"Had us a busy, busy little day, didn't we?"

Henning instinctively looked over his shoulder. Was there someone here, someone else coming close to them?

But ahead, and behind, there was no one.

Just this man, and him.

And then Henning knew who he was.

His heart began to race.

Even being so old, one could feel such fear. At no age are we ready to give up hope, to abandon the lifesaving adrenaline rush of fear.

"It's you, isn't it?"

The man laughed, but he didn't move—keeping the distance between them.

"You," the man mocked. Then again. *"You.* So nice to be so well known to be called simply . . . *you."*

Henning took a step back. At the same time, he reached his hand in his pocket to feel for his phone. But he felt nothing. So careless with it, but then what did he really expect that he was going to do? Call some Singapore 911 to come here, to help?

Then, in his other pocket . . . feeling for his rosary, for the reassuring string of beads.

His hand closed on it.

Still, the man did not move. "You, on the other hand, Father, can't keep your mouth shut. It's not like I bother you and your men in your dresses, hiding in Rome. Not like I make your world any more difficult than it already is." Another laugh. "You have enough trouble without me."

Henning took another step, now calculating what might happen . . . *if he turned, if he started to run, looking for an open door, a shop, a place to get away.*

Calculating the possibilities.

"Hmm? Cat got your tongue, Brian?"

In answer, Henning took out his hand with the rosary.

The man shook his head. "If this was a cheap horror movie, this would be my cue to recoil. But it isn't, is it? And your string of worthless beads is just a string of worthless . . . beads."

In answer, Henning said softly, "Hail Mary full of Grace, the Lord is with thee—"

But immediately Henning thought—*Is the Lord with me? Is the Lord here?*

And—

He had known what risk he was taking. He shouldn't be surprised.

"Blessed art thou among women."

The man shook his head. "You had to reach out to the world of science. Will wonders never cease. The Holy Roman Catholic Church reaching out to the atheistic world of science. Why? I am curious."

"Blessed is the fruit of thy womb, Jesus."

"Okay. Don't answer. I can guess. Good thing I was watching. The sleeping cat catches no mice, hmm? Now I have two mice. You, her—and trust me, Father, I know what to do with mice."

Henning turned. If he was going to run, it would be now—now, when the man hadn't moved any closer, when there still was a good twelve feet between them.

"Pray for us . . . sinners."

Henning turned, and started running.

RUNNING.

Except when you are old, that word has no meaning anymore.

None at all. Not when the muscles can't make your legs do more than a slightly faster walk, not when your knees seem to threaten to pop out and fly onto the pavement like bony Frisbees.

Still, Henning had no other option. He turned as fast as he could and started running.

But as if it were a joke, some illusion, a dream run that had no power to take him anywhere, the man was *there*, right behind him.

He grabbed Henning around the back of his neck.

"Normally, I would like to take some time with this. You . . . deserve it. But circumstances—"

Henning turned his head as much as he could. He could feel the man's skin against his, feel his breath on him, his lips close—

Then the sharp pain. A blade sliding into some soft spot in his side. His eyes exploded in an array of white-hot agony.

"—dictate—"

The blade slipped out.

"Otherwise . . ."

Like an animal feeding, it slid in again, this time twirling, twisting as it did. Henning's mouth filled as if he had just taken a deep drink, a mouth-filling drink, something thick and salty.

He tried to say a word, but his mouth just sputtered and made small foamy bubbles.

Reddish bubbles.

LISA froze. She had stopped just where the winding alley curved sharply to the left.

She stopped when she saw the old priest being held by someone as though he were an oversized ventriloquist's dummy, knees oddly bucked forward, head tilted back awaiting the next words to come from the wooden mouth.

And the *mouth*, full of blood, dripping blood, bubbling blood. And Lisa, now shivering by the side of this building, now icy cold even with the humid temperature well above ninety, could see the man behind him only slightly, the hair with a slight sheen, a crisp white shirt that surely had to be getting stained with blood, but mostly the man's arm . . . moving slowly away and back, digging, sawing in.

As if they now performed some secretive sex act in the dusk, not caring who saw them.

The man's arm moving back and forth, holding the knife. And then—something on a wrist, like a bangle.

Almost distracting her from the blade.

It took only seconds for Lisa to take it all in.

Three, maybe four seconds.

And after that time, she backed up into the shadows, back to the twisting lane.

Her breath weird, ragged, like a mongrel dog choking on some meatless bone, air tube blocked.

She stood there only a second.

Then she turned, and began to run as fast as she could.

12

THE cell phone rang, sitting on Mari's small couch right next to her as if it too was watching TV.

She blinked awake; she realized she had dozed off when whatever was happening on the screen, in the world of HBO and *Rome*, became too confusing.

She looked down at her phone, the small screen glowing with each ring—and now also showing who was calling.

David . . .

She picked it up, and didn't make any effort to keep the sleepiness out of her voice.

"Hello."

"Mari. It's David."

She told him the obvious. "I know. My phone tells me who calls me. Bet your phone does too."

She was surprised at her bite considering that she had just woken up from a deep TV-induced sleep.

"I'm back," he said.

She looked over at the clock on the set-top cable box. 9:45. Kind of late to announce he was back.

"You just got back?"

"Well, no—had some stuff to do, then I—"

"You know, David, I'd love to hear all about your wonderful

weekend getaway to Block Island, but you just woke me up so maybe I can take a rain check?"

Yeah, she thought. Definitely harsh. But she didn't hear any other voice inside her urging some restraint as she laid into him.

For a few moments he didn't say anything.

And in that small window she suddenly could feel the real possibility that she could lose David forever.

"Uh, David—you still there?"

"Yes. I just wanted to let you know—"

Mari heard her call-waiting beep on her phone.

Shit. Quiet all day, and now—

She looked down at the screen. Her editor.

"David, I have a call from Joann Gully. I have to take it."

"Right. Catch you tomorrow."

"Maybe later—"

But he was already gone. Mari hit FLASH, and in a minute she heard the cigarette-ravaged voice of the editor that ruled her world.

"**MARI,** sorry. Got no damn service out here."

Mari knew that "out here" meant the Hamptons, where Gully probably whiled away the weekend with other monster editors from New York, hitting a David Geffen cocktail party or hanging with Billy Joel after his DUI classes.

"Thanks for getting back to me. It's just when I saw—"

"I know. You saw that story and you want in. But there's some stuff you don't know about that. I don't want to talk about it over the phone. Hate the goddamn phone. So tomorrow. Nine sharp. And we'll see."

"I'll be there."

"Good. In the meantime, Mari—don't talk to anyone about this, okay? I mean anyone. Just get some sleep, and be there on time."

"I will, Joann, and the—"

But the woman was gone. Mari immediately hit the CON-TACTS button on her phone and scrolled down to David's cell.

She pressed the SEND button, and saw the information that it was ringing.

Until it went on too long and the voice mail kicked in.

Simple and straightforward . . .

Please leave a message.

But Mari killed the call, and scrolled down to his landline. He'd said he was home, probably sitting there, stewing.

She hit that number, but then again listened to the phone ringing until the same voice mail instruction came on. And this time—

"David, Mari, Sorry . . . my editor, I—"

She was about to tell him about the story, about what happened over the weekend. But then she remembered what Gully said.

Best to do exactly as Gully instructed. Keep her mouth shut until they met.

"—I had to talk to her. Maybe we can talk tomorrow?"

Funny, she thought . . . how things change. A few minutes ago she had been freezing him out and now, heart racing, a little scared, she was ready to talk.

Women . . . we are so weird.

She looked back up to the neglected TV screen. Someone wearing a laurel wreath, some young emperor, someone who was a kid last season, walked to the edge of a balcony overlooking an arena. He looked out over a crowd and then quickly stuck out a closed fist, and in the next beat, the closed fist bloomed into a thumbs-down.

The camera seemed to swoop down from the imperial balcony to two gladiators, one on the ground looking like bloody roadkill, the other not looking much better, but brandishing a short, blunt sword over the body of the first one.

Then, with a brutal swiftness, the camera went tight as the standing warrior raised the blade and brought it down hard.

And the thoughtful producers showed the slash into the bull-like neck of the fallen warrior.

Credits appeared.

Brutal.

Like this weekend's killing.

But then a thought—

Not the first time she had the thought.

What is it really like?

To be killed, to be butchered like that? Then another thought that made her feel as if the frozen entrée she had eaten, empty of calories but filled with salt, might not sit well at all.

What does it feel like to do that?

To take a life so directly, so viciously, so—

Primal. That's what it is, she thought. *Ancient, and primal. One person knowing they have to kill the other.*

She found the remote, and switched to the mindless babble of what these days passed for the Channel 5 ten o'clock news.

13

LISA slipped into the tiny noodle shop, the smoke so thick she could hardly make out the dozen patrons sitting so close together, some loudly slurping up bowls of noodles while others swigged Tiger beer and smoked Chinese cigarettes.

No Marlboro country here—the American product was far too expensive.

Through the haze, she searched for an empty chair, and then spotted one next to an elderly man and woman who sat facing each other but whose eyes struggled to look anywhere but at each other.

She walked over to the chair.

The couple looked at her, eyes wide, maybe grateful, she thought, for something to look at in the packed little restaurant.

Lisa smiled at them.

A young girl, the waitress, looking tentative, came over to her.

Lisa smiled at her too.

"Um, a bowl of chicken rice with noodles, please. And"—she looked at the two beers already on the table—"one of these."

The girl nodded, and hurried away.

Then Lisa, the smile fading from her face, turned to the front door.

Had she run far enough, fast enough? Was it crazy for her to sit here after what she saw?

She felt beads of sweat running full out, and her lungs ached. Smoking didn't help things.

Then a quick, panicky thought—and she opened her purse. She took out Henning's phone and looked for the latch to remove the battery. Where the hell was it? she thought as her fingers traced the smooth clamshell design.

Then she felt the tiniest indentation, and dug a fingernail into the crevice.

The back popped open, and she quickly dug out the battery.

Should have done that right away, she thought. How long had it been on, sending a signal to who knows where?

These days carrying a cell phone around was like carrying a personal spy device—only it spied on the owner, telling whoever could access the account where you were.

Then—another thought.

Her phone!

That could be traced also. She pulled it out of the purse, and found the latch that opened the battery compartment. Her new BlackBerry phone did everything but the dishes—but for now, until she thought things through, she'd have to do without it.

The battery fell into her hand, and she slid both parts back into her purse.

The wide-eyed waitress came back with her beer and a steaming bowl of rice dotted with stringy chicken.

She didn't really want the food, didn't really want to eat anything—but you don't come into a Singapore restaurant like this and just order a beer.

She checked the door again, half expecting the man to walk in.

The man . . . she thought.

A chill raced over her body.

If Henning was right—God, if he was right—then she had some idea who the man was.

She knew just how scared she should be.

Lisa took a swig of the Tiger beer, not really that cold, almost room temperature. But the biting beer taste felt good on her tongue, and she was so thirsty. She took a couple of good hard swigs.

The front door creaked and she looked up from the table to see a pair of workmen, in overstuffed overalls, walk into the small restaurant. They stood there, scanning the place for some seats . . . but none of the current patrons, even those sitting with empty bowls and bottles, gave any indication that they were about to move.

Lisa looked at her rice.

She picked up the chopsticks.

When you didn't know when you'd eat next, or where, best to take advantage of the food, of the quiet, of the smoke . . . of the time.

And she ate, as she tried to think, tried to plan.

FINALLY it was dark, and the winding alleyways seemed oddly safer.

They might hide her.

Lisa made sure she stayed with groups of people . . . to the point that if a group suddenly veered off in a direction, she followed them.

Her goal was the City Hall train station.

From there—surrounded by people—she could get a cab to the airport.

She had toyed with the idea that she could go back to her apartment.

But she knew that was impossible.

What a crazy idea . . . to think she could go back there, even to grab a few things and bolt.

All she had to do was imagine that man's arm moving, so mechanically, sliding the blade in and out of Henning, digging into him in such a relentless way.

And what does that feel like?

To feel the metal, the pain, the thousand nerve endings screaming at the horror of being killed.

She had once gone eyeball to eyeball with a twelve-foot blue shark—and during those terrible moments below the aquamarine waters of Abaco, she briefly allowed herself to imagine what those teeth would feel like as they resolutely bit down.

Resolutely began to move, to grind, to tear.

The thought—one hundred feet under the water—kicked her adrenaline into overdrive. A near-giddy rush of chemicals flooded into her, and she braced for the shark attack that never came.

What happened to Henning must have been like that.

But no amount of adrenaline could save him.

No, the apartment was out of the question, though she wanted to get her notes.

And she thanked whatever bit of paranoid thinking told her to grab her small purse with her wallet, phone, and passport as she chased after Henning.

Never leave the house without a purse.

In this case her wallet with her credit cards, magic cards, might get her the hell out of here.

They'd leave a trail. But there was nothing she could do about it. Getting away was the important thing.

And more—based on what Henning had told her, what he had revealed—there really was only one place she could go.

The family she currently walked behind stopped at a door. They were home, Lisa guessed. The father of the group, wearing a short-sleeve beige shirt with bright orange stripes, looked back at her.

Lisa nodded, and passed them, aware that in a few seconds she would be by herself.

While the man fiddled with the key, Lisa looked around for somemore people she could attach herself to. . . .

But the alley was empty.

She was still a distance from Commonwealth Avenue.

The door opened, and the family streamed in while the watchful father stood by the door, his suspicious eyes locked on Lisa.

In seconds she'd be alone.

She took a breath, feeling the shallowness that a pack of cigarettes creates so well in one's lungs.

The door shut; the family gone.

Another breath, and then, she started running.

LISA exploded onto Commonwealth, cheeks flushed, coughing, bending over for a second as though she might keel over from her sprint.

But now she was surrounded by a moving sea of people.

Still—was that completely safe? She did a quick 360 to check the surging crowds flowing in both directions.

But all she saw was the amazing array of people that made up this island city . . . this island state. Malays and Indians, Chinese and Indonesians, all hurrying so fast.

But not him.

Not the man who'd killed Henning.

She let herself melt into one stream, heading toward the train terminal, towering over most of the people. She walked slowly, paying back the oxygen debt for her mad sprint, her thin shirt stuck tight to her, probably even looking provocative to any male eye that took a glance.

It didn't matter.

She felt just a bit safer.

Even as she knew that she would never ever really feel safe again.

And another recognition:

Her life had just turned incredibly strange; strange, dangerous, and—oddly for someone who lived so irresponsibly and freely—important.

And as her breathing struggled to return to normalcy . . . she kept walking and thinking.

14

A young woman slid into the crowded elevator clutching a stuffed attaché. As she rushed in, the attaché swung back and clipped David square in his left kneecap.

Nicely sending a brilliant spike of pain firing up his leg.

If the elevator hadn't been packed, he might have even moaned. The pain was *that* bad.

The doctors said that it should get better—eventually. Better, but not perfect.

It would never be perfect, never really be good enough so he could walk any faster than an amble, at least without excruciating pain. And the pain medicine they gave him—

He tried not to use it. He hated the fog it threw over his thinking.

That was one thing he knew he didn't like, and couldn't afford.

Get foggy, get careless—and he might have more than a bum kneecap to worry about.

The elevator stopped on the eleventh floor, current home to the SID—Special Investigative Division—at One Police Plaza. If the Puzzle Palace, as it was called, had a dead-letter office, a place where the unsolvable crimes ended up, then this was it.

He walked out.

"Yo, David—Biondi's looking for you. Got a late start?"

David nodded at the younger detective, some detective third grade who had only been with the division six months but immediately assumed that he was one of the crowd . . . part of the group overnight.

The kid didn't know yet that there were some major dues to pay to get into this club.

"Thanks, er . . ."

He didn't remember the kid's name, so he let the sentence trail off.

Biondi was waiting for him. Couldn't be anything too damn important. Ever since the Warehouse Murders—ever since David lost his partner to something that nobody really liked to talk about up here—there didn't seem to be a rush of urgency in *any* of the assignments David got.

He had entered a funny shadowland.

A place where, sure, he was still a detective, where he was still given cases to follow, things to look into . . .

But somehow he had become a brand-new one-person department in charge of flaky events.

He didn't see any of the other detectives smirk at him. But he sure could imagine that they did. And any detective who lost a partner . . . well, you entered a special realm whenever that happened.

The realm of cops who lose buddies.

Biondi was waiting. . . .

But David still walked to his corner desk, turned on his computer, looked at the Post-its from last week stuck on the monitor, and the new one telling David to "Come see me pronto!" on Biondi's personalized Post-its stationery, dead center on the screen.

From the desk of Captain Frank Biondi.

For a moment David wondered: Could something actually be . . . as they say . . . *up*?

Only one way to find out.

* * *

WHEN David walked into the surprisingly cramped office, he saw a chair waiting for him.

There was a time when he wouldn't have taken that chair, when he would have stood just to show how really okay he was.

But now he nodded at everyone, and walked over to the chair.

"Morning, Rodriguez. Car trouble?"

David looked at Biondi, thinking, *Man, what the hell do I have to do to get you to ease up?* Biondi wasn't there that night, didn't see the slaughterhouse, didn't shoot the maniac, then—

(And what was the killer really? What had David really seen that night?)

But everyone forgets when you've eaten that kind of meal. Yes, business goes on as usual, and it's all about being a cop, getting the job done, and don't give us any whacked-out stories about the shit you've seen.

"All's fine, Captain."

Now David looked around the room. He saw Izzy Karp, another homicide detective, an old-timer who had to be ready to retire, had to be way past the twenty-five-year mark. But David knew that Izzy was separated, and living with a doll who was half his age.

That kind of stuff got expensive.

And Izzy had a tired, worried look.

Who wouldn't?

Just don't tell me I have to partner with him, David thought. *Those tired eyes miss stuff, and they are absolutely crap at watching anyone's back.*

And in the corner, standing behind Biondi, a woman—what was she? Asian, Hawaiian?—not young, midthirties maybe? Someone David had never seen before, dressed in khakis and a crisp white shirt.

Interesting little setup, David thought.

Something definitely up *here.*

And only one way to find out what they wanted.

David didn't bother keeping the sarcasm out of his voice.

"So, how can I help you fine people this morning?"

Biondi looked at Izzy, then to the woman.

Then he tossed the front page of the *Daily News* at David.

The headline, SLAUGHTER IN THE MEATPACKING DISTRICT, was up to the *News*'s usual standards.

David grabbed the paper. "Yeah, I saw it. I assume you had guys all over this during the weekend."

Izzy coughed—back to smoking, David guessed. That and successive shot glasses of Seagram's at O'Reilly's near J&R Electronics. Around the corner from the Puzzle Palace.

"We were there within twenty minutes, David. The scene was a mess. The *News* got their pics from someone with a crap camera phone." Another cough.

David nodded, thinking, *Why are you telling me this?*

He glanced down at the photo. Didn't tell much.

Biondi spoke up. "We got more detailed pictures, and all the forensic stuff you might want."

You might want?

Am I getting a case? Is that what this is about?

Why wouldn't they leave it with Izzy? A bit ragged around the edges, true, but at least he didn't have a history of facing down killers who—

Go on, he thought. *You can admit it to yourself. No matter how you cut it, the facts were damn clear. You stopped a killer who could enter people's dreams. Yeah . . . and nobody wanted to talk about that.*

"You have pictures for me?"

Biondi pulled his rolling chair closer to the desk.

"Yes. But that's not all. Izzy here had been looking into— well, there's been other killings."

David tapped the paper.

"Like this?"

"Different places, different victims, but yes. We've been able to keep them quiet. Under the radar."

Izzy interrupted. "Not that I could see any pattern, David. I mean, me and the guys have not been able to find anything—"

Biondi interrupted. "Except—" He let the word hang there a moment. "Except . . . one."

"And what is that?"

And now the woman finally spoke.

"How they were killed, Detective. The way they were stabbed, the way the knife was used—absolutely identical."

David looked up at the woman.

He waited.

Biondi jigged his head in her direction.

"David, this is Detective Susan Kunokine. New to the SID. She has a medical background. Nearly finished her internship—"

And the woman spoke up. "Which is when I decided that I didn't want to be a doctor. Useful training, though. For this."

David smiled.

"I bet."

He tuned back to Biondi. "You said that there have been others . . . and no press coverage? Nice trick. How the hell did you keep it out of the papers?"

"A couple we could just keep the lid on. And one I called in a favor with the editors, a favor that is—obviously—about to expire." Biondi licked his lips. "But there's another thing, David, why I called you in, why I thought of you—"

Biondi looked at the others. He looked . . . almost nervous. *Something secret is about to emerge,* David thought. And what could be so secret, so strange, that it would make Biondi— who ran a tight ship with everyone's balls on the line— actually nervous?

But Detective Kunokine answered. "We have found the same pattern of murders in other places. Los Angeles, for one."

"You mean the killer was there, came here—and started up again?"

Biondi put up a hand.

"That's not all. Right, sure it was Los Angeles, but—you know everything's computerized now, all the data, every god-damn thing. It's all there. So it found these unsolved killings. And they're kind of famous."

"Yeah?"

"And it's not just that they were in L.A., David. They took place"—a big breath—"sixty goddamn years ago."

Full stop, while he looked David in the eye.

And in that moment, David knew why this bit of juicy business had come to his desk.

Why it had come to him.

Ever since the Warehouse Murders, anything odd drifted over to his corner, a Sargasso Sea of weird disappearances and strange killings. Most easily resolved or, in some cases, completely irresolvable—nobody seemed to care much.

But all with their odd touches.

David grinned. "Nice. Sixty years. But that's—"

"Impossible?" Biondi said. He grinned, not at the humor of it but from something else, something darker. "Right, totally fuckin' impossible. But there you are. Sixty years ago."

Detective Kunokine scooped up an envelope from the table.

"We have pictures here. Of course the forensics back then were terrible. But all the illustrations, the entry wounds, the ligature—"

"Ligature? Some of these people were tied up?"

Biondi nodded. "Yes, sorry. Thought I mentioned it. Not all of them. But some."

"The knife entry wounds, though—all the same," Kunokine said.

"A copycat?"

Biondi looked up at David.

"Could be. Might make sense."

David shook his head.

"But what else could it be?"

And no one answered that question.

What the fuck else could it be?

And now both the question and its answer were David's baby.

He looked at Kunokine. He could anticipate the next card to fall in this cleverly managed game of poker.

"Detective Kunokine is new here, David. But she was an

amazing street cop and precinct detective. And she knows more about what this guy is doing with a blade than anyone else I could give you."

A cough from Izzy.

"I can give you all the stuff I got so far, Dave—"

Which will be worth absolute shit, David thought.

So we're partners, he thought, looking at the woman. *What a pair,* he thought. *Me, with a leg that is barely functional, and this woman who—forgetting forensics—still seems mighty wet behind the ears.*

But she was obviously smart.

She knew her knife wounds.

And he thought, *What the hell— it's as good a way to start a Monday as any.*

He smiled at Biondi.

"I guess . . . we'd better get started."

And grabbing the arm of the ancient wooden office chair, David stood up, and started gathering the assorted files and envelopes that he guessed wouldn't tell him much at all.

15

JOANN Gully stubbed her cigarette out in what had to be an ancient beanbag ashtray on her desk. Then, a wisp of smoke still streaming from the butt, she opened a drawer and put the ashtray in it.

It was, of course, illegal to smoke in the office.

But it would take more than a Bloomberg law to get the editor of the paper to quit smoking before she finally left the world of publishing and other less-colorful characters took over.

She looked up at Mari.

"Not much I can do here, Mari. Hands tied, and all that."

"I don't get it. There's a story; I'm a good fit—why can't I have it?"

Gully turned on her swivel chair and looked out the window. She was backed by a row of nondescript high-rise office buildings with one gleaming exception. The top of the Chrysler Building, the brilliant spear, towering over them all.

Must be part of the reason you wanted a job like hers—to get this office, this view, to feel that you have all New York before you.

"It's complicated."

"What's complicated?" Mari said. "A girl is killed, you run the story on the cover, pictures, and—"

Gully turned back. "You are making this harder than it need be, you know? Just . . . let it go."

Mari took a breath.

Then—

"No. Tell me why. I've put my . . . life on the line for this paper. You know that."

It was a card she knew she could play. Gully owed her, the paper owed her—and though Gully had only given her insignificant stories lately, she knew she could turn the screws.

"God, you are a tough one. Be easier to just fire you."

"But you won't do that."

In Gully's eyes, Mari could see that she took no risk in saying that.

"No, I won't." A bit of a smile. "You are too good. Almost as good as I used to be." A grin. "Real persistent. Okay—I will lay it out for you."

Gully got up and went to a stand of file drawers. She turned a key, and the lock on one tray popped out. She slid it open and pulled out a plastic folder, held tight by a drawstring.

She turned back to Mari, who instinctively held out her hand.

But Gully shook her head. "No. I am not . . . giving this to you. I am telling you what is inside. Telling you what's really happening here. As much as I know."

She sat back down, her hands firmly placed on the folder.

"That girl, killed on Norfolk—well, she wasn't the first."

Mari leaned closer.

"And the others?"

"In here. Some reported as disappearances, others down as random unsolved murders. But the police don't doubt it was the same person. So the nice people at One Police Plaza asked me to sit on the details. People just don't disappear—but information can be hidden. All the city editors agreed, reporters moved to other stories, until—well, I guess this folder is the only place where it comes together."

"So there's a killer—a serial murderer out there—and the paper is not covering it?"

"Pretty much. It improves their chances of finding whoever it is, of sifting out the random killings. Call it being a good citizen. And maybe a crappy editor. But I have no choice."

"But then—what happened that you ran Sunday's story, with pictures, details?"

Gully laughed, a phlegmy sound that turned into a hacking wheeze.

"Details? Take a look again, Mari. There are no 'details' in that story save where the girl was found and what happened to her. And we ran the story, like every other paper, because it was all over the Internet, the pictures, everything, thanks to whatever lucky drunk guy found the butchered body."

Mari nodded.

It made sense—everything Gully was saying. And yet, seeing that folder . . . something about it made her feel chilled.

Chilled in a way she hadn't been since—

(Since that night.)

"So you see, Mari, I'd give it to you if I could. I can't, and that's that. Forget all about it. Look for some nice, safe story. Lost puppies found, the new subway tunnel, the latest plans to build goddamn something at One World Trade Center besides political bullshit. *Anything*. Pick of the litter. As you say, we owe you."

But Mari was only half listening.

That chill she felt did more than scare her. It suddenly had her thinking, planning—and she knew that she wouldn't let this go that easily.

"Okay. Hold on a sec."

"Yeah?"

"Last time you let me run with that story, knowing you couldn't publish anything until it was all over."

"And that worked out real well, right?"

"It did." Mari realized that she said the words too forcefully. "I mean, I had the story that no one else had, and then you finally could publish it."

"Except you were in the center of it. Nearly killed. Planning the same thing this time?"

Mari stopped.

Planning the same thing this time . . .

Of course she wasn't. But was that . . . possibility somehow driving her? To become part of the story rather than just report it? The strange fear somehow strangely attractive?

"No. But—"

"You still with that detective?"

"Um, yes."

"You don't seem too sure."

"I am. I mean, we hit some bumps, but it should—"

Gully stood up and took the file back to the cabinet. She tossed it in, closed the drawer, and pressed home the lock.

"You know, there isn't much in that folder, Mari. Either way, I can't tell you what's there or show you any of it. But how about this . . . since you seem to want this so much—"

"I do."

"You get your detective, Rodriguez, to work with you. One of my spies says it's going to go to him anyway. You see what you find, do all that stuff that good street reporters do. We print nothing until we can—and when we do, the story is all yours. How's that sound?"

It sounded impossible, but Mari wasn't going to back off now.

"Great. Fair enough. At least I have one victim to work with—"

"And whatever you can wheedle out of your Detective Rodriguez. Use your feminine wiles. Used to work for me, kiddo."

Another cough-filled laugh. Mari found it hard to imagine Gully with anything closely resembling female wiles.

But she had seen pictures of Gully when she was a young desk reporter, the wavy, puffed-up seventies hair, sparkling eyes, and—in the words of today—she looked hot.

On the other hand, Mari would have to build some bridges with David if anything was to happen.

And what if he didn't have anything to do with the case?

That . . . seemed unlikely.

He had become the department's go-to guy for the NYPD's

weird tales. And now, even knowing so little about this, Mari could see this one was definitely weird.

She stood up.

"Thanks, Joann."

Gully nodded, a small smile at the corners of her wrinkled lips.

"Don't thank me yet. Let's see where all this takes you first, okay? Then—maybe a nice bottle of gin for your soon-to-be-retired editor."

"Deal."

And Mari turned and left the office, the smell of Marlboro clinging to her clothes.

16

LISA looked up at the departure monitor above the Singapore Airlines ticketing counter.

A young female agent with a swirling yellow and purple scarf carefully arranged around her neck waited patiently for her.

What must I look like? Lisa thought.

She had spent the night in an all-night cafe near the train station, waiting until the first light of dawn.

Then she grabbed a cab to Singapore's Changi Airport, wondering all the time if her paranoia had slipped out of control.

I'm a scientist, she told herself. Amazing how quickly logic could go out the window, vanish in the face of something as primal as fear.

When she got to the airport, yellow-suited cleaners were spraying water on the walkways outside the main terminal.

Singapore was nothing if not clean.

They also did a great job of hiding the fact that it was a police state.

Finally, the agent at the counter spoke, her voice small, sweet . . . birdlike in its gentle trill.

"Excuse me—but may I help you with something?"

Lisa nodded. "Yes. I wonder—when's the latest I can

purchase a ticket . . . on the next New York flight—and still get on the plane?"

The agent's smile didn't fade, but her eyes seemed to widen. A strange question, and people at the airport were probably well trained to take note of strange questions. Throw in the fact that Lisa needed a shower, her face washed, the smell of sweat scraped off her—

"Excuse me," the agent said again. "But you need to know—?"

Lisa smiled. "I'm, er, trying to plan. So I was wondering . . . when would be the latest that I could purchase a ticket—say, on that 9:30 A.M. flight—and still be able to board."

The agent nodded, radiating a false sense of *oh, now I got you.*

When in fact the woman probably had little alarms going off.

Lisa looked around for a moment. She saw some Singapore police walking around, machine guns slung over their shoulders. Not so many that you might become nervous.

But still there.

Nice men armed with submachine guns. Find them in every airport.

But in a place like Singapore . . . any unusual requests could elicit unusual requests back.

Would you mind coming with us?

She knew that if she had told anyone about what she witnessed, she'd be stuck in Singapore for a long time.

And that couldn't happen.

Not after what Henning had told her, what he had died to tell her.

The young agent was joined now with another woman, older, dressed in the same impeccable way, also with a warm, inviting smile.

But there was no question that Lisa's request had bumped things up to some supervisory level.

"Good morning," the supervisor said.

Lisa nodded. "Good morning to you."

"Your question . . . about flying with us—"

The supervisor was too polite to say that she didn't understand the question. Or rather, she did understand it, and such a question was a cause for alarm.

"Yes. I am waiting to see if I need to be in New York as soon as possible." Lisa dangled her BlackBerry at them. They nodded as if the supercharged cell phone explained all. "So— I wanted to know the latest I could actually get a ticket and still board."

Lisa risked a quick glance around, a quick check to see if someone was watching her and if all this planning was useless. But no one seemed to take notice of her.

The supervisor nodded, and she moved into position in front of the terminal, gently easing the younger agent out of the way.

"I will check for you, miss."

The sound of fingers tapping keys.

To the right, Lisa saw the two guards—more like soldiers— looking at the people in line, staring at others streaming toward departure gates.

The supervisor nodded at the screen as if in a dialogue with it.

Then, after what seemed an excruciatingly long time—

"Yes, you want the 9:30 nonstop to . . . Newark?"

Lisa nodded, then: "Yes."

"That boards at 8:30. Which is an hour from now, yes? Boarding closes twenty-five minutes before takeoff. So you would have to have your ticket, and any luggage, then clear security—"

"I have no luggage."

Maybe the wrong thing to say, Lisa thought. *Fly halfway around the world with no luggage.*

At least it should reassure them that I don't have any bombs or box-cutters hidden.

"No luggage," the woman repeated. "Then, if you have your ticket by 7:45 A.M. and you are at the gate by 8:05, then—"

The supervisor looked up from the screen.

"Then you should have no problem."

Lisa smiled. "So 7:45 A.M.? Thank you. Now I, er, just got to check if I have to go to New York."

Both of the women nodded as Lisa stepped away from the ticket counter, ignoring the stares of the other customers behind her who obviously had decided she had taken way too long at the counter.

LISA looked at the clock, wishing she could light up here.

Probably a capital offense. Blindfolds at dawn.

Her idea had been simple. Keep her credit card information out of the system for as long as possible. Buy the ticket at the last minute, and leave the smallest amount of time for that information to pop up anywhere.

And while she waited, she bought a clean blouse from a store, and some basic toiletries to use before boarding. She then slid into a handicapped toilet, and washed and changed . . . until she felt that whoever was lucky enough to sit next to her wouldn't be completely grossed out.

Then she found an electronics store selling digital cameras, iPods, and portable DVD players. Her BlackBerry battery was half gone. And the charger was back at her room.

But though the electronics store didn't have a charger, they steered her to a travel store that sold a universal charger. Lisa planted herself by an outlet and let her BlackBerry soak up some needed juice.

She watched the time . . .

7:15. She bought two yellow pads and a pen.

7:25. Feeling hungry, she picked up a baguette from an Upper Crust franchise—mozzarella and tomato on fresh-baked bread, washed down with a small bottle of OJ.

Had anything tasted so good?

7:35. Plugged in the BlackBerry for ten more minutes of juice while she ate. If she was lucky, she'd have one of Singapore Airlines' new planes that came with an outlet under the seat.

Then—

7:45.

She returned to the ticket counter, hopefully looking fresher in her new pink top and with a washed face.

The young woman nodded at her, but acted as though this was their first exchange.

"Yes, may I help you?"

"A ticket to Newark, please. The 9:30 flight."

Another nod. "Round trip or—"

"Sure, round trip."

Though Lisa doubted she'd be back. At least for a while. "Next Sunday," she added.

Best to give the illusion that a return was planned.

The agent looked up. "Any luggage?"

The agent definitely didn't remember her. Or maybe was just being polite. Lisa shook her head. "No luggage."

She slid the credit card and passport to the agent. The woman looked at it carefully, flipping through pages filled with stamps from around the world. Speeches, seminars, research trips, diving in Hawaii, Sharm el Sheikh, Abaco . . .

Lisa looked at the clock heading close toward the 8:00 A.M. mark.

Then—the sound of a boarding pass being spit out.

"Gate C-5," the agent said.

Lisa took the boarding pass. She looked around for the sign pointing to departures. Wondering—

Had she cut it too close? Security could eat up precious minutes.

The agent saw her craning her neck. "That way, please . . . and now. You must hurry."

"Thanks."

I know I do. . . .

And Lisa ran toward the departure area, security, and the plane that would take her—

Well, for someone who was an expert in the great unknowns of the physical universe, she realized that this flight was about to take her into something way beyond any unknown she had ever researched.

The line at security was thin, and she sailed through the electronic surveillance scanner, just slipping her BlackBerry into a tray.

Something to be said for traveling light.

A plane trip into the unknown, maybe the unknowable.

A trip into something ancient, dark, deadly—

The experience of my fucking lifetime, she thought.

I just hope—

(Because . . . I sure don't believe in prayer.)

—that I survive.

Then, once through security, she bolted for Gate C-5.

17

MARI made the call standing outside the *News* building, standing a dozen feet from the corner of the building used by the unrehabilitated smokers, those who kept at their cigarettes as though there might be only one thing that would pry them away.

Daring death to make them stop sucking in the smoke.

She heard the cell phone she called ring twice, then go automatically to message.

Too damn common in this city. No matter who supplied your signal, a call could vanish inside any of the mammoth stone office buildings. And all signals vanished completely while in the subway.

London had installed relays so their Underground got cell phone service.

Never happen here, she guessed.

"Please leave a message."

David didn't waste any time on his message. Blunt and to the point.

Mari took a breath. "David, I think we should talk. About us, of course. I mean—the shit I gave you. Sorry, I mean—"

She always winced when she cursed. But Mari grew up in a house of brothers who talked like drunken sailors, and the editorial room of the *Daily News* retained a healthy respect for the rough talk from the days when it was a good old boys' club.

"Yeah—we need to talk. But also, I'm working on something that I figure . . . well, I'm guessing it's on your agenda. I don't have anything to offer this time. Not yet. But—"

A beep.

Damn, what an incoherent message. What was she saying to him? She could use his help on this story, or—

She thought of calling back, but she imagined that she'd make a mess of it again.

She debated going back into the building.

Gully gave her nothing from the secret file—but there was no reason Mari couldn't dig around for stuff that was published.

Mari went back into the building, the sky behind her beginning to darken from a light blue to the azure of an early fall twilight.

ELAINA Suro leaned over the main pool of the Coney Island Aquarium. All she had to do was splash the water lightly, and Susie was there.

Susie, the Aquarium's oldest dolphin, popping up her head, bottle nose pointing to the sky, chirping away like an oversized water bird.

"Hey, girl, how are you?"

But she could look at the dolphin's eyes, filmy, lined with red, and know that despite Susie's quick response, she still hadn't responded to the antibiotics. The other dolphins seemed to be avoiding her.

Classic behavior.

As if they sense something.

Not a good sign.

Elaina patted Susie's nose. "Still not good, hmm, girl?" She reached behind her and grabbed a small codfish and brought it close. Susie took it between her small serrated teeth—but then did nothing with it. No kicking back the head to send it slithering to the back of her throat.

How old was she? Too old—older than maybe any dolphin in captivity in North America. Maybe she just wasn't strong enough to fight off the infections that inevitably swirled in the seawater, the small bugs and parasites that attacked any creature that lived in a submerged environment 24/7.

Susie didn't let go of the fish—almost as if she didn't want to let Elaina see that she just didn't have the will to eat it.

Then—in a moment that broke Elaina's heart—she reached out and took the fish back . . . and whispered . . .

"Good . . . girl."

Another pat to Susie's nose, and Elaina stood up.

The sun had vanished behind the apartment buildings, and the sky above—a beautiful blue September sky, forever to be a special kind of late summer sky for New Yorkers at least— had deepened to a royal blue.

She felt a hand on her shoulder.

"You should go home, Elaina. You can check her tomorrow . . . as early as you want. But for now—"

Elaina turned to the director of the Aquarium, Dr. Derrick Kemp, a bald, bespectacled man who looked more like a fussy accountant than a respected oceanographer, a man who had explored more of the Atlantic Ridge up close and personal than anyone else in the world.

"I know. Just—she looks so bad."

Dr. Kemp nodded. "Yes. And I'm not sure what we're doing is helping."

"It isn't."

Kemp took a breath. "It's age, Elaina. She's old. Susie isn't a kid anymore. Just doesn't have the strength."

Elaina shook her head. They had had this discussion before. "So I just forget about it? Let her slip away?"

Kemp said nothing. The answer—as always—clear, obvious. Then:

"But for tonight, there's nothing you can do. Get home. Get rest. Get here as early as you want in the morning. But you're no good to Susie or any of the rest of them if you're completely exhausted."

"Yeah," Elaina said, not bothering to hide the sound of resignation in her voice.

"Please?" Kemp added.

And Elaina nodded, and walked away from the pool. On some days Susie would chirp to her as she left, loud shrieking chirps of good-bye.

But not today.

"WOULD you like another . . . gin and tonic?"

The Singapore Airlines attendant seemed to have noticed that Lisa's glass had suddenly become empty.

She'd have to watch the alcohol if she was to get all these notes straight.

Could she afford another g and t?

Hell, yeah.

"Sure."

Though what she really could use was a cigarette. Thirteen hours was a long stretch for her. Time to quit?

Funny how many times she'd get asked how could someone who was so smart, who knew so much—how could she smoke?

She had a pat answer for that one.

I smoke the killer weed because, you see . . . I do know a lot.

But when she woke up with that foul taste in her mouth, it was easy to resolve that the time had come to give it up.

In fact, in some alternate universe among the . . . millions, maybe she already had.

She looked down at her pad, having already filled a half-dozen sheets.

What else? she thought. She had to capture everything Henning had said before some of it started fading, slipping away.

She flipped back a page to the simple time line she had

drawn. She looked at the dot that represented today, 2007. Then to the other dots with notes attached, tied to the different events mentioned by Henning.

Events, places . . .

1974, Chicago. Los Angeles, 1947. Berlin, 1933. And 1927, aboard the *Mauritania* somewhere in the North Atlantic.

Then, the dots spreading out until she hit a big one. Something key.

1888, London.

She let her finger rest there. What that dot represented— that alone was enough to send chills racing up and down her spine.

It was stupid, crazy . . . absolutely impossible.

And yet—at the same time—it made perfect sense.

Perfect sense, she thought.

Then she let her fingers trail through the other dots, sparse now, skipping hundreds of years, a thousand, until her time line ended at some approximate time thousands of years before Christ.

Not a precise date. An estimate, give or take a hundred, or a thousand.

Before Christ.

Before nearly everything.

We were barely out of the caves, barely had some mastery of farming, some rules, the beginning of communication, a simple society, money, people living together, for trade, for . . . protection.

The attendant came back.

In fact, she must have been standing beside her for a few minutes, hovering, while Lisa was lost to her squiggly line.

Lisa looked up.

"Your drink, miss."

Lisa smiled and took the plastic glass topped with a neat crescent of lime.

"Thank you."

"You're very welcome."

So polite on this airline. Must be an order from the police state. You better be nice to people who fly our airline, or it's back to the rice paddies with you.

She flipped back to a clean page of the yellow pad.

Flipping past the list of names. That had been the hard part. Did she remember them correctly? Did she get any of them wrong? If all this was true, she'd need these allies and fast.

There was an opportunity here.

She thought—for some reason—of the sea.

Opportunity for one creature, and danger for another.

Like when a crab molts and has to scurry around with a soft shell so easy to bite through. Or a hermit crab who has to jettison its shell, and find another pronto before it's snatched up by something hungry.

An opportunity here . . .

If I don't screw it up.

And on the blank page, Lisa now started writing down an account of her meeting with Henning in prose. She wasn't the best writer—without her amazing editor, her physics books would have been nearly incomprehensible.

But if anything ever happened to her, these next pages might be the only thing that explained what happened to Henning on that Singapore backstreet, what happened to Lisa herself . . . and what was going to happen.

If it wasn't stopped now.

During this period of—

Opportunity.

She began writing, as though for a stranger's eyes.

My name is Dr. Lisa Griffino. . . .

MARI dug in her purse, looking for her wallet with the cab door open.

Her digging sent out a spray of keys and a Tic Tac box falling to the curbside of Rivington and Ludlow.

"Shit," she said while the driver, wearing a puffy woven hat that made him look like the captain of the invading mushroom people, waited . . . probably not so patiently.

She found her fat red wallet, an object filled with every discount card, credit card, bank receipt, and semi-important slip of paper that had entered Mari's life in the past year.

She zipped open the main vault—the billfold—and pulled out a twenty.

"Um, just give me five back." The driver gave his head a small shake, not pleased. And Mari realized that she did the tip math wrong.

"Oh, I mean . . . no, just three. Yeah, three dollars."

The driver handed her three bedraggled-looking bills. Mari took them, and then the cab sped away.

She had wanted to get here just at sunset, figuring that whatever work the police were doing at the site would be done. She could see it . . . the place where the killing took place. Maybe walk to the bar on Rivington, at the hotel, where the girl had been partying.

Talk to people there—

But the traffic had sucked, and now the sun had already slipped below the craggy apartment cliffs of New Jersey, slipping out to the west, to the other coast . . . just like in that famous *New Yorker* cover where the USA is just New York and L.A., with a whole lot of nothing in between.

She walked down to Norfolk Street, and turned left. She saw the yellow tape stretching out to two crooked poles the police had placed on the sidewalk.

But there was no cop on duty.

That was good.

Means that they had done whatever they were going to do here.

She could get as close as she wanted.

Not that it would tell her much.

It wouldn't be like when she first saw the handiwork of the Dream Killer, his subterranean room set up like a torture chamber. That said . . . volumes.

This would just be a stretch of pavement, stained a bit, but revealing nothing.

But as she got closer—

She saw that she was quite wrong about that.

18

MARI stopped about twenty feet away from the scene.

The yellow police tape had lost the shimmery brightness, now a muted color in the twilight.

She tried to imagine what it was like—

To walk down the street, streetlights spaced to form milky pools that should have provided safety. No lights were out that night. So the entire sidewalk should have been lit, should have looked safe.

But—

Mari turned and looked to the left. A building with a narrow loading dock; no sign indicating what was to be loaded, what product was made here or arrived here.

Just a narrow dock with a small platform.

But the hulking building also had a zigzagging fire escape cutting back and forth on its front and, beside the platform, a recessed doorway.

One might say . . . perfectly recessed.

Like an animal, someone could lurk there, waiting.

And while waiting, what would be going on? Had the killer seen the prey coming, planned this spot, made it all ready for the attack? Was his heart racing, thumping in his chest, as the prey came close?

The photos showed the victim's pointy-toed stilettos.

There would have been an eerie shoe sound as she walked closer. Click-clack, click-clack, unaware that just outside the pool of light, that milky light on the sidewalk, there was a hidey-hole with a nasty surprise.

Did she try to run?

Or—

Was she lured?

The very word . . . ominous.

Lured . . .

Had the predator, the human monster, somehow lured her closer? Like the events in an old fairy tale, tricking the tipsy young girl, flush from the trendy cocktails and the chatter and buzz of one of New York's newest hot spots. Had she some-how been made to stop, then step closer?

That's right. This way. Over here, young girl. See what I have for you, see what I found, see, see—

Until—

Mari licked her lips, her imagination running at full speed, making the event come to life.

Until—the trap was sprung, and she was caught.

And what does that feel like?

But Mari knew that.

She had been caught. She knew very well.

The sun was well gone behind the stone hills, behind the apartments of New Jersey. A breeze blew from the west, from the river, making prickly gooseflesh sprout on her arm. At least—she thought it was the wind.

To be caught.

To first struggle, then realize that all struggle is hopeless. And your mind, now an animal thing, searches for a way out, some hidden exit. There must be an exit, must be a way to es-cape, until . . . like some dark black sopping wet chunk of sackcloth, it falls over you, smothering all hope.

There is no exit.

There is no escape.

And now you have only one thing to look at, to think about.

What will happen next?

Thoughts that you wish you could banish.

But the mind, this very human brain, simply doesn't work that way.

That's exactly where it goes, and there is nothing you can do about it.

Mari took a breath, and now, with the yellow tape only meters away, she took some more steps . . . right up to the spot.

JULIO, one of the night crew at the Aquarium, part custodian, part watchman, and—as he was quick to remind everyone— someday to be just like them . . . *a real oceanographer* . . .

—came into Elaina's office.

"What, Elaina? Still here?"

Elaina, sitting at her computer screen, turned and nodded.

"Yeah, Julio. Just checking on some things—"

Julio nodded. "You should go home. Get here early, leave late. Not much of a life, Elaina."

When he first arrived, Julio spoke Spanish to her and addressed her as Doctor.

But then Elaina took the man aside, not knowing anything about him, what country he was from, or whether he was legal or illegal. But she told him—

"Speak *English*. It's the way you will get better. And if you plan on staying here, I'm Elaina. I'll need your help in this place—so Elaina will be fine."

Of course, she was alert to his misreading of her advice, to his taking it as an opening to some stupid machismo flirting.

But Julio was smart. He heard her message, and appreciated it.

Her own father had been illegal, a refugee from the DR— the Dominican Republic. Some people here treated him well, some like dirt, but he worked hard to make sure Elaina could reap all the benefits of this country.

The opportunity that—even in these days—still held true.

Julio picked up her small trash can. "I think—you are worried abut Susie."

Elaina nodded. "Yes. Guess I am. But I didn't get to check some things I should do. Look, I'll be out of here in fifteen minutes; then it will be nice and quiet."

Julio laughed. "Never quiet at night here. The whales—they like to talk to the stars. And to me too!" He laughed. "So noisy."

She also knew that Julio would throw some of the cetaceans a fish, so that they knew they had an ally in the night. He had watched the staff feed the whales, and as long as he kept it to a fish or two, it was okay.

Maybe Julio's kids will grow up to work here.

Or do some other thing that would have been unthinkable for them in Guatemala.

"Good. See you tomorrow then," Elaina said.

"You bet."

She turned back to the screen.

With her worrying over Susie, she had neglected looking at the project.

That's what she called it: *the project.*

The Scripps-Howard Institute had given her a hefty grant based on some early intriguing data. But they would like a real report before too much more time went on.

But what did her data show?

She flipped through the screens, showing each dolphin, with a reading of their brain activity over a weeklong period.

And while it was all very interesting, she didn't quite understand what she was seeing.

Except—the dolphin brain showed none of the anatomical structural characteristics of more evolved brains such as those of primates. But the strange thing was that the regions of the dolphin neocortex could be differentiated by electrophysiological methods. In fact, they were arranged in very much the same order as in any common hypothetical ancestor of the higher mammals.

Their memory and intelligence worked differently. But

there were secrets in the dolphin brain, areas that so far defied mapping or understanding, sections where we didn't know what they did.

And if there was something secret there, her proposal was to uncover that secret. Her proposal argued that much of what dolphins do, whether it was communicate, navigate, learn, had something to do with this black hole in the middle of their memory center, their neocortex.

Her proposal was to see what triggered activity there, and to get a clue to what the dolphin still hid inside its brain.

And this question: How ancient was that secret?

How far back in evolution does that memory "black hole," this uncharted area, really go?

She took a breath. She didn't know much about it now. But she knew it was important. And communicating with other scientists around the world, she hoped that she might be close to a breakthrough.

Might be . . .

If she wasn't so distracted by poor Susie.

Stupid, she thought . . . to get attached. Not a very good detached scientist.

She stood up, leaving the screen on.

Maybe she'd come back in the A.M. and something would leap off the screen to suggest other possibilities, other theories.

In the meantime, e-mail would flow into her in-box all evening from supportive (but equally confused) colleagues around the world.

She grabbed her navy backpack, stuffed a spiral notebook into it and a half-finished bottle of water.

And then Elaina turned and left her office, sailing out to the now dark Coney Island evening.

19

MARI let her hand touch the tape. Not that the tape could hold her or anyone back.

But the tape outlined where it all happened. The pavement directly in front of her wasn't stained. But just to her left, she saw the now brownish-red stain, looking like the dried spill from ice cream, coloring the speckled stone of the sidewalk.

She tried to imagine the position of the body when they took the pictures, somebody wandering by with their camera phone and seeing this—

Stepping back probably. But then thinking—

Shit . . . gotta take a picture of this.

The woman's legs curled back, head resting right at the door.

Even now the shadows had deepened so the small alcove had little light, the black door, the stone already turning into the hidey-hole that led to the girl's death.

Mari felt her stomach tighten, and she was glad that it had been hours since she had eaten anything.

"Thought you'd be here . . ."

She spun around.

And there was David.

* * *

ELAINA walked down the hallway, past the row of tanks holding crustaceans from every ocean in the world, all perfectly maintained for temperature, pressure, and salinity.

She saw Otto look at her as she walked by.

Otto. A Bathynomus Isopod Giganticus, a giant three-foot-long albino crustacean dragged from the bottom of the ocean, miles deep. A completely new species found two decades ago, looking like it had come from Venus.

So alien and weird, no matter how many times she looked at it. Your worst nightmare of a cockroach, only it was the size of a small dog and it lived miles deep.

Otto had thrived, living quietly, eating a variety of earth foods, though he was five miles above his home environment.

And he proved something to all the oceanographers in the world, at least the ones who hadn't accepted it yet.

This idea: We know only a fraction of the creatures in the sea.

We don't have a clue what waits for us down there.

Elaina pushed opened the doors that led to the main entrance hall, past the giant mural of the sea showing a somewhat dated family tree of the creatures that fill the oceans.

If only they could get some money, it would be a great idea to rip that off the wall.

She walked past a pair of cleaning women, twinlike ladies who smiled and nodded.

"Buenas noches," Elaina said.

And then back: *"Buenas noches, señorita."*

Señorita. Another thing that should be addressed. My social life, or lack of it.

Elaina pushed open the door, out to the cooling night air of Coney and the sea.

Summer has somehow slipped away.

So surprisingly . . .

And already it was dark.

"DAVID—"

"Can't stay away from crime scenes?"

Mari saw the Asian woman next to David looking her up and down.

"You have business here, miss?"

Business.

Mari started to answer.

But David turned to the woman. "Detective Kunokine, meet Mari Kinsella. The reporter." He waited a beat, searching. Then: "A good friend."

Mari saw a light go on in David's partner's eyes.

The reporter. Oh, *that* one. Who nearly got killed. With you. With the others.

The woman seemed to chill a bit.

"Okay. Yeah."

"Can I have a few words?" he said to Kunokine.

David's new partner nodded, and she walked back to a car, whipping out her cell phone.

Then David moved closer to Mari.

"So—of all the gin joints in town—"

Mari smiled. God, how she loved how he could just say something and take the weight off. *Note to self,* Mari thought, *stop being such a drama queen.*

"My editor gave me the story."

"How nice of her. And is there a story?"

Mari nodded at the dried blood pool. "You tell me, David."

"I wish I could. But I am afraid—"

Mari reached out and touched his arm. "I know. I mean—I know you can't say *anything*. The editor told me that there are others—"

"Oh, she did, did she?"

"Don't worry. We're not going to do anything with them."

"Nice to hear that you and your editor are going to act like good responsible citizens."

A beat.

"But this—it's horrible. Why did they give this to you?"

"You mean why did they give me a brutal killing when I'm supposed to only get all the wacko cases?"

"I didn't say that."

And now he smiled. "I know you didn't. I did. All I can say . . . for now, is that Biondi thought it a good fit."

Kunokine called out to David.

"About done there, David?"

He turned and nodded.

"Just a minute." Then back to Mari. "Look, I—"

But Mari grabbed his wrist again.

"Stop. No apology from you. I was the jerk. So jealous. I can be pathetic."

Another grin. "You're beautiful when you're pathetic."

Mari smiled back. And waited. Thinking:

Would he just turn, sail away . . . the sweet moment somehow fading?

But instead—

"Hey, after I get back . . . why don't we meet for a drink. Maybe combine some business with it."

"What do you mean?"

"The Hotel on Rivington. Right down the street. Expensive bar, but we can have a drink, talk to bar staff. It's where the victim was last seen. Do some off-duty nosing around. Then we can put any apologies behind us. How's that sound?"

Mari smiled. "I think it sounds great."

"One hour. Meet you there."

Then David turned and walked back to the dark gray unmarked car, still hobbling, the man who saved her life and who—right now—she knew she loved more than anyone she had ever loved in her life.

THE earplugs reduced the roar of the giant twin jet engines to a low-level rumble, almost soothing.

And Lisa's eyeshade blocked out what light was in the cabin for the long night crossing the Pacific.

She should have known that she would have dreams.

After everything that had happened, dreams and nightmares would be eagerly waiting to invade her sleeping mind.

And there was this: Dr. Lisa Griffino was a vivid dreamer.

She could move and act in her dreams the way most people did in real life, totally aware that she was in a dream and yet capable of making decisions, and seeing where those decisions took her.

Playing with dreams.

Like now . . . standing on a dark New York street. Wind whipped a newspaper into a frenzied dance in the middle of the street. A misty night, the streetlights had a gassy glow around them, nearly like fluorescent lights. Lisa felt that same wind whip at her coat, a simple Burberry raincoat, kicking up the hem, as if trying to sneakily make it fly up, and then away.

She stood alone.

The dark, nearly foggy street. No cars. No people. Of course, this is the way it would be in the nightmare.

Lisa could act. A vivid dreamer, remember. It was all under her control.

Save one aspect . . . she could not end it.

No, that last bit of control, which some dreamers do in fact possess, was not allowed her.

She could think, decide, move, act, but not end it.

Alone. On the street.

When she heard the cry. A cry from—

She had heard *something* like that before.

A wail from a Wagner opera, a low guttural sound manufactured by a burly soprano trying to capture some special agony, so false, so theatrical.

But this wail was none of those things.

This wail was real, the agony no playacting. The only human sound here, and it came from—

(The building right next to her.)

She looked at a door, open about an inch, a pale light inside. The sound again, but now shallower, feebler.

She knew, of course, what this dream was about.

Not every day you watch someone get murdered.

That guarantees you some special nightmares.

She could walk on.

Down the street to see what next this nightmare might

manufacture for her. But the street was empty, a lonely stretch of a foggy New York street, and—

No.

She looked at this street, the cobblestones, then at the lamps.

Not electric at all.

Gas. Gas lamps. And when she looked around, she could see it wasn't New York at all.

A European city. But with no street signs nearby, hard to tell what city.

But if there were people here, the men would surely be in top hats, the women wearing bustles, and the night filled with the clopping sound of hooves, horses pulling carriages.

The moaning wail again, lower, fading, time running out.

Lisa could decide, could act; she turned to the door and walked in.

Inside, a wooden stairway leading up.

Pale gas lamps on the wall giving just enough light to show the splintery steps leading up. Then those stairs turned at a small landing and went in the other direction.

Lisa put a hand on the wall, feeling the wood, painted so many times, her hand sliding smoothly as she took step after step.

Until she got to the top of the stairs.

And at the top, another closed door, one that might lead to a bedroom. It wasn't open. Wasn't inviting her. So she turned and walked back down.

(That is, if "down" still existed. Lisa could decide on actions, but the nightmare had no rules that made it play fair. The whole staircase could simply vanish, an exit out of the house simply disappear. Since she had entered it, the building could now turn into some kind of dream trap.)

She grabbed the doorknob, twisted it, and pushed open the door, leading out of the dream.

20

THE screech of the door was suddenly matched with now the faintest of moans. What surely had to be a last moan, a final, fatal moan.

And she entered—a room.

Looking like a dimly lit butcher's shop, with just one item on offer, the item on the floor, the object still *twitching* on the floor.

Dressed in layers of cheap sateen, a bodice open, white flesh smeared in red, and other openings exposing parts of the body, like a massively difficult operation gone horribly wrong.

The brown wood floor . . . no longer brown.

The sickly yellow walls were spattered, resembling a giant piece of random art.

The woman looked up at Lisa.

(And she expected this next part. Of course, you didn't dream as much as she did, and think about them, without expecting this. . . .)

The woman looked like her.

Eyes locked, then shut.

It was over.

The door screeched, the reverse of the sound before.

The door closing gently behind Lisa.

Lisa thought: It isn't over.

She turned to the door still closing in this room that, yes, of her own will, she'd decided to enter.

Now that door—shut tight.

And she turned to see who'd closed the door.

ELAINA walked down the boardwalk, preferring the rhythmic crash and swoosh of the nearby ocean to the always car-clogged Surf Avenue.

The sky had now deepened to true black sky, with stars beginning to appear as if by magic, dotting the darkness. In winter, the boardwalk would be deserted. But even now, there were only a few people as far as she could see, and one arcade open, going through the motions until the first fall winds would finally roar off the Atlantic and turn this boardwalk into a true ghost town.

And that thought gave her a chill.

She knew the Coney winters—and sometimes she wished she didn't have to leave the light and warmth and the creatures of her aquarium.

She came to West Sixteenth Street, and took the ramp that led off the boardwalk. The new Stillwell Avenue subway station, an amazing bit of architecture that might just be the first round in a Coney Island renaissance, was only a few blocks away.

When she hit the sidewalk, she could see—at the corner—Nathan's.

Nathan's Famous, the original, home to the best hot dogs in the world, and here in Coney at least, equally delicious clams, corn on the cob, and Nathan's own distinctive fries with whole swatches of the peel left on the fat, unbelievably tasty fries.

She had eaten it all.

Because Nathan's was the place where her illegal father had found work, starting as a cleaner and then graduating to a cook, getting to wear a crisp rhombus-shaped hat, a hat he wore with all the pride of a general's cap.

He worked hour after hour, tirelessly, until he had almost as much overtime as straight time. Saving, always smiling, building a future for his two kids.

It was hard to believe that he was gone. Harder still for Elaina's soft-spoken mother, the love of her dad's life, who seemed a changed person once Elaina's father passed away— where else—at work, collapsing one day, his work done.

She didn't go there anymore.

But somehow, she always liked to take this street that took her past the place.

Reaching the corner, she glanced in, the windows steamy from all the cooking, an Edward Hopper collection of people standing and eating.

It was her own show of respect, her walk past this place.

Then—she crossed Surf Avenue.

DAVID walked in, and saw Mari sitting at the glitzy bar. A man in a blue shirt with a white collar, tie loosened, sleeves rolled up, stood behind her, talking to her.

Not surprising. She's a beautiful woman. Even in a jaded New York City, she's going to get attention.

David walked to her left.

"Sorry. Got held up a bit."

Mari turned.

"Oh, David—didn't see you get here."

For a Monday night, the hotel bar was full, bustling. The tables all filled, the bar stools taken. He guessed such trendy places were immune to any beginning-of-the-week doldrums.

The man with the two-tone shirt, his foot—David now noticed—lodged on a rung of Mari's stool . . . didn't back away.

Sizing up if his chances were now completely done.

David turned to him, saying nothing.

But he guessed his own body language indicated that he could, if he wanted, make that foot come sliding off the stool rung in a rather painful fashion.

"I had to write up a quick report. A new procedure. Every day filing something. More words for the troops to digest," David said to Mari.

"Very smart lady you have here," the two-toned shirt said.

David ignored him.

Mari looked at David and did a quick roll of her eyes, obviously glad for the rescue. David laughed.

"How about some food?"

"Only if we go Dutch. This place is incredibly expensive."

"Deal."

And David watched her slide off the stool, and they walked to the hostess podium, where a too-slender young woman in the tiniest black dress studied the chart before her as if prepping for the organic chemistry final.

LISA felt her whole body shake. Then something grabbed at her midsection.

Her eyes opened, but she realized that she still wore her eyeshade.

Another terrific shake, the awareness coming quickly.

Turbulence.

She reached up and pushed the eye mask to her forehead.

Turbulence wasn't the word for it.

One of the attendants was just pulling herself out of someone's lap. The plane had an odd tilt, as if the pilot might be banking.

The seat-belt lights were on.

Another lurch; this time a sickening drop that only reminded Lisa how much she hated roller coasters. All that crazy dipping and climbing, screams from everyone.

No screams now.

Though she thought she could feel the tension rising in the business-class cabin.

The attendant, now standing again, wedged her arms on the overhead bins, and started walking down the aisle, checking that everyone had their seat belts on.

Fact is . . . if anyone didn't have their seat belt on, they'd probably be rolling in the aisle.

The plane bumped again as if it had hit a curb, the force of the contact sending Lisa's head hard against her seat back.

I hate this, she thought.

She knew what came next.

"Folks, I'm afraid we—"

But the reassuring homily was interrupted by another lurch, and Lisa could well imagine even the captain holding on to the plane's wheel, very thankful for the gyroscopic system that kept the plane steady.

"—we're in a bad stretch of turbulence. Some storm system north of Hawaii. So we're going to—"

The plane drooped; a crazy elevator with wings.

"Um—going to climb and see if we can get out of it. So just sit back—" Another bumpy hit, and then Lisa heard a wet hacking noise. Like a cough.

The pungent smell that filled the cabin told her that this was no cough. Someone had tossed their cookies. And that smell would probably only trigger more of the same.

"—while we try to get above all this."

The engines kicked into a higher pitch, a shrill whistle as the turbines went into overdrive. Now the nose tilted up, and Lisa saw that the attendant had slid into one of the fold-down seats and strapped herself in.

Whoever was hacking away in the cabin kept on doing it.

Nice . . .

Lisa felt the slightly acid taste of bile, just there at the back of her throat.

The plane screamed upward.

And she had—of course—only one thought.

If something were to happen, if my notes—and what I know—got lost . . . well, then, this . . . opportunity, this . . . chance would be lost.

Her hands closed on the armrest. She closed her eyes.

She waited.

21

ELAINA walked past the shuttered carousel, usually open all the time, even well into the late night, when one can only imagine who might be wandering onto the ride to try and snatch a silver ring.

The silver ring . . . always returned at the end of the ride, valueless but full of a giddy symbolic importance.

Like a lot of things, Elaina thought.

Still, she found it odd that the place was closed. Always open, and now, for some reason, shuttered.

Strange.

She hurried now, the unlit letters that announced the carousel catching some of the streetlight but not enough to show their true lacquered color.

Then, at the corner, she started down Fifteenth Street, a little shortcut to the new station, moving down this smaller side street rather than going down Stillwell.

And only a few feet into the block, two quick and unwanted thoughts.

First, that there had to be a reason the carousel had been closed. Something must have happened for this extraordinary event.

Then, a feeling she never got, even in a place like Coney where one would expect to feel such a thing.

Somebody's watching me.

But a look around showed that she was all alone on the block.

She picked up her pace, noting the lights ahead, the stores on the other side of the street that appeared open, the reassuring signs that told her not to worry.

Which is when she felt a hand cover her mouth, a perfect mask of skin locked on her face.

That hand dragged her backward.

And at the moment when she would use all the things a New York woman learns, the twisting, and kicking back with her legs, the elbows shooting sharply backward, she felt something sharp, painful cutting through the material of her blouse, pressing tight.

And she smelled him.

The smell of smoke, and beer, and something sweet on his face, that face now close to hers, now whispering.

"Nothing funny, eh? And nothing fancy, and it will all turn out all right."

An accent . . . at first she thought . . . British. But then layered with something else, as if the English language had been learned, acquiring odd little ticks.

The man pulled her into an open doorway, a waiting doorway.

The smell of urine.

The door kicked shut.

Elaina waited.

"HOW are your shrimp?" David asked.

Mari bit another body off a coconut-coated shrimp.

"Crispy. Good with the—what is it?—pineapple/mango sauce? Very good."

"At four dollars a shrimp, they better be." His salmon was

just okay. But it didn't matter. Food was not the real issue here.

"So, first things first—you accept that we can't do anything together this time?"

Mari smiled. "*Accept* is maybe not the word I would use. But I understand. But you know—"

She let the unfinished sentence dangle while she brought up another shrimp to her lips.

Driving me a bit crazy with the shrimp eating, David thought.

She's certainly a lot more than a good reporter.

"I know—what?"

"My editor didn't tell me . . . what she couldn't tell me. But I know that there have been other killings, disappearances." Her face lost the girlish glow of flirting for a moment. "You're dealing with a pattern."

David looked away.

He couldn't say anything; she was a reporter.

"I can't comment."

Mari nodded. "I know. But who knows? Maybe I can bring something to you that will be useful. Maybe things can change."

David reached out and put his hand atop Mari's, her fingers on the stem of her wineglass.

"Some things I don't want to change."

"Really?"

"This weekend. I knew you were upset. Johanna, going to Block Island."

"I'm past that—"

David gave her hand a small squeeze. "But I'm not. I want to see you, keep seeing you. I don't want that to change. Ever."

For once, she just looked at him and didn't say anything. New York women, he knew, grew hardened from the dating and relationship wars. No matter how much she cared for him, she would have to keep her guard up.

She released the stem of her glass.

"Me too. And I really am past that."

David smiled. "Good."

Her eyes lit up, as if some amazing flash of inspiration had just come to her.

"Why don't you . . . get the check. Then we get a cab . . . to—"

"Your place?"

"No. Yours. It's closer."

And just those words alone . . . excited David.

"THAT'S it," he whispered. "No moves; do not do anything to make me mad."

Elaina's mind raced. The horror of her situation had her frozen, but at the same time thoughts were starting to connect that might let her do something.

Because she knew . . . anyone would know . . . the hopelessness of where she was.

This doorway, this building. Abandoned.

The event planned.

But why me?

The first coherent thought. She tried to reach for another.

"That's it. Nice and still. You see, I just want to tell you something."

The next thought, as false and cheap as can be.

He just wants to tell me something.

"You have been doing some interesting things with . . . that animal."

Animal?

"Susie. The one you love so much, probing what's inside her, what is the black hole in the center of that dolphin's mind. Such interesting work. But—unfortunately, nothing I'd want to ever see the light of day."

He tapped Elaina's head.

"There are secrets in there."

The man laughed. A silly, wheezing laugh. As if the idea was somehow humorous.

Then:

"My work can't allow that."

Then the next true thought, a rational idea.

This man with his strange inflection, his odd combination of smells, his *knowledge* of Susie . . . will kill her.

It was the only impulse she needed.

And signals were sent out to her body, deep, primal messages that have told bodies for millennia that they either moved now . . . acted now . . . fought now. Or this would be the last few seconds of life.

INSIDE the door—

They stopped, and kissed. Mari immediately pressed against David, and felt how he was hard already. Boldly she reached down, her hand teasing, coaxing.

Now they kissed and stumbled their way to his bedroom, the bed so ready for them.

Her hand left off caressing him through his pants, and now both hands went to his belt. She felt him fumbling with her blouse buttons.

They undressed each other ravenously, the hunger intoxicating, the lust driving them so fast.

Close to the bed, David stumbled a bit, and Mari remembered that he still had pain there, and this awkward dance to the sheets could hurt him.

But no matter—

They fell into the bed, David kicking off his pants, Mari wriggling out of her skirt—both of them madly pulling at what clothes were left on the other.

She felt David as he gently guided her back as he slid down, kissing her stomach, then lower, as if his hunger could be fed by doing that.

Mari let the waves of pleasure take her away, immediately

moaning with his sweet licks and kisses, the world and everything else but this bedroom vanished.

Her fingers went to his hair, not to guide or control, just to feel him there and wishing this moment could just go on . . . and on.

22

THE man's odd voice was right in her ear.

"You haven't been seeing me watch you at all, have you? A scientist, so observant—and yet you notice nothing."

She squirmed just a bit then, testing his hold on her, but that only seemed to make him tighten his grip. Tighten, close, the feel of his muscles so strong against her, the feel of his hand over her mouth, the strong, rough fingers.

A large powerful hand.

And, she thought, a practiced hand.

She knew her eyes screamed panic.

But inside her mind she was forcing it to follow everything, to notice every detail. The feel of his skin, the rough texture of the fingers, the strength of the arms, the smell—

The smell, the smell—

She tried to place it. She had smelled this before. The mix of smoke, ale, something sweeter too. A cologne perhaps. Something from some other place.

Some other place, she thought.

"And what dark terrible place are you going to in your mind now?" he whispered.

A car horn honked outside. A voice. Then gone.

He must have known this hallway would be vacant. A

condemned building, empty perhaps, or maybe filled with people who would hear such noises and very carefully, very quietly, slide the locks on their doors.

"Oh, I know that place. All the thoughts you have. The animal-like searching for a way out. But"—his voice lowered, a coo now, a whisper—"there is none. None. But maybe—"

She tilted her head to try and see his face again, and as she did Elaina felt, so slowly, the blade slip into her midsection.

In, then *twisting*.

Her brain became an explosion of white, her scream muffled, as he began his work.

MARI rested on top of David, astride him, looking down.

The lovemaking leaving them with a summerlike coating of sweat.

She hesitated a moment, and then leaned down and kissed him.

And when she pulled away—

"Welcome back," he said.

"Was I gone?"

"I was afraid so. Or we both were."

"It will take more than an ambitious ex to lose me, *capiche*?"

David's teeth caught the light as he smiled back.

"*Capiche*."

Then he reached up and pulled her down to his side, pulled her close. And when she was curled up as close as she could be to him, he whispered. . . .

"Got a secret for you. I don't ever want to lose you."

Mari thought of a dozen things to say in response, all corny, all so sappy.

So like a good New York girl, she just accepted the words, and held David tight until their breathing was almost in sync, and they fell asleep.

* * *

THE blade came out of her, and Elaina could feel her blood beginning to gush out. She noted how the man held her, how she couldn't really see him, and how that blood wouldn't trail down to his clothes at all to add a new scent to the smoke, the sweetness, the—

A pub!

London, pubs, beer.

That smell!

But different, thicker somehow—

Without Elaina even being aware, her legs began to kick, the animal struggle kicking into a higher gear with her very life beginning to dribble to the ground.

"Yes, that's what they all do. With the realization, with life . . . sapping away. The legs begin to kick. Your arms, if you could move, would do that too. The same response all the time. But always . . . exciting."

And in the horrible moment, as he spoke, she tried to check everywhere he held her, touched her, pressed against her—

Bile filled the back of her throat, her tongue tasting the acid.

"Which is why the legs have to be next. Before I continue. The tendons and the muscles—need to be rendered useless. One cut will do that. Then I'll return to our journey together, I promise you."

She felt his right arm move, bringing the blade down to her uselessly kicking legs.

Then—something on the wrist, a dull gray, but sending a shaft of prismatic color at her eyes.

To the other arm, the other wrist. Another circular piece of gray metal.

So odd—

When the door flew open.

"What the goddamn, what the goddamn *hell*—"

Elaina's eyes looked up and she saw some wavering figure holding a brown bag, a gristled gray-black beard against black skin, a skullcap on his head.

The man tried to turn and leave, still muttering—

"What the hell shit—"

When he walked into the edge of the door that had only closed partway behind him.

Into it, then bouncing back, a woozy boxer taking a knockout punch. Falling back, slipping, sliding—

On the blood.

Back, down onto Elaina, falling hard. Onto the hand with the knife, the dead drunken weight now peeling that arm away, then pinning it to the steps.

And in that moment, Elaina felt the man's other arm, the hard muscle, the meaty tight fist, *loosen.*

Just a bit.

But enough so that Elaina's gym-trained legs could kick again, the drunk rolling to the side, now Elaina kicking up.

Her midsection felt as if something had exploded in it. The pain immense, nearly making it impossible for her to see from the white fireworks exploding in her brain.

But she was up.

The man's hand started to close on her ankle, but then the drunk must have moved, pulling that hand again away. She kicked back, hard, heard the man swear.

He'd be on her again in mere seconds.

Only seconds.

That's all she had. To grab the edge of the door. Lock on to it. Grab it, hold it, and pull it the hell open, all the way open, so that she could—

Yes.

Stumble out to the sidewalk.

Was the drunk dead, killed even as he let her escape?

Then, if there was no one there, on the street, the man could simply drag her back in, like some spider assured of his work, pulling a scurrying insect morsel back, pulling it back, wrapping it in the gauze again.

She saw a cab.

No one would stop. No cab seeing her like this, no car.

Not here, not in Coney. The cab was moving, moving past her.

Moving, and Elaina saw no other choice.

She stumbled out to the street, right into the cab's path, turned, her hand holding her oozing midsection. Enough strength left in her legs to throw her body up a bit—

As the cab cruised slowly into her.

Her body fell forward onto the hood.

The screech of brakes. The cab stopped. Elaina only on that hood for a moment before rolling off, onto the street, landing hard.

But the yellow cab, now with a bloody smear, stopped.

It stopped—

—after Elaina had tumbled down to the black and litter-filled asphalt.

Landing so hard.

Blissfully hard so that the blow to her skull made the whiter lights, the screaming pain, the memories, the fear, all of it end—

Just . . . like . . . *that.*

IT was still dark morning.

But Dr. Lisa Griffino could see that the cabin lights had come on, the fluorescent glare penetrating even her sleeping mask.

She pulled the mask up to see the Singapore Airlines attendants retrieving what remained of the breakfast service that Lisa had missed.

Then she pulled the mask back all the way down. The captain started talking from the cockpit, the sound muffled.

Lisa reached up and removed her foam earplugs.

"Folks, we're about a hundred miles from Newark Airport and look to have an on-time landing at 6:15 A.M. The weather is a bit chilly, about forty-seven degrees, and overcast."

Funny, Lisa thought, *the captain for Singapore sounds like he's a good old boy from Texas.*

"Flight attendants, please make the cabin ready for landing."

Lisa rolled her shoulders, trying to unloosen the kinks

from a night's sleep, achy even in the roomy business-class seat. She heard the dutiful sound of tray tables being slapped into their "locked and upright position," and seats popping out of their recline position.

Lisa leaned forward. She had slipped her yellow pads into the seat back pocket in front of her.

It starts tomorrow, she thought.

Christ.

Then—

Not tomorrow. Tomorrow is here. Starts today.

She looked around the business-class cabin, people ready for a day in the canyons of Wall Street, or midtown boardrooms.

Nobody's going to be doing what I will be doing, she thought.

There's only one crazy person on this plane.

Crazy. That's what they'll say.

And it will be her tough job to convince them that she's anything but. . . .

BOOK TWO

Then . . .
and Now . . .
and Here

23

IT is autumn.

That much remains the same. And the month too. And the unseasonable chill . . . all the same.

But everything else is different.

Soar through the skies, through the clouds down to the man-made smoke and smudge below, hiding the gas lamps, the crazy jumble of buildings, down to the bustle and the squalor . . . and markets of Spitalfields.

There would be a few things you would notice immediately.

A few things that would make your senses react on a physical, visceral level.

But none more than the *smells*.

All that smoke and soot and stench of a city seemingly intent on choking itself under its own foulness, its own desperate pollution.

It is London, September 8th, 1888, at 5.00 A.M.

But of course it is.

A black and white dog, the name forgotten, tugged at a piece of meat thrown to the floor by the owner of The Ten Bells Inn.

Annie Chapman sat in her chair quietly watching the dog,
feeling the eyes of the drunken men, the men with their
grabby hands and foul gutter breath, watching her.

None with any coins to pay for the privilege of using those
hands on her, or digging in their filthy pants to see if they
could still do anything after so much drink.

All that drink always meant that Annie had to work harder.

Cohen, the owner, turned to Annie as he cleaned glasses,
getting ready for the morning workers to arrive at the market.

But morning still seemed so far away for Annie, with dark
and fog outside.

"Annie, you best be going home, lass. Give it a rest for the
night."

Annie could feel the drink in herself too; that, and the des-
peration of getting some shillings. When the workers arrived
for their first ale, they'd be drinking fast, no time for a whore,
hurrying to the market and work.

"I'd like another, Mr. Cohen."

Cohen shook his head, and pulled back on a spigot releas-
ing another half pint of warm dark ale.

Annie popped open her purse. Easy to find the few coins
she had, gathered there, lonely, waiting for others.

She stood up, steadying herself with the chair back.

She walked to the bar, as steady as she could. She put down
the few pence for a half ale, then forcing a smile, hurried back
to her chair.

It was 5:00 A.M.

The night was nearly over.

But it wasn't over yet.

The ale nearly gone, Annie looked up to the tall windows
that faced Commerce Street.

Not that she could see anything but the strange glow made
by the lamps and the fog. As if the pub was smothered in a
dark gray cotton.

Smothered . . .

Mary liked to stand just outside. Some of the girls fought
over the best places to stand, but Annie liked being in here,

catching someone's eye, rather than planting herself outside, vainly trying to snag someone.

She took another sip, the ale gone, her money nearly gone.

There could be the stray bloke wandering outside.

Certainly drunk. Might be easy to relieve some drunk of his coins.

Not that she ever stole from the customers.

Well, maybe a few times. If they fell down. She was ready to perform her duties, and sometimes the blokes would just collapse.

What was a lady to do?

And she might, truth to tell, even help herself to more than her share. For her trouble, she'd tell herself. Going out with them only to have nothing happen.

Few times then, leaving them with nothing but the aching head they'd have in the morning.

That's all.

That is, if some slit-purse didn't come up, take whatever else they had, and leave them with a cut throat.

Leave no witnesses, that was the way things were done around here.

Dead men tell no tales.

And was she scared? Despite the girls who had been killed, Annie felt safe. Some of the girls could do things to get themselves in trouble, get themselves into situations where they'd get hurt.

Not Annie. Even with drink in her, she made good decisions. She was safe.

She opened the latch of her small purse and looked at the few pence and shillings sitting there. Really all she had.

Back to the tall windows of the pub, the glow outside, thinking perhaps there was some promise in that glow outside.

She got up. The chair tilted back, almost ready to fall.

Couldn't go outside straightaway.

Not all full of piss. So much ale . . . filling her.

She headed toward the curved stone staircase, leading to the basement of The Ten Bells, down to the toilet.

Her arms went out to the side to support her unsteady walk following the tight curve of the stone staircase.

"Cor, these steps will be the death of me. . . ." she said to herself, carefully lowering one foot, then the other, her hands sliding along the stone.

The smell grew more powerful, more disgusting with every step. Did Cohen ever clean down here? Or was it left to the rats and other vermin to guard this place, where the real drunks often didn't even bother to use the trough to relieve themselves?

And some of the other girls would find a corner down here, a place where—rank as it was—they could earn their money.

Right now, Annie's insides ached with the pressure of all her drinking.

She walked to the cold porcelain toilet, filthy as could be . . . but a welcome sight nonetheless.

She hiked up her skirt, and pulled aside her underpants— need of a wash, they were—and took care to squat but not really sit on what must be a filthy, slimy seat.

The blessed sound of her water hitting the toilet.

"You . . . you all right then, missy?"

Annie looked up. One of the men from the bar. Some drunken codger hoping he'd get lucky, that perhaps this was his night to get something for free. The man stood just outside the stall, blocking her way, wavering a bit.

"I'm fine, so now let a lady do her business in peace."

The man stood there, not moving.

Annie stood up, done.

"So you go now or I'll tell Cohen on ya, and you'll have to find another place to drink yourself into a stupor."

She saw his eyes widen; nobody liked to have to find a new place, not when one was all settled and made a home where they could drink undisturbed.

The man nodded, then turned and trudged away, stumbling to the room with the giant porcelain sinks and the big pissing trough.

Annie moved quickly back to the spiral steps and went back up.

The room had lost a few patrons, the night crowd leaving before the noisy and burly workers arrived.

But it was still dark out, still thick with a smoky, smudgy fog.

Annie kept walking, no one taking any notice of her. She went to the pub's double doors, with thick colored glass that could make the inside so inviting, glittering in so many colors and light.

But now showing nothing of what was outside even a few feet away past the open door.

"G'night, Annie. See you tomorrow."

"You can be sure of that, Mr. Cohen," she said. He did, after all, get a bit of her earnings now and then, on a good night. They were, she realized . . . connected.

She pushed open the heavy door. It sent a creak through the now somberly quiet barroom.

The fog seemed to back away as she stepped out to the night.

Taking a breath, she took a few more steps, pleased with how steady they were, out to the night, turning to the right . . . toward Mary Kelly's favorite spot.

This was likely as not a hopeless effort.

But maybe, she thought . . . *maybe* something would happen.

24

DAVID heard the buzz of something vibrating, then, in clarification, the ring of his cell phone. No musical tones, no songs, just a ring that even he had to admit sounded harsh in the morning.

He saw the phone on the other side of the bed, past Mari, curled up and sleeping close.

Another ring, and she shifted her weight.

As carefully as he could, he reached over her and picked up the phone.

"Hello?"

He turned to the alarm clock on the other end table.

7:15. He still had another fifteen minutes of sleep coming that someone had now just stolen from him.

"David, it's Biondi. Can you get here as fast as you can?"

David rubbed his eyes.

"Yeah, sure. What's up?"

"Tell you the whole deal when you get here."

The phone went dead.

Mari turned to him, the sheet sliding away from her body.

Forget any thoughts of something sweet in the morning, he thought.

"What's wrong?" Mari said.

She didn't make any attempt to cover up, . . . which would make leaving only worse.

"That"—he stood up and, as he talked, walked over to his dresser—"was my captain. Telling me to hurry."

"Something happen? Where's your TV remote?" Mari said.

David pointed. "Right next to you."

New Yorkers expected anything these days, and TV news would be the place where the information would appear fast. A bridge gone, an explosion, whatever new and terrible thing had just happened to the place that always gets its Homeland Security money cut back.

Geez, who'd ever want to hit New York?

David pulled on some briefs, a black T-shirt, and snatched his pants off a chair where they'd ended up being tossed the night before.

The TV came to life.

"—another beautiful September day. So get out there, and enjoy that New York sunshine."

"Guess everything's okay. In the city, I mean."

David nodded. "Yeah, just not okay at One Police Plaza."

"He ever do this before?"

"No. Police work runs on doughnuts and time—some clichés are true. So why the rush today? Who knows. I'll find out."

"And maybe tell me?"

David sat on the bed, pulling on socks, tying his shoes, then—

He turned back to Mari, stroking her dark hair.

"Maybe I'll tell you. Okay, Nancy Drew?"

"Okay."

He leaned forward and planted a kiss on her forehead. But that wasn't enough, so he slid down and gave her a hard kiss on the lips.

Yeah—it was hard to leave this morning.

He stood up.

"See you tonight? Dinner somewhere?"

Mari nodded. "Sure. That's when you'll tell me everything that's going on."

He smiled, and grabbed his wallet, keys, then sailed to the door outside. Coffee, minus the doughnut, could be scored at the pushcart that hung out at the entrance to One Police Plaza on Center Street.

MARI finished dressing, then dug out her lipstick and mascara. She hated showing up at the office so obviously having not been home the night before. A coating of makeup might throw the scent off.

Doubtful . . .

But part of her thought—she didn't mind. As if she was saying: I've got a damn good life. A lover, in man-challenged Manhattan.

How about that?

The national news was finishing, and the few minutes of local news began.

Something about an attack in Coney Island.

The image cut to WCBS's Lou Young standing on a street, the blue sky in the background, wind blowing his hair.

"Police have said nothing about the young woman attacked last night."

Probably some quarrel in a tenement, Mari thought. Drunk husband whales on some drunk wife, one of those stories that churn through the city every day.

But not this time.

"But Channel 2 News has learned that the woman, Elaina Suro, worked just blocks from where she was attacked, at the Coney Island Aquarium. Apparently she was walking home, after dark, when the attack happened. Authorities have confirmed that she was taken to Kings County Hospital and is in critical condition. No sign of who the attacker might be so far, or a motive."

The reporter signed off. And the national feed kicked in with barbecue hints for an Indian summer cookout with Bobby Flay.

And sitting there, the remote in her hand, Mari had to think—

Is there a connection between David's call this morning, and that story? And if there was . . . would he tell her?

Mari started moving fast, hurrying to the *Daily News* building.

DAVID waited outside the ICU at Kings County Hospital. Susan Kunokine talked on her cell phone.

"I don't care what you want to do," she said. "You're to come home right after school. I'm not there and—"

Kids and police work. Always a rough mix.

A nurse walked by and pointed to the cell phone. "Sorry, we don't allow cell phones anywhere near the unit."

Kunokine rolled her eyes. "Okay. Just a minute."

Back to the phone.

"I can't talk now. But I will see you at home. Bye."

The nurse moved on.

"Kids. Don't know what ever possessed me."

"I've dodged that one," David said.

His partner turned to him. "No, not that I ever wished that I didn't have kids. I love both of them, crazy about them. But God, being on my own with them—it's a lot of work, a lot of rules—"

"And they don't like rules?"

"You got that right."

It was tricky getting to know a new partner, David thought. Here was someone who was supposed to have your back—literally. So very quickly they had to become your best friend in the world, someone hopefully endowed with near-supernatural powers of thinking the way you do, second-guessing every decision. . . .

So how much could he trust this woman's abilities?

He didn't have a clue—yet.

But despite having two kids, she had been in Biondi's office ahead of him, the conversation already started, and David playing catch-up.

Not that there was a hell of a lot to catch up on.

A woman attacked on Fifteenth Street in Coney Island, and somehow escapes. Hit by a cab—or as the driver reported, she *threw* herself at the cab. And the only witness . . . what looked to the cabbie like a drunk homeless person stumbling away from the scene.

No sign of any attacker.

Not a lot to go on.

Until the woman was able to talk. Right now she was sedated after two operations to repair the holes that someone had drilled in her.

The door to the ICU opened. The nurse, white-haired and with a smooth moon face, whispered, "You can come in for a few minutes. But try to be quiet."

David nodded, and he and Kunokine followed the nurse to the bed, to the victim.

For a moment they stood there, both looking at the woman in the bed. Tubes and wires surrounded her; oxygen mask over her mouth, liquids flowing into her arms.

Even like that, David could tell she was quite a beautiful Latina.

"Worked at the Aquarium," a voice said behind them.

David turned to see Foster; that's all anyone called him. A forensics expert, the guy who could look at wounds and say exactly what happened, what kind of knife, how deep, how good the steel was.

Foster had the gaunt physique of someone who—no matter how much he ate—would never get any real weight on his body. To perhaps compensate, he dressed nattily . . . a three-button vest under his tweed sport coat, a bow tie, his thinning hair combed back and lacquered down flat.

"She didn't just work there, Foster. She was the director of Marine Mammals."

"A job's a job."

Foster took a step closer.

Foster had been here since a few hours before dawn, watching the operation from a distance, getting a look at the wound before they stitched the woman up.

"So what do you think?" David said.

"It's interesting. I expected—I dunno—someone stuck a shiv in her, fast and dirty, after stealing her purse, after . . . you know—maybe a rape attempt or something."

Rape or something . . . Foster was an odd bird.

"And not so?"

Foster pursed his lips.

"No way. Not at all. Whatever was used to stab her, he slid in clean, but not too deep. Whoever used the knife damn well knew what they were doing. Caused enough bleeding to cause a lot of pain and stop her cold. But he didn't gut her. No hack and slash here."

"That's what kept her alive, she was lucky?" Kunokine said.

Foster smiled, amused at what he was about to show was an incorrect assumption.

"No. That's *not* what kept her alive. Whoever did this kept her alive intentionally. Like I said, he knew what he was doing. Where he cut her—not too deep. It would have been all too easy to kill her."

The nurse walked over, checked the readouts of blood pressure and heart rate on the monitor above the bed. Then she turned to the three people standing beside Elaina.

"I think you best wait outside. We generally like it nice and quiet here."

"When will she become conscious?" David asked.

The nurse looked at Elaina.

"Hard to say. At the very least, not till the sedatives wear off. Then we will watch how she reacts. It might be a good idea to keep her under another twenty-four hours. After that, well . . . when her body says she's ready to open her eyes."

"And you'll call?"

The woman seemed to bristle.

"Yes. We understand we're to call the moment she's awake. So we will."

David nodded. Then he thought he should add something to those instructions . . . and maybe try to get this woman on their side.

"Thanks. The sooner she's up . . . the sooner we might stop whoever did this from doing it again."

"I understand."

"SHE'S a tough number," Kunokine said.

"Just doing her job," David answered.

But he knew the sooner they could speak to Elaina the better. They could get a description, details, vital information to help them hunt whoever did this.

Foster showed no indication that he was leaving.

"So you think they're connected?" he said.

"Hmm?" David said, turning to him.

"This one, and the one in the LES, and the other one a few weeks back?"

"Too early to tell."

Foster gave him another smile and laughed.

"Oh, they're connected."

Kunokine shook her head. "Then why the hell did you ask us?"

"You're the homicide detectives. You should know, shouldn't you?"

"Look, Foster." David said, "why not just tell us what the hell you're talking about, okay?"

Foster looked from David to Kunokine. "Come on, guys. The wounds are all the same. Done with the same . . . skill. Clean, smooth. Of course, the other two people had been killed. But he got interrupted here."

"The others were eviscerated," David's partner said.

"O-kay. That's one way to put it. But skillfully done. The guy—I'm assuming it's a guy due to the strength issues—knows what he's doing."

"How reassuring," David said.

Foster nodded.

"One other thing. He sure ain't no homeless person, no drunk. But I'm guessing you knew that already."

David turned to his partner.

"Ready to go to Coney?"

And they walked down the hallway to the elevators.

25

"SO early? Can't you let an editor get some caffeine into her?"

Mari shut the editor's door behind her. "Who do you have on the Coney story?"

"On it? No one really. Ralph filed the basic story since it's his turf—Brooklyn, I mean."

Mari shook her head.

"No, it has something to do with the other killing—you know that."

Joann Gully took a sip of coffee from a massive mug. "Really? Except—not to put too fine a point on it—no one was killed. The woman escaped, so I'm guessing she was probably attacked by some homeless weirdo who—"

Mari grabbed a chair and sat down facing Gully.

"No, okay, see—I was with David last night."

"All well in Tahiti?"

"Everything is fine in Tahiti."

"Glad to hear it. Romance has such a hard time in this town." A small grin with—Mari thought—a bit of a sadistic edge to it. "But you know that."

Mari chose to ignore the comment.

"So this morning he gets a call," Mari said.

Gully opened a drawer and pulled out an ashtray and pack of Marlboro filters.

"Do you mind?"

Mari shook her head. It might be totally illegal in this new New York. But she wasn't about to lose her audience.

Gully lit up.

"So—Detective Dave gets a call. Go on."

Mari nodded. "His captain tells him to get to One Police Plaza immediately. And he moves."

"To deal with this stabbing, this random attack?"

"I'm betting it wasn't a random attack."

Gully took a drag of her cigarette. "And what did your David tell you?"

Mari looked away.

"He told me nothing."

"You must be losing your touch."

"Just as you haven't told me anything."

"I told you what I could. The rest—is sealed. Gave my word as editor to the commissioner." Another big drag. "Can't screw with that."

"So can I follow up on the story?"

"I doubt very much it *is* a story. But you want it, it's yours. Somewhere down the line, do try to bring me something print-able? You know, something to fill all the white pages they have sitting in the factory waiting for words?"

Mari smiled. Gully was an old-school battle-ax, no doubt. But there was something refreshing about her. She sure as hell didn't hold back.

Mari stood up. "That is the idea."

Gully waved her hand at her. "And close the door quickly behind you. Keep the smoke in here while I get one of these damn windows open. The mayor has smoke spies every-where. . . ."

"Sure." Mari turned, quickly opened the editor's door, and slid out.

* * *

"AH—yes, Ms. Grifffino, I see that your room is ready."

"Doctor," Lisa said without much enthusiasm. "Dr. Griffino."

Not that the title meant a great deal to her. But she hadn't suffered the long road to the academic peak to be labeled a *Ms*.

"Yes," the man behind the registration desk said. "*Dr.* Griffino. I see you prepaid for last night, so you are"—a big grin—"all set."

And getting that room locked in for the night before she arrived—so she'd have a bed in the Soho Grand this morning— set her back close to four hundred dollars.

Could she even sleep?

She felt exhausted, but she was also so wired that she might just end up lying there, staring at the ceiling.

"And your bags . . . ?"

Lisa shook her head. "No bags. They're"—she fabricated something on the spot—"lost."

The man seemed personally crushed. "Oh, so sorry to hear." Then a reassuring grin . . . no cloud lingers long in the lobby of the Soho Grand, Lisa guessed. "Don't worry—the airlines are so good about getting people's bags to them."

"Yup—except when they don't."

His palliative rejected, the man behind the reception desk—Paul, according to his badge—fiddled with something below the high desk.

"Will one key be adequate?"

"More than adequate."

He slid a plastic key into a small envelope, and put a tiny key on a small ring atop the envelope. "It is Room 338 and this"—he pointed to the small key—"is your minibar key. I assume you do not need a bellman, not having any bags . . . or maybe perhaps to show you the room?"

She laughed, and the man looked personally wounded.

"No, I've stayed here before. I'll find the room just fine."

She picked up the small envelope and the small key.

"And thanks for your help."

* * *

"SO why such an early meeting with the bear?"

Mari looked up from her desk to see Julie Fein hanging over the cubicle divider.

"I asked her to let me follow this Coney Island thing."

"Really? Doesn't sound like much."

"I think it is."

"Reporter's instincts?"

"Something like that."

"And then she said—?"

"Gully felt pretty much the way you do. Didn't get why I wanted it."

"Nor do I."

"But she gave it to me. Now I'm trying to see what precinct that is."

"I can check that for you. I have this list I found somewhere—matches all the city streets to a police precinct."

"That would be great."

"I'll get it."

"Lunch today?"

"Sure. I mean unless something pops up. Let's hit Madison Square Park . . . bit of a walk but not too many great days like this left."

"Brrr . . . tell me about it. Now's about the time I start dreaming about working in Miami.

I'll e-mail you that list. . . ."

Mari smiled.

"See you later . . ."

And Julie slid back to her side of the dividing wall.

DAVID turned down Bath Avenue, and pulled the car to an empty angled spot, right in front of the Sixty-second Precinct.

"Maybe we can hit the beach later," Kunokine said, smiling.

David turned to her. "It's not that nice a beach. Or it didn't used to be when I was a kid. Who knows . . . maybe it's gotten better. Everything in the city is getting better these days. Or at least cleaner."

"If you say so."

David turned to get out when his partner touched his arm.

"Before we go in there, how you want to play it?"

"I think—we just act as though it looks like what it is . . . one of those wonderful random acts of violence. Best if we keep any other ideas to ourselves."

"So if the locals want to talk about it?"

Locals.

Kunokine meant the precinct detectives looking into the case. "We can talk—but I don't want to plant any ideas in their head. That way . . . we can see what pops up . . . what is real—"

"And what ain't?" Kunokine said.

"Right."

David popped open the car door and performed the always painful maneuver of sliding his leg out and standing up.

He looked up: the crystal blue sky, the smell of the ocean not far away, one of those last beautiful days of late summer.

Then he followed Kunokine up the steps.

LISA came suddenly awake, in the shadowy room with the thick blackout curtains pulled tight.

Awake, and for a few seconds, completely unaware of where she was.

Then—

Right. A bed. The Soho Grand.

She searched for the alarm clock, a trendy squat black box with eerie green numbers.

A little after eleven.

She had slept . . . what, an hour? Maybe more?

She took a breath.

Thinking: time to get going.

Time . . . to get started.

Had to be a coffee machine in here somewhere. Small packets of coffee, creamer, an array of sweeteners. The essentials.

Then—she had a stray thought that seemed to come from nowhere.

What if someone had followed her . . . all the way from Singapore?

Followed her, and was following her still.

Could she be bringing something very bad to these people?

And—she'd be completely unaware.

Not that she had any choice. But lying there, atop the bed-clothes, what had been the comfortable temperature being pumped out by the AC suddenly turned chilly.

She rubbed her arms.

Quickly she moved off the bed to hunt for the light switch.

26

"**WHERE** did you get these guys?" David asked the lieutenant, who held a paper coffee cup like a lifeline.

This precinct was so far away from NYC, these cops might as well be working in another country, a land with roller coasters, seagulls, and the smell of an ocean all summer.

David looked through the one-way mirror at the lineup of what in the old days people called "bums."

The lieutenant, a good ten years younger than David, shrugged.

"Where'd we get these guys? Hey, fellas . . . where did you round up these gentlemen?"

Everyone in the room laughed. Kunokine looked at David, clearly not happy with the level of frivolity in the room.

The lieutenant walked up to the one-way glass, looking into the room with its row of homeless men.

"These guys live here, Detective. They *are* Coney Island. Pretty harmless, but also pretty useless as eyes and ears. It would be good if the victim—what's her name—?"

Christ, David thought, *a woman gets stabbed and they can't even remember her name.*

"Elaina Suro."

"Right. Well, if she came to, could look at them—that would be a great help."

"That's not likely to happen for a while," Kunokine said, doing little to hide her irritation.

"Like I said," the lieutenant went on, "with that help, we might be able to figure out if one of these yokels saw anything. Without it—"

A resigned shrug.

David stood up. He noticed the lieutenant studied him when he had difficulty getting up.

His eyes going to David's leg.

Probably dying to ask, *What the hell happened, Detective? Work-related? Racquetball injury? Age?*

David walked to the window.

"Tell you what I'd like to do. With your permission."

"We're all ears."

David nodded and looked around. *This might be the Wild West of NYPD precincts, but fuck that,* David thought.

"First, can we clear this room except for you, Detective Kunokine, and me?"

The lieutenant pursed his lips ever so slightly, as in, *Oh, you're one of the hard asses.* But he nodded to the cops behind him, and they filed out, the muttering beginning even before the door was shut.

"Great. Now, we could talk to each of these rummies one on one. But my guess is that wouldn't tell us a thing. But now—"

David turned and looked at the room.

"Now—they're like rats in a box. Shake the rats up, and maybe something interesting might happen."

"Be my guest. Want the mike on now?"

"In a minute."

David turned back to Kunokine, and leaned close; a whisper.

"Susan, I'd like you to trust your instincts. If one of them does anything strange, feel free to jump on them, cut me off . . . okay?"

Kunokine smiled, clearly pleased that David guessed exactly how she'd like to function in this unusual interrogation.

"Okay. Turn on the mike and let's have a chat."

MARI sat with Julie Fein in Madison Square Park, the pigeons creeping closer as if maybe if they took their time, they could come close enough and snatch a bit of panini.

Julie stamped her foot.

"Damn, I hate those fucking birds. Flying rats."

"And some people insist on feeding them."

"We need more hawks. You know that a hawk uptown's been picking off pigeons? We need a couple hundred hawks."

"Might cut down on the rats too."

"And do we ever need it. There's a figure I heard—New York has, like, a hundred rats for every person."

"I know what I'd like to do with my hundred."

They laughed, and then Julie tapped Mari on her knee. "Hey, see that guy on his phone there—he's checking you out."

Mari looked toward the sidewalk and saw someone with sleeves rolled up, tie loosened, and indeed looking at her.

"Great. Got myself a park stalker."

"Hey, he looks cute."

"Don't they all? Besides, I am involved."

"And a few days ago you were 'uninvolved.'"

"No, we're good now."

For a moment Julie said nothing, the changing of gears. "I just don't want you hurt. You don't need it. Hell, I don't need it."

Mari turned to her friend. Could anyone really do this New York thing without friends?

"Thanks. But I'm okay." A breath. "We're okay."

"*We're?* Now I'm really worried."

And Mari laughed again.

"And how's your story going, that girl—"

"That," Mari said, rolling up the sandwich wrapping paper and stuffing it back into her brown paper bag, "is going absolutely nowhere. David says nothing, the police say nothing, and all I know is what the public already knows."

"Maybe you should drop it?"

Mari looked her friend in the eye.

"You're worried," said Mari.

"I mean, there are stories you could play with that don't involve people getting brutally killed. It's an idea, hmm?"

"Like—"

"Like what I do. Movie interviews. Fashion openings. Restaurant reviews. All very safe. Fun even."

"Your turf. And I like mine."

Julie shook her head. "You like it? Different strokes—"

"Exactly. We best get back—not that I have much to do."

They stood up.

The man with the cell phone had vanished, perhaps not that interested at all.

But someone else was watching her.

Watching, waiting—

"ALL right, gentlemen," David said. "We have some questions for you. The sooner we get through them, the sooner we get some answers, the sooner you guys get back out to the sunshine and work on your tans."

Truth was, any of the men could have asked for a lawyer and gotten out immediately. But they'd learned that if they played ball with the police, the police would cut them some slack. And guys like this could use all the slack they could get.

"Something happened last night. To a young woman."

David waited.

Kunokine wasted no time jumping in. "Hey, you on the right there. Look this way when the detective is talking to you."

A skinny skeleton of a man snapped his head around as if he had just been caught by his mother doing something really disgusting.

David smiled at his partner.

That's the way . . .

"Someone was seen near her. Someone . . . maybe one of you . . . saw something. And we're going to take all the time we need to find out who."

David studied the movement of the group. They more or less stood still under the bright lights, but there were small shifts, bits of movement. The lights made their filthy street clothes look like costumes, as if they were actors hired to portray the homeless, drunks, bums, whatever—

And the costume and makeup departments had absolutely nailed it.

"Now, we don't think this person last night had anything to do with this. We think he saw something, ran away . . . someone was seen running. But for us to help him, whoever he is . . . he has to talk to us."

More movement.

Kunokine leaned close to David. "Hmmm . . . they all look guilty."

He nodded. "Because they are. No stabbers there, but God knows what else."

One of the men leaned against the wall.

Kunokine spoke up again.

"Hey, stand up straight, you, No leaning against the wall. Nice and straight and listen to the detective."

"Okay. Question one . . . the first step to getting you all back out on the street. Was anyone on Fifteenth Street last night?"

One man coughed. A few shook their heads. No one volunteered anything.

Exactly as David expected. Probably they *all* had been there last night, doing their rounds, gathering soda cans and shooting for the target price of whatever poison was their nightly drink.

"We know where you hang. Don't try to bullshit us or it could be a long day."

Finally one man, then another, raised his hand.

"I—I was on that street. I'm always on that street every night."

Another man cackled. "Yeah, he's like a regular."

The first speaker turned to his associate, his face angry. Could have a nice brawl in there. That wouldn't help things.

"Think we can take those two off the list," Kunokine said.

David nodded.

"All these guys are harmless, Detective."

David turned to the lieutenant, in the shadows at the back of the room. He clicked off the mike.

"I'm sure. But someone in there saw something or knows someone who did." He turned the microphone on again.

"So, we know . . . we *know* one of you saw someone attacked last night. Now you don't want to have more questions, a lot of waiting. And let me tell you, it would be a lot better if you talked now. A lot better."

Kunokine tapped David's shoulder.

"Check out the one on the left."

David leaned close to the glass.

The man's eyes were wide; not only that, they darted around the room as if they wanted to pop out of their sockets.

Everyone else was treating this like someone's birthday, minus the cake, presents, or party.

But this guy—

"Yeah," David said. "I think we have candidate number one." He turned to the lieutenant. "Can you put him in a room and let him chill? I think about an hour or so should have him in good shape for an in-depth conversation."

Either that, or the man would be completely bug-eyed. These guys probably didn't do so well when they had to wait for their next drink.

But if any one of them looked guilty, if anyone looked like they might know something—it was that one.

"Sure," the lieutenant said.

David shut the mike off. "I've got to make a call."

He walked out of the suspect identification room.

27

"**YOU** want whipped cream on that?"

Lisa turned back to the man in a green apron holding her mocha. "No. Just like that. No cream."

The man snapped a top on the cup, and Lisa turned to look out the window of the Starbucks.

She saw the two women she had followed now sitting in the middle of the park, the trees still green, framed by a deep blue sky and snow-white clouds.

The park full, and everyone enjoying the sun.

God, she was tired. Though she had rested on the airplane, it had been a big mistake lying down for an hour in the hotel. Now she felt pained by the deadly combination of jet lag and fatigue.

And today was not the day to be dragging her heels.

She took the cup with the protective cardboard sheath to prevent dropping it like the hot potato it was.

She walked out of the Starbucks, and stood to the side by the building.

The two women had stood up.

Moving.

Lisa took the tiniest sip of the scalding coffee.

She'd have only one shot at this. One.

And as she stood there, she realized how ridiculous the whole thing was going to sound.

DAVID walked down the steps of the precinct house.

The street was quiet and he could just hear the low rhythmic rumble of waves hitting the shore.

He dug his cell phone out of his pocket, and pressed number 4. The speed dial displayed Mari's number, and David held the phone to his ear.

It rang three times—and then he heard her voice.

JULIE Fein walked next to Mari. "I told him . . . I don't date people in relationships. I think he thought—"

She stopped when Mari's cell phone rang.

Mari dug in her purse for her Razr, so small that it easily got lost in the sea of stuff that floated in her purse.

"Hello?"

She heard David.

"Hold on a second, David."

Mari lowered the phone. "Why don't you go back to the office? I'll see you up there."

Julie nodded. "Okay. Say hello to your lover for me." A grin, and she was gone.

Julie kept on walking out of the park, while Mari turned back to the center, away from the street, the sidewalk, the jumble of people and cars that made this park an island of sanity.

"Hi, David—how's your day going?"

"Not sure yet. Look, I'm in Coney Island."

"I figured. How's the girl?"

"Still drugged up. They think she'll surface tomorrow."

"Then you talk to her?"

"Yes. But I'm here now—at the Sixty-second Precinct. Have a potential witness cooling his jets. Making him sweat a bit. Then going to talk to him. Not sure how long it will be . . . how long, I mean, before I get back into town."

"So dinner is off? That it?"

It seemed like they did three steps forward, and two back. She had to wonder: Was he keeping her at a distance, or was she just being a paranoid New York female?

Somehow she had to be able to deal with this without thinking that whatever they had could so easily fall part.

"Okay. So we can the dinner."

"Well, yeah. Maybe. I just don't know when I'll get in."

"Fine," she said too quickly.

But David knew her too well to let that go. "Look, Mari. When I'm done, when I'm finished here, can I call you? Maybe we can meet later." A beat.

An important beat, Mari thought.

"I really want to see you."

"Sharing secrets yet?"

He laughed. "No. No secrets to share yet. But that doesn't mean we can't share other things."

"Like a John's pizza?"

"Exactly."

"And anything else we think of we might want to share."

His voice . . . deeper, more intent this time. "Exactly."

"Great. Well, that's just fine 'cause I have work to do too, you know. You're not the only one chasing crazy killers."

He laughed. "Oh, we have a bunch of them now? Thought there was just this one."

"See? You're falling behind."

"I should get back in there," he said. "But we will see each other tonight."

"Absolutely."

"Good."

Then an odd thought: appearing from nowhere, it seemed. Not really fitting in with their flirting conversation.

"David? Be careful, okay?"

"I am—and I will be. See you later."

And then he was gone.

Mari turned back around on the path that led out of the

park, the crowd thinning out as people hurried back to their offices for the last few hours of work.

She had only taken a few steps when someone touched her arm.

Like any sensible New Yorker, Mari spun around, quickly taking a few steps away, ready to face whatever begging homeless person had crawled out of the pavement.

But instead she saw a woman, with long auburn hair, jeans, blouse, and dark brown eyes locked on Mari.

"Mari Kinsella?"

Mari's guard immediately went up.

As a reporter, you write a lot of things, cover a lot of stories. And sometimes you could get people mad. And months after a story was written someone could pop up who was not happy.

It was one of those things to be careful of . . .

So Mari kept her distance.

"Yes. Why?"

The woman looked around the park as Mari watched her.

First thought: The woman is scared.

Then another: If she's scared, maybe I should be too.

DAVID walked up the steps, and back into the precinct house.

Susan Kunokine waited just inside.

"Time to talk to our guy?"

David shook his head. "Let's let him sit a bit more."

Kunokine nodded, but David saw her eyes looked to the right, and he guessed she might have hoped that they'd finish here fast.

Her kids at home, David guessed. Those pressures to be in two places at once. Juggling the various obligations of job and parent.

Couldn't be easy.

"So," she said, "what do we do now?"

"Let's go take a look at the scene. Not that it will have any great secrets to reveal. But—you never know. And it's a gorgeous day. Let's enjoy it before we get locked into a room with Mr. Nervous."

"Mr. Nervous." Kunokine laughed, and shook her head. "Sounds good to me."

28

"THIS is going to sound crazy—"

Mari debated walking away. Anyone opening with that statement probably had a good shot at fulfilling that promise.

"I'm sorry—but if you want to talk with me, you can call my office, it's—"

The woman shook her head, and now Mari's alarm system was on full alert.

Instinctively she looked down to the bag the woman carried—some kind of leather satchel.

And what surprises could be lurking in there?

"I can't do that." The woman again reached out and touched Mari's wrist. "*We* can't do that."

Mari took a breath. So far the woman hadn't whipped out a hunting knife. The bag didn't *look* as though it contained a gun. There were people all around, and, and—

But it was really the look in this woman's eyes that made Mari pause for a few moments.

Thinking . . .

Hear her out.

One of the key rules of journalism, for Mari at least, was you just never know where something interesting might come from.

You never know—and so you have to take chances.

The woman, not missing a beat Mari could see, smiled, sensing that Mari was willing to stay, to stand here.

She looked around the park. "How about over there? That bench. I have a lot to talk to you about." A small laugh that had nothing to do with humor. "A lot. But in a few minutes you will hear enough to decide if you want to hear more."

Mari looked at the bench. Empty. Now just an old couple sitting on the opposite bench like props, facing the empty bench, the early afternoon sun now tinting the scrawny trees with flecks of gold amidst the green.

"Okay. Sounds like a deal. A few minutes—but then I really have to get back."

The woman nodded, and they walked over to the bench.

"**WELL**, what does it tell you?" she asked.

David had pulled open the door to the building, the door still unlocked, leading to a bunch of other broken, unlocked doors.

"Not a hell of a lot," he said to Kunokine. "And upstairs?"

"The lieutenant told me when you were outside—he said there's just a bunch of storage rooms. Some sweatshop operation used to be here. They broke it up. But now it's empty, rat-filled. Wow—you smell that—?"

David nodded. Even from the sidewalk, even way out there, the stench was overwhelming.

"Nice joint," he said.

He held the door open, and now Kunokine walked in.

"Breathing through my mouth, that's what I'm going to do."

"Good idea."

David followed her. The light from outside provided a subdued glow inside. If there was a light switch, he guessed that the power would be off.

"Hard to see much," his partner said.

"The only blood they found was the victim's. Would have been a lot more blood if she had been killed."

"Lucky girl."

"Very. But what saved her?"

"When she wakes up, guess we can ask her."

"If she'll remember. Always the chance—"

"I know. The whole thing blocked out by shock."

"Exactly."

David reached into his back pocket, and pulled out a small three-inch flashlight. He turned it on.

"Hey, good thinking."

"Yeah. Always be prepared."

He pointed down to the ground, then around the wall. This wasn't like the site on Norfolk Street. No slaughter here, some blood spatters, a small smear on the wall—all the victim's blood, and—

"Hold on."

David crouched down and pointed the light at a spot on the wall, surrounded by islands of flaking paint. At first it looked like any other blood drop. But as he leaned close, David saw that this was different.

"What do you have there?"

"Take a look."

Kunokine crouched down, as they both got close to the pool of light neatly focused on the somewhat circular smear.

"More blood?"

"Yes—and look—a fingerprint."

His partner leaned even closer.

"Hell, if you aren't right. Good eyes. And the locals missed this? But the print, it still could—"

"I know. Still could be the victim's. Probably is. But that print, if it was missed, and if it doesn't match the girl's, well, then"—he turned to Kunokine and smiled—"then that could be something, couldn't it?"

In turning he had moved his light, catching part of Kunokine's face, a bit of the light letting David see her eyes. Which is when he noticed another pair of eyes, right next to hers . . . looking right back at him.

* * *

FOR a moment Mari and the mystery woman sat on the bench.

"Sorry," the woman finally said. "I'm jet-lagged, exhausted, frazzled."

Mari watched her dig out a pack of cigarettes and light one.

"Maybe we should start with . . . who you are?"

The woman took a puff, nodded, and pulled out a business card.

DR. LISA GRIFFINO PH.D.

And underneath, a variety of e-mail addresses and phone numbers. One of the e-mails was an *.edu*. An institutional address. So she's a teacher, Mari thought, a college prof, a—

"Dr. Griffino?"

"Aka Lisa. And yes, just got in from Singapore. Fifteen hours nonstop."

Mari nodded. "And you teach there?"

Lisa laughed. "You wouldn't want *me* teaching. I've tried. No. I'm a physicist. And an author. My new book came out six months ago."

Mari nodded.

Lisa looked around the park, thinning out even further. Mari could see that the woman wasn't just tired, she was scared. *Furtive* was the word that came to mind, as if the physicist was being stalked.

Lisa said, "Want to see? Here. Take my BlackBerry. Type in my name. Might even get a nice head shot."

"That's okay, I—"

Lisa's voice turned a bit edgy. "Go on. At least then you'll know that I am who I say I am."

Mari entered the name in the small version of Google. In seconds, a bio appeared, a list of a half dozen books. Then— halfway down—a picture.

A picture of the woman sitting next to her on the bench.

"None of my books did much until the last one. That one caused a stir. And the world of physics doesn't like getting stirred or shaken."

Mari scrolled back up to see that title . . . from 2006. *The Reality Revolution: The Truth About the New Physics.*

"Can't say I read it."

Lisa laughed. "Not a lot of laypeople did. But in my world, it was akin to publishing the Anti-Bible. Found myself pretty much out there by myself. But I didn't mind. What I wrote was true and other scientists will have to deal with it."

"Like Galileo?"

Another laugh. "You mean because I challenged the establishment? Yeah, maybe a bit like that . . ."

Mari sat there wondering what on earth this obviously intelligent and talented scientist would want with her on this beautiful afternoon.

For a few moments she thought that Lisa must have mistaken her for someone else, maybe the science reporter, someone who could help her career—

Mari looked at her watch. "Look, I really need to get back. There's this daily roundup for reporters, not that I—"

Lisa turned to her sharply, the small laughs and smiles quickly vanished. She tossed her spent cigarette butt to the ground.

"I know you do. I didn't come here to talk to you about physics, about my books, about any of that . . . not really."

She pulled out a yellow pad.

Mari saw that the pad's pages were puffy from words written in ink, pages flipped over, flat and then morphing into something else.

"Then what did you come here for? Not to see me. All the way from Singapore . . ."

Lisa looked Mari right in the eye. A quick turn to look at the old couple across the way, the couple not talking, just sitting until whatever quitting time arrived and told them it was time to go home.

"Oh, yes, I did. All the way from there to here to see you. To talk to you and—"

She held up the yellow pad.

"Tell you all about this."

A breeze blew through the park. The leaves of the under-nourished trees rustled, and a few leaves—getting an early start—began a slow tumble to the ground.

THE eyes . . . smaller, of course, then a brownish face, the whiskers, and David realized that Kunokine didn't know that she now had a rat the size of a giant house tabby sitting on the step, inches from her head.

David didn't move the light.

Rats have such bad eyesight. Makes them jumpy. You don't want jumpy rats.

Shit, you don't want any kind of rats.

But Kunokine could see David's eyes darting away, slightly to the left, looking at something.

And before he could whisper something like, *Stand up, slowly now, nice and slow* . . .

She turned her head, and her cheek brushed the rat's whiskers.

The rat squealed, a high-pitched shriek that sounded alien. . . .

David moved fast, at least as fast as his bad knee would allow him to move.

He stood up, letting his right leg do most of the work. His free hand reached out and grabbed Kunokine, pulling her to her feet.

The rat moved.

Without the light on it, David couldn't see what it was doing. But then he felt this deadweight hit his leg . . . *thump*.

And if that wasn't bad enough, he felt a small . . . *bite*.

Shit, he thought, *the goddamn thing bit me!*

He backed up, pulling Kunokine, now moving under her own speed, to the front door.

David looked around, and he could see the rat again, this time walking right into the edge of the open door, hitting it, then turning to the foot-wide opening leading outside.

All that brightness made the rat circle around crazily, like some jacked-up dog chasing its tail, which in this case was as long as the rat itself, until—

Together, in the shadowy light, they watched the rat go thumping back up the stairs, scurrying, sticking so close to the wall.

"You okay?" he asked Kunokine.

She nodded. "I think I'm going to be sick."

"The thing bit me."

"What? It broke the skin?"

The thought made David's stomach go tight.

"Yeah . . . I better get back to the station house. Get whatever you get for rat bites."

"And the fingerprint?"

"We can have them send someone, make a copy."

"And warn them about the rats."

"Right."

And David, both legs now operating with difficulties, walked outside.

29

"THE priest came to see me. From the Vatican no less. Someone named Brian Henning, SJ. I imagine you might find something about him online. Then again—maybe not."

Mari saw the woman rub her bare arms.

"Did it turn cool all of a sudden?" Lisa asked.

Mari nodded toward the buildings behind them. "Once the sun starts going down, it turns chilly."

"Never gets chilly in Singapore. Only hot and muggy . . . then hotter and muggier."

"He came from the Vatican?"

A nod. "He had an official position there. God knows"—a small smile at that—"what his title *was*."

Mari noted the use of the word *was*.

And now she too looked around.

"Something a bit left of center. Some secret subgroup. Like that Da Vinci Code book stuff. But not so mundane as whether Jesus had any offspring."

"Never read it."

Lisa smiled. "Neither did I. Saw the film on the plane, though. Henning was some kind of historian. But not just of Christianity. How did he put it . . . 'the evil that transcended the mundane.' "

"You mean *Exorcist*-type things?"

Mari still had to wonder what all this had to do with her. Could this woman have flown halfway around the world just to see her? It made no sense . . . so far.

"No. I mean, maybe, perhaps that too. Who knows what kind of ancient divisions and subdivisions there are in the Vatican. But this was not about possession and Satan. I got the feeling that whatever it was . . . *his* division was pretty secret and anything but"—she searched for a word—"moribund these days." She looked at Mari. "Guess you're still confused why I came to you, hmm?"

"Go on—what else?"

"Right." Lisa tapped the pad. "He told me about one thing. One continuous thing that the Vatican had been following, watching, studying for as long as there was a Vatican. Except it didn't begin with Christianity. No. It began long before that. Thousands of years before that."

They were completely in the shade now, the shadows lengthening. The old couple stood up, slowly, creakily, together—rising in tandem as if they were one.

"I'm rambling. I know," said Lisa. "It's a lot to just dump out there."

"How long did he talk to you?"

"Six . . . seven hours. Until I got the full importance of what he was saying, and long after he mentioned . . . your name."

Gooseflesh sprouted on Mari's arm just like that.

"HOW'S that?" one of the precinct sergeants asked David, pulling the bandage tight.

"Good. Thanks."

Kunokine stood beside him. "You know you still have to see a doctor. Get to a hospital. A goddamn rat bite."

"I will. But the rat barely broke the skin. Kids get bit by rats in their cribs all over the city."

"Nice thought."

The sergeant, an old-timer who had to be near retirement age, stood up.

"Yeah, I'd get that checked out, Detective."

David nodded. "And I think we left the guy inside on ice long enough." He looked up to his partner. "Shall we?"

Kunokine nodded, and they followed the sergeant to a locked interrogation room with a uniformed patrolman outside.

And the crisp young cop stood to the side and unlocked the door.

"MY name?"

Lisa nodded. "See. That's why I'm here. You—and what's happening, and the other things Henning told me. I think we would have spoken more. There were plans."

Two pigeons landed across from them, heads bobbing as they looked for any crumbs left behind, perhaps bits of a sandwich shared by the old couple.

Mari didn't say anything, because by now she knew what was coming. She knew the reason for the haunted look in the scientist's eyes. She knew what kind of event could propel someone to run . . . *run* . . . half a world away.

Finally, Mari said it.

"He was killed?"

"Yes. After he met with me, I followed him; he had left behind his cell phone. I followed, and just as he said—"

Just as he said . . .

"—I watched him get killed."

The woman turned away. Another cigarette emerged from her bag, but she didn't light it. Mari had seen her own share of horror. But still—she could see that whatever Lisa had seen she still carried with her.

"Did the killer see you?"

Lisa turned back. "Did he see me? No, I don't think so. I mean, perhaps afterward he knew—"

He knew. . . .

"—I had been there. And I knew I was as good as dead if he came back to my apartment. So I left. I came here."

A big breath.

"To you."

"And my other question. Who was he?"

"Who was he? Who is he?" Lisa shook her head as if pondering one of the great secrets of the universe. "Who will he be?"

"You're losing me."

Lisa looked around at the increasingly deserted park. People still streamed by on the sidewalk that girded the small park. But here, the park was quickly being reclaimed by the pigeons.

"I can tell you everything else. But not here. Not out in the open. I'm a bit . . . jumpy."

"Understandably. And I . . . well, I should get to the office. Catch some of that staff meeting. Otherwise there will be questions."

"Okay."

"So . . . my apartment . . . tonight?"

Lisa shook her head.

"No. Not there. Not someplace he might follow me."

Mari stopped. She reached out and touched Lisa's arm. "Wait. You said he might follow you? You think he followed you from Singapore?"

"I wish it was that simple. Wait till tonight, please? But no—not your place. Maybe something downtown, someplace small, where we can talk, no one paying attention. Maybe see if anyone walks in."

"I have to tell you—you're scaring me now."

Without a smile—"Good. That's a good thing. So, know a place?"

Mari thought a moment.

"Yes. Opens after six. Down some weird stairs. Looks a bit—what's the word the Brits use—dodgy. But it's okay. I'll find a table inside."

A small smile returned to Lisa's face.

"I like the way you think."

The scientist stood up.

"What are you going to do now?" Mari asked.

"Oh, don't worry—I have other things to do. Before we meet. Someone else to see. Maybe get some things from on-line that will help me—help you."

She stuck out her hand.

"Thanks, Mari. For not running away like I was completely mad."

"I reserve the right to do that later."

And—for a moment—they both laughed.

THE man—the nervous homeless guy—sat on a wooden chair at a desk as if he were about to take the homeless person's entrance exam.

His head shot up as David and Kunokine walked closer.

"I didn't do nothin'! You don't know anythin' 'bout me. Nothin'! I just get my cans and mind my own *bizness*."

David nodded.

The man seemed in an appropriately jumpy state of mind.

"We know."

His partner spoke up. "We're not accusing you of anything . . . yet."

The well-placed last word produced a snakelike effect in the man, as his tongue came out and tried to wet dry, cracked lips.

"But, sir," Kunokine said, "we will need to know some things. A woman was attacked."

"I didn't—"

Kunokine put up her hand. "We *know*. We know you didn't have anything to do with that. We heard you the first seven times."

The man's head bobbed like, well, a head-bobbler.

This much fun should be illegal, David thought.

Easier being a dentist specializing in root canals than trying to pry information from this shambling wreck.

David leaned close.

"So—you didn't do anything. We know that." He looked
up at Kunokine as if seeking her agreement with the next
proposition. "We believe you. But you saw something. We
need you to tell us *what* you saw. Everything you saw."

Again the tongue came out—and up close David could see
what a nasty piece of work that bit of meat was. . . .

More head-bobbing.

"I dunno. I dunno."

"Look," David began.

The trill of a cell phone.

Kunokine pulled her phone from a sheath attached to her
belt.

"David—I have to take this."

He nodded, then turned back to the man.

"We'll be right back, sir." A stretch using that word. "You
just review everything in your head. Go over it, okay, so you
can tell us everything."

Another nod.

Kunokine left the room—and David followed.

"YES. All right, I thought I would and—I'll see if I can get
someone there."

Kunokine flipped the phone closed.

"Problem?"

The woman nodded. "My kids. Home from school. I have a
girl with them till I get back—but I thought we'd be done
earlier—and now she says she has to leave. Teenagers. I have to
see if I can get someone to come. Might take a few."

Tough, thought David again, doing a job and being a single
parent. And he guessed that this woman, who just scared the
beejeezuz out of the man on the other side of the door, did
both jobs with a lot of care.

"Look, this guy is ready to open up. He's going to tell us everything we need. I think"—David smiled, aware that a compliment here would go a long way—"I think you got him a little scared."

Kunokine grinned at that.

"So—go home. I'll finish this. Call you later. No real need for the both of us here. Take the car. I'll grab a cab home."

"Are you sure?"

"I'm sure, and I will fill you in. So—not to worry."

He held out the keys.

"You're really sure?"

"I'm sure."

"David. Thanks. Parenting, you know . . ."

Actually, he didn't. *More my loss,* David thought. Though maybe that door wasn't quite closed yet.

"See you tomorrow, Susan."

And his partner turned, and walked out to the precinct's front desk.

While David turned back to the door, the young patrolman on guard standing to the side as if he might be guarding the president.

"At ease, Officer," David said with a grin. "He's not going anywhere . . . I don't think."

And the young cop smiled back.

It will take him a few years to really become NYPD, with all the good and not-so-good that brought.

David opened the door, and returned to the small interrogation room.

30

THERE are those, in the highly unreliable process of remote detective work, investigating mysterious events from even a century before, who maintain that someone called to Annie Chapman on that night, on what was really an early morning in 1888, to come out of The Ten Bells Pub.

Some "drunken sod," as the Metropolitan Police records would show, reported that Annie had been called out of the pub, that the man was someone that he—at least—had never seen before.

Yet Annie stepped out quite willingly, just a little after 5:00 A.M.

That is wrong.

Like much that surrounds this murder and so many others. Faulty memories, suppositions, rumors—a mélange of bits and pieces that all worked well to cover the events with what could have turned into a permanent fog.

Like the fog that shrouded the streets of London that morning.

And you might be excused for thinking that this fog was simply an ordinary London fog, the warm water of the Thames hitting the cool air of the night and morning and creating a surface cloud that would slowly begin to burn off.

But not then.

No, the fog then had another element, the thick smoky pol-
lutant that filled the air of London, a foul, brownish, noxious
mixture that surely had something to do with the short life
span of most of the residents.

The people who never got to the rolling hills of Kent, or to
the lake country to the north. Those who might as well have
been trapped in this poisonous smoky jar that was the city of
which Samuel Johnson said, "When one is bored of London,
one is bored of life."

Poisonous, yes.

Boring . . . no. Not now . . . not certainly then.

So we slow down those moments.

Since we are about to witness what really happened, free
of so many layers of untruth.

Annie Chapman, who only moments before had relieved
herself down the winding stone stairs of the pub, was now
desperate to have something to show for the evening.

Thinking . . .

Soon the workers will come to the lanes and alleys of the
Spitalfields Market, just across Commercial Road. And some
of those workers—the ones with money, the ones without
wives, or the ones whose wives had long ago given up the idea
of sleeping with them, fucking them, and risking another baby
to strap their already tight finances—

—why, they might be open to the notion.

Of a lady of the evening, now in the morning, promising a
jolt of adrenaline, some fast excitement that would certainly
wake them up for the hard work to come.

It was a possibility.

And while Annie couldn't actually walk those lanes, stroll
by those stalls . . . if she stood outside, the workers—
especially the early ones, especially the ones looking for just
that—would see her.

On offer.

Ready.

A distant vision that, from that distance, masked the pow-
dery makeup, the eyes bloodshot from too many ales—

So Annie, unnoticed by anyone in The Ten Bells, walked outside.

It was morning. The sun had started its creep over the hills. But the buildings masked that first crescent, and the fog that wasn't really a fog rendered whatever early light there was so that it wasn't much more than that produced by the feeble gas lamps.

Those lamps themselves were beginning to shut down.

It was dawn, after all.

Though you would never know it.

Annie walked along the side of The Ten Bells, up Commercial Road, then took a position at the far corner of the building, away from the big windows.

It wouldn't do to have anyone inside telling Mary Kelly that Annie had occupied "her" spot. She liked Mary, and Mary was no one to trifle with. They all had their place, and Annie knew hers.

But Mary was long gone for the evening. No one inside could see.

And with a bit of luck, Annie might not go back to her cramped room empty-handed.

She heard the voice from behind; not from across the way as expected, from where she could hear the sound of a workman's feet trudging up to the marketplace entrance.

But from behind, up a bit further on Commercial, where there was a narrow alley.

It startled her.

Annie had been waiting, expectant, eyes scanning. So to be surprised like this felt strange.

It was as if the voice had just *appeared*.

And what a voice.

Deep, velvety-sounding—but almost foreign. Not at all like any of the jumble of cockneys and brogues that filled The Ten Bells, or even the foreign voices, the occasional French or Italian worker who found his way to the markets.

This voice was completely different from any of those.

He had said:

"Good evening."

Then, even before she turned!

"Aye, good morning, y'mean . . ."

She turned and saw the man. Ten feet away. Close enough so she could really see him, but still with a bit of the foggy haze around. She noticed that he looked well dressed. Not a worker at all; but well dressed in a strange way.

One thing stuck in her mind—his shirt, open at the collar. It looked odd.

But he had seen her, greeted her.

She smiled.

"Indeed. Yes, it is morning, isn't it?"

The man nodded.

"Daylight soon. Everyone off to work."

"And what is it you do then, sir, a nice gentleman like you . . . hmm?"

She pursed her lips together when she said "hmm," brazenly flirting, hopefully planting an image of those lips in the man's mind. The thought of what those lips could do, so quickly, so expertly.

"I travel," the man said. "Always . . . traveling."

"But"—Annie took a step closer, a coy step, with just a hint of sway in her hips—"you're here now. You're not traveling now. Maybe—"

Another step, and she could touch him. And she did . . . her hand pressing gently against the collar of his jacket.

The material—smooth, fine—and she immediately imagined how much she could charge.

"—you need some entertainment. A bit of rest for such a hardworking bloke."

She looked up at his eyes.

Deep, dark—and his face chiseled. Someone fit, strong—

She let her hand trail down, slowly, her eyes on his, eager to feel whether she had provoked a reaction.

But when she got down below his belt, she felt nothing there . . . yet.

No matter. She knew how to resolve that.

The man seemed to hesitate for a moment.

"I think I could. Some entertainment could be enjoyable. If you can be quick, that is—maybe back here."

Annie leaned out a bit and looked down Brick Lane, leading to Hanbury Street and an alley. She knew that the lane opened to a small courtyard, surrounded by a few shops, but also small buildings where people lived.

"Cor, not very private down there, sir, don't you think?"

"It's private enough. There's still fog. And"—his hand came up to hers, closing on it, a gentle squeeze—"and I know you can be . . . so fast."

Annie smiled, lips open, grinning, agreeing. "You best hope I'm not too fast, eh. Now the price—"

But the man nodded. He pressed some coins into her hand, a fistful, and Annie knew that now the whole night had been worthwhile.

And still holding her hand, cradling it, he led her down the alley.

They reached the courtyard.

They were unseen.

What follows, if seen, would be for most unwatchable. And if seen, unforgettable.

In the true sense.

Something not to be forgotten.

Ever.

In the interest of establishing the facts, we must see the various—steps. The sequence. But you can be sure that to have been there would have been unbearable.

As merely a witness.

Unbearable.

And so . . .

A light was on on a nearby second floor, a flickering lamp for the morning, or perhaps from the night before.

It shed a little glow.

Annie looked around. This was so open, not at all private. Wasn't good to have people complain. The police might come, chase the girls away.

They'd blame Annie. . . .

"Good," the man said. "Here."

Annie smiled, her professional smile, as the work began.

Her hand trailed down again and she began rubbing, sliding up and down, through the material, again the material so much smoother than the coarse trousers that most of her customers were forced to wear.

And now—some reaction.

"Ah, there he is," Annie said.

"It has been a—frustrating day."

More rubbing.

"Do you know the meaning of the word, Annie? Frustrating?"

"Cor, now, 'ow do you know my name?"

"I just do. You're famous."

She laughed. "Famous for what . . . this?"

She brought her fingers up to the zipper—no buttons here, and opened his fly. Her hand quickly brought him out.

"Bet I know what you like, sir, I do."

She started to go down to her knees, knowing that the stones were wet with the morning, cold, uneven—

And as she lowered, she heard the man say—that accent so strange—"Bet you don't . . ."

31

ANNIE looked up, even before her lips touched him.

And it had been a frustrating day for her too.

Whatever a *day* meant to him, to this traveler. Probably so much of a difference in their meaning of frustrating.

His hand went to her chin and caressed it. Her fingers were locked on his zipper, but his hand had stopped her.

She must have thought: *What does he want then?*

Some stand-up, in and out, leaning against the building? Or did he want to go someplace? That could still be done, and surely would mean more shillings for her.

She started to get up from her kneeling position.

Annie heard voices from out on Brick Lane. The clatter of horse hooves. The day slowly building. But they were shrouded just enough back here, in this alleyway near the market.

"I didn't intend to return here so soon," the man said. "I really wanted someplace new. Something new. And I think I have found it. But this can be so dependable."

He smiled at her.

And Annie, her confusion mounting, thought . . . nutters were always a problem. That, and the drunken boyfriend who could kill you.

The thought crossed her mind:

*I should get up. Get up fast, and move away. This one's . . .
a strange bird. Who knows what he wants?*

But she had already taken his money. He might get mad.

There was that moment's hesitation.

She didn't even see the move.

It was that fast, that practiced—

She felt it first, then saw what it was seconds after.

All of a sudden, there was this curving gash in her throat.
She felt liquid fill her mouth. Fill it, as if someone had pried
open her jaw and just poured something in, salty, slick.

The gash sent bolts of agonizing pain straight to her brain.
Instinctively her hands went up to the opening as if somehow
they could stem the flow of blood.

She looked at the man, and saw the knife in his hand, the
blade catching the pale light, smeared with something, with
whatever filled her mouth.

She gagged. She coughed.

The man had moved to the side. Practiced, experienced.

Annie fell forward, heaving, spitting . . . incapable of making any sound but a low gurgle.

The man spoke again.

"I must take a trophy, Annie. You know how much they will
like that. The people and their newspapers, the ones that read.
How it will excite them. And it's all about excitement, isn't it."

She felt him behind her, a hand on her bottom, turning her,
then sliding up her frayed dress and petticoat.

He would work quickly.

It was morning after all.

But Annie would be awake, aware while it all happened.

And that—as one can well imagine—was the true beauty
of it.

LATER . . .

A workman walked by the alleyway and saw a shape. He

stopped. Took a step, and then wisely, as he told the story hours later, he called for the police.

"I yelled as loud as a bloke could, eh? Screamed out for the coppers. Never around where the real stuff is 'appening, what?"

He became a hero. The man who found her.

The bobbies, already alarmed that something odd was happening here, that the papers' coverage of two dead tarts might not all be hysterical journalism, didn't really examine the body.

That was beyond their training, their ability.

What they saw, lying there, required the eyes, the hands of a man who could deal with such things, look at such things, touch such things.

One might think of a butcher.

In this case, they waited for a doctor, a retainer of the Metropolitan Police.

His report, written so carefully and dryly, can be read today. It's all that there is, all that's left of Annie.

She died from loss of blood, her open throat a life-seeping gusher. But the report said that she didn't die before other cuts were made in her abdomen and, finally, something removed with a skill that would lead to other legends, other rumors, other myths. . . .

All false.

Her uterus was gone, neatly incised and removed.

Fueling more mad speculation of the killer and his motives, his imagined trophies, the wrongs done to him . . . all the typical thinking that fueled the mystery.

When that was all merely part of the game, all that speculation.

There really was only one objective from the beginning. It had been, as he said, a frustrating day.

And what did the people see? What did anyone see?

Did anyone stumble upon the scene? See someone running through the streets, perhaps something wrapped in a bit of material cut from the dead victim's dress?

Nobody saw anything.

No steps, no one running.

Nothing.

Though the alleyway only emptied out to Brick Lane and onto the Spitalfields Market, nobody in the slowly building crowd of early morning workers saw anything. . . .

Nobody saw anything.

The killer was nowhere to be found.

Nowhere.

It was as if, the Scotland Yard inspectors would say amongst themselves, as if he had up and disappeared.

Though what in the world could the odds be of that happening?

BOOK THREE

Nowhere

32

THE man's name was Eddie, David found out.

Eddie . . . what? Nobody at the station knew. Or cared. Homeless slobs like Eddie stood in the way of the long-planned-for Coney Island redevelopment.

Rumors were now floating that it would turn Coney into a resort to rival Atlantic City, with luxury oceanfront hotels, sparkling casinos . . . all the old decrepit rides replaced with a new family-safe theme park.

Would the old Cyclone roller coaster have to go too?

All that wood, and its rickety sound?

Of course it would.

And Coney would finally become part of the new New York. Clean, safe, and fun.

David guessed it might be a good thing, but part of him longed for some of that edge the old New York had—when you knew it was the biggest of big cities.

And guys like Eddie?

They'd all be gathered up, tossed on a bus, and dumped somewhere else. Guys like Eddie hated the shelters—they loved the freedom of Dumpster diving and scouring their neighborhood for the poor man's gold strike, the deposit on nickel cans.

David sat down and faced Eddie, as eager to have Eddie get back to his life as Eddie was.

David smiled.

"Now, where were we?"

Eddie's tongue attempted to wet his lips.

"Can I—can I have some water?"

"Sure. No problem. Soon as our chat is done. No problem at all. Maybe even have a few bucks for you. Since we burned some hours on you."

The thought of money made Eddie's eyes widen. Every dollar meaning that much less time gathering cans, that much sooner he could start pouring some kerosene-grade liquor into his stomach.

"How's that sound?"

"Uh, that's good. But I tell you. I mean, the guys here know me . . . I didn't do anything."

Guilt. It's a funny thing, the way guilt can just take hold of someone. You could be perfectly innocent, David thought, and then every bad thing you ever did comes bubbling up, making you look guilty as sin.

"We know that, Eddie. You're a good guy. Never a problem."

Eddie's dry lips attempted a smile.

David looked around, as if checking whether anyone was watching what he'd do next.

But to Eddie—it might look like David was making sure that they were all alone.

"But even though you're one of the good ones . . . no stealing, no hassling the nice people out for a day at the beach . . . we also know that . . . *that* night you saw something. We can see it in your eyes. Your face. The way—"

David pointed an index finger at Eddie's grimy forehead, and then touched him, wiping.

"All that sweat. Just doesn't look good."

Eddie nodded, the inevitability of his fate becoming clear.

"So—all we want you to do is tell us. What you saw."

Eddie's bloodshot and rheumy eyes finally fell full square onto David's.

Then, taking a breath in this purposely airless room, Eddie said the words David had been waiting to hear.

Like a gummy oyster opening to reveal a tiny pearl inside.

"I'll tell ya." Eddie rubbed his chin. "I'll tell ya what I saw."

LISA Griffino plopped down into an ornate couch, in the outer extension of the Soho Grand Bar. It was quiet now, no DJ, no flirting couples yet, and just a few hipster-business types having tea, coffee.

In an hour, she imagined, it would all change.

A waitress in a black sheath, the top cut so low, Lisa imagined, that when she bent to serve someone, they could see a nice view of the swell of her breasts.

"Just a pot of tea," Lisa said.

She waited until the girl had left, then dug out her Black-Berry.

And as was becoming a habit lately, she looked around the room. No one looking at her. God, not even the trio of males looking her way, checking her out.

Guess a shower and change of clothes might be in order.

But what clothes? She guessed there had to be a Gap or Banana Republic nearby. That should do.

Back to the BlackBerry.

She used the browser to get a number. At the same time she checked her watch.

Shouldn't be too late there, she thought.

Good half hour before five. Everyone should still be there.

Unless—

Was it Monday? Lot of museums closed on Mondays. Some archaic blue law.

She thought—what day was it?

No. It was Tuesday.

She pressed SEND to dial the number.

She probably could have gotten a direct line—but the general number would probably be fine.

Three rings, a fourth—then:

An automated message. "Hello, you've reached the main information number of The Morgan Library, please listen—"

Screw listening, Lisa thought. She hit 0.

A gamble that didn't always work, but this time:

"Please wait for the next available operator."

Some Vivaldi came on. Not bad for phone music.

Then, after a minute:

"Hello, how may I help you?"

"I'd like to speak with Museum Director Dr. Kirkland Mathews, please."

"And who shall I say is calling?"

"Dr. Lisa Griffino."

Lisa hoped that the "doctor" would nullify any attempts to prescreen the call any further.

And it did. . . .

"Hold on, please . . ."

And Lisa did.

EDDIE started slowly.

"I was—I was just looking for a place to take a swig and a piss. You know, they don't like you doing that in the street anymore."

"Really?"

Eddie nodded as if it were a real question.

"So there's this old building, a small—I dunno, warehouse or something. I go there, other guys too. Usually it's okay unless some crack heads are in there. Then . . . man, it's not safe even for me. And ya have to watch out for the rats."

"I'm sure. So you go to that building."

"Yeah, yeah, the door is always open. I mean, it's abandoned, right?"

"Appears that way."

Eddie stopped. For someone who lived on the streets with crack heads and other unsavory characters, he seemed about as nervous as a schoolgirl.

"Go on. Tell me what you saw."

Eddie looked up. "You're gonna give me some money after this, ain't that right?"

"That's right."

He rubbed his beard.

"Okay then. I pushed open the door. And this girl was there, on the steps. I saw the knife right away. And this guy— damn, he had cut her already, I guess. Some blood on the floor. But she was still alive."

"What did you do then?"

David wondered how much of Eddie's memory could be relied on. Some, none, all? It was a crap shoot, but for now it was all he had—that, and a fingerprint.

"I-I like fell back. I mean, there was blood."

"And then?"

"The girl—guess I startled the guy. She did something. Kicked him. His face was bleeding. Then she ran, or something. All cut up too. I backed away, started to turn. I mean, I didn't want to see any more. But the girl—she ran right out onto the street. Shit, a car was coming."

"And that freaked you?"

The man nodded. "Sure did. Sure the hell did. But that wasn't all. Even though—shit—I was really scared even then, and I don't get scared easy, mister."

David guessed most "scary" things flew well under Eddie's radar. *Was that a real rat, or just a blurry spot moving on my eye?*

Eddie stopped, looked down.

"You saw something else?"

Now Eddie slowly raised his head. And David saw in his eyes a near-sober look as he nodded.

"I'd stopped and turned. Only a second, to see. The girl, the car, then the man—coming out. Guess he saw her run out to the street. Lost her, and, and—"

Was that a tear in Eddie's eyes?

Had he seen something that could slip past his layers of drunken encrustation, his armor against the real world?

David figured he didn't need to nudge him again.

"The guy, he ran out. He turned. Saw me. Christ, and he smiled. Like it didn't fucking matter. *It didn't . . . fucking matter*. And then—"

Eddie shut his eyes. The whole thing too vivid for his wet brain to deal with.

David could hear his own breathing. The hum of a fluorescent bulb. The feeling in the room that something was about to happen.

Eddie's eyes opened.

"He disappeared. He just . . . fucking . . . *disappeared*."

33

"DR. Mathews?"

"Yes, this is Dr. Mathews."

"Dr. Mathews . . . I'm Dr. Lisa Griffino. I'm a physicist, writer . . . and, well—"

"Yes?"

Lisa looked around the Soho Grand lounge. People were arriving and tea service was giving way to the first onslaught of cocktails.

"Um, I was wondering if I might meet you in the morning. To see—discuss certain items in the Pierpont Morgan collection."

The man made a polite laugh.

"I would love to, Dr. Griffino, but I'm afraid this week is all booked with meetings. Fund-raising never ends. Barely have time to attend to the exhibitions. Perhaps in a week or—"

"No."

Lisa realized that the stress of the past twenty-four hours was taking its toll.

"I mean, I'm sorry, Dr. Mathews. But—"

Lisa tried to process in her head how much of this she could tell him on the phone. She had hoped none of it. But that obviously wouldn't work. A *week*? It would be too late, time up.

Game over . . . she thought.

How . . . apt.

"I am very busy, Dr. Griffino. Perhaps I could switch you to my secretary and she could find—"

"Dr. Mathews, I have just come from meeting Father Brian Henning."

A pause.

A name he knew.

Then cautiously . . . "Yes?"

"It was in Singapore. I understand . . . you have communicated with him."

"We have."

Lisa could feel the shift in Mathews. The affable curator suddenly on guard. The tension palpable even over the phone.

"He sought me out. He thought I might help."

Mathews said nothing in response to this.

"And—" Another look around the lounge. "I watched him get killed."

"Good God!"

"So, Dr. Mathews . . ." A breath. "Trust me when I tell you that there is no time to postpone our talking. We can't wait a week."

For an eternity of seconds . . . nothing. Then:

"I understand. I can see you first thing. I will clear the whole morning."

"It may not take that long. But Father Henning felt you may have something that would help them . . . help me understand."

Another pause.

Then: "I'm not sure I believe it all."

Lisa laughed, a small chuckle born equally of fear and confusion. "Nor do I."

"I get to my desk early. 7:30 A.M."

"Then I will be there. Will someone let me in?"

"There will be a guard at the main library entrance. Just tell them who you are."

"See you in the morning. And Dr. Mathews . . . thank you."

"Good-bye," the curator said.

When the line went silent, Lisa guessed that her call hadn't brought happiness into the cloistered world of The Morgan Library. Unless she was wrong, Mathews was about to take a giant step out of the museum's cosseted past . . . and enter a very grim, very real present.

She stood up and looked at the time on her BlackBerry. Time to grab some quick clothes at the Gap. An even faster shower, then on to a place she had never been, but under the circumstances, sounded weirdly ironic . . .

Double Happiness . . .

DAVID walked out of the interrogation room. The precinct house had grown quiet, the evening shift not kicking in, and the few officers in the building just marking time.

The captain, a short round-faced man named Keller, came up to David.

"So you want us to hold him?"

David shook his head. He knew that—for now—he wasn't going to tell anyone what Eddie had said.

That would go over big with the department. Disappearing killers.

Just my kind of stuff.

"Yes and no. Got everything out of him that I could. So no reason to keep him here. But he did see the guy. Not too sure he'd be able to guide a sketch artist at all. But it's worth a shot."

Keller nodded, then looking up at David, who towered over him, said, "If he saw him, Detective, then where did he say the guy went?"

David smiled.

"Look, I'm not sure how much faith you can put in Eddie's version of what happened. He saw the guy, he saw the victim stagger to the street. Then"—a small lie, but almost true—"he didn't see anything else."

"You want some of my homicide guys to talk to him? You know, they got history with these bums."

David figured he better not make too big a deal about *not* having them talk to him.

"You can. But I doubt they will learn anything. More important is trying for a sketch—and checking that fingerprint."

Keller nodded.

"Oh, yeah. We dusted it, then brought that bit of paint back here. Pretty clear print, and it's not the girl's. We took a scraping to see if the blood maybe isn't hers too."

"So, if the guy did anything, we'll find out."

David thought about Eddie's words—*he just disappeared*—and wondered whether a fingerprint, or a blood type, could have any meaning at all.

"Want to wait for the sketch guy?"

David nodded.

"Yeah, and maybe if you look for a print match . . ."

"That should come in fast."

So now David had a little downtime in Precinct Sixty-two, Coney Island.

"How about some food while you wait? Got a good clam place right around the corner and they deliver."

David smiled. Fried clams as only you can get them here.

"Sounds great."

MARI sat at a corner table in the dark confines of Double Happiness. She guessed it must have been a while since her last visit here, one that left her with wobbly knees from too many green tea martinis and the memory of kissing someone a lot that she had just met.

Not my finest hour, she thought.

New York was littered with places like this that could turn into a maze of strange entanglements and lost inhibitions.

But she had also been to small parties here . . . for her friend Julie, whose novel came out last year (and vanished immediately), and her friends at Scholastic, who had a going-away party for one of their group who was able to escape.

The stone walls themselves seemed full of memories.

But the setting was perfect for whatever Lisa Griffino was bringing Mari. Quiet alcoves, everyone minding their own business, lovers, friends . . . everyone in their own little bubble.

The bartender brought over a cup of tea sans martini.

"Sure that's all you want?"

Mari smiled. "For now. Maybe something stronger later."

He turned away, and Mari awaited the mysterious physicist from Singapore.

LISA looked at the number she had written down: 173 Mott Street.

Well, that was here. But the stone steps guarded by a green iron railing at 173 Mott looked like they led nowhere, except maybe to the storage basement for one of the Asian food shops nearby.

Place would fit in well in Singapore, she thought.

Mysterious, a little intimidating.

She took a breath and walked down the stairs.

Mari saw the door open and Lisa Griffino walk in, scanning the bar, looking to the back of the room.

She got up and hurried to her.

"Hi—everyone does that."

Lisa laughed. "Oh—look lost. Yeah, I felt like I got off the wrong floor of an elevator."

The bartender hovered nearby.

"Like something?"

"Um"—Lisa turned to Mari—"what are you having?"

"They make great green tea martinis . . . but I'm having plain old tea for now."

"Me too then. For now."

Mari led Lisa over to the small table, around to the side.

"Looks like a person could get shanghaied here," said Lisa.

"Who knows? Maybe it's happened."

"Spooky. A little romantic."

Lisa's tea arrived, a tiny cloud of steam floating upward.

Mari pulled something out of her purse, a book.

The Reality Revolution: The Truth About the New Physics.

"My book."

Mari flipped it over, to a head shot of the author.

"Did a little homework?"

"I always do my homework."

A trio of young women in business attire pushed their way in past the swinging doors, laughing, already clearly in party mode.

"Good then. We have a lot of ground to cover. And I'm not sure how much time."

Mari had her reporter's notebook out, pen ready.

"Best start then. So—this priest was killed, he told you things. About a killer and—" Mari hesitated. "Wait. Does it have something to do with what's been happening here, the killing on the Lower East Side, the attack in Coney, the others that are still sealed?"

Lisa nodded. "I'd say yes to all of that."

"That's hard to believe."

"But that's not why I'm here. Not really."

"Hold on—" Mari said.

She dug in her purse and pulled out a small digital recorder.

"Do you mind? I'll still take notes. But—"

"Go ahead. Will it pick us up"—Lisa waved at the surroundings—"here?"

"It should. It's good at picking up just the voices at close range."

Lisa smiled. "Okay. Let's begin . . . because, you see—it doesn't have to do with just those killings, Mari. My guess—is it has more to do with you."

Mari felt her breath catch. The cup of tea in front of her had lost its steamy cloud.

She reached down, and pressed RECORD.

34

THE time is 1947.

For this beautiful dark-eyed woman, that is.

1947, a balmy evening in Los Angeles.

And the woman—stunningly beautiful, you would say. Jaw-droppingly beautiful in that way that only a movie star can be. Especially a movie star that hasn't been discovered yet.

Hasn't been used.

But she's not a star yet, and the person who will certainly be discovered, who will become that most incandescent of stars, sits across from her in the quiet lounge of the Biltmore Hotel.

That other woman's face you might recognize, but not the hair, not yet platinum blond, not yet colored to that white gold that would perfectly match that smile, those eyes.

So it's this other woman, not more than a girl, who gets the second looks, the attention. And she too has come here, to Los Angeles, to seek that stardom that somehow she must have thought was her birthright, her destiny.

It's a funny thing about destiny.

We can think one thing, and it can deliver another.

Destiny. It's what will happen, what is happening, and what has happened.

All three, with such small things shaping each little fateful twist and turn.

Destiny, made of small things, and sometimes, as we well know, as we all understand—some very big things.

But for now, the evening for these two young women is near ending. . . .

"Look, Beth, I know how these guys think. . . ."

"I know you do, Norma," the dark-haired woman said without any sense of rebuke. "But I don't think it's the only way to break in."

Norma leaned close, the bottom ringlets of the sandy-brown hair brushing the tabletop.

"Maybe it's not the only way—but it's a *way*. You're crazy not to use what you have."

"Like talent?"

A bit of teasing there.

"All right, ignore me. But if you never get a shot, never get your face in front of the cameras, all that talent will mean nothing. You might as well be a soda jerk."

"Or just a jerk."

Beth watched her friend look at her watch—a gift, she imagined.

"You got to go?"

"He's picking me up in fifteen. I could still ask if he has a friend."

"No, thanks. Not in a 'friend' mood tonight."

"I'll give you"—a little wink that Beth had to admit looked irresistible—"the battle report tomorrow."

"Can't wait."

And then she watched her friend walk out of the Biltmore Hotel, moving in a way that she had to admit looked incredibly sexy.

Could use some of that myself, Beth thought.

And—maybe a new name. Elizabeth—or Beth—not sounding like a movie star. Certainly not Betty. There already was a "Betty."

Nothing like Lana or Rita . . . both made up, both perfect.

Maybe a new name might be good.

She sat there finishing her glass of wine, nursing it actually because she really didn't have anywhere to go tonight.

It felt safe in the lounge, safe . . . and quiet.

While only steps away from Beth, someone watched.

He watched with the eye of connoisseur. Someone who recognized quality. And more importantly, someone who knew how legends are created.

She was beautiful, that was undeniable.

And her beauty and what happened to her would become the stuff of legend.

He had seen enough for now. No need to wait.

No need to stay here *for now*.

No need to stay here at all.

35

DAVID sat in the wardroom of the precinct house, dipping clam strips into a red sauce and then eating each strip like a bird.

Probably a taste you could only get here, he thought, by the sand and salt and gulls of Coney.

Keller walked in.

"We got the results, David."

David wiped his hands on a napkin. "That was fast."

"Even here we got broadband. Zapped it to VICAP, they zapped it back in minutes. We'll keep the chip, the print on file—"

"But nothing? No match?"

Keller nodded.

And somehow David knew that was what was going to happen.

A nameless print.

A print with no history.

Like it was the first fucking time the attacker had done that.

As if . . .

Then he thought of what Eddie said. Could have been a euphemism—*guy just disappeared.*

If anyone asked, David would certainly play it that way.

Guys disappear all the time.

But when he had leaned closer to Eddie, ignoring the stench that wafted off him, looking right into those rheumy eyes, it was clear that this was no goddamn euphemism.

The wardroom felt chilly. The clams suddenly settling into their greasiness.

He thought of what had happened in the spring. The so-called Warehouse Murders.

Where suddenly he was playing with something that was miles beyond the strangest cases of the department, out there, all alone except for Mari.

While someone used . . . dreams . . . to lure, to kill.

The department's chief shrink seemed mostly interested in getting David through his mandatory counseling sessions, and out the door,

That kind of weirdness rubs off.

And now . . . *this.*

And you didn't get to be a detective for a decade or more— a good detective—without gaining some life-preserving in-stincts.

Thoughts, hunches that surfaced. Thoughts and hunches that could sometimes mean the difference between life or death.

Like the one now.

That those murders in Manhattan and this attack . . .

That somehow they were connected.

Maybe not in the sense that one victim had something to do with the other.

No. David had looked into the bullet-ridden body of the dream killer. As they aver in *The Wizard of Oz,* he was truly dead.

No coming back home for that one.

But this instinct was about something else . . .

That this killer knew about those murders, about the dream killer, *knew* about David, and in a strange way—that was all part of it.

There are no accidents in life.

Something he learned a long time ago. Everything has a reason, the good stuff, the bad stuff, the deadly stuff, the stupid stuff—all of it.

"Hey, Dave—you okay?"

David looked up. "Yup. Just thinking what's next."

Keller nodded.

"Sounds like this time, he just got away."

David stood up and gathered up the remaining, now unappetizing clam strips.

"This time. Yeah. Thanks for letting us come out."

"Anytime, Detective, anytime."

David looked around for a convenient trash can to drop the clams in, and then he would head back to New York, to perhaps the only person he could really talk to about this.

To Mari.

THE digital recorder ran silently.

Lisa leaned close, eyes on Mari.

"I'm going to have to cover a lot of ground fast. I'll try to cut some things out that Henning told me. I mean, it was just so much. And I don't think we have the luxury of time."

Mari held her pen, ready to fill the steno page with good little reporterlike notes. The words, though . . . so disturbing . . . *we don't have the luxury of time.*

"Okay, first, I am not religious. God and me—well, we split a long time ago. I am a scientist. So I file religion in the 'bullshit that has screwed up civilization' folder. And Father Henning came to me knowing that."

"Because of your book?"

"Yes. They knew that. They knew—I might be the only person who understood."

"Something religious?"

Lisa shook her head. "No. Not religious. But then again— it's like Clarke said. Science carried to its extreme would appear as supernatural. So I guess they thought that there is a

place where science and religion do meet. It did a few days
ago, in my apartment."

Mari emptied her tea.

"More?"

Lisa nodded. "Yes. We best still hold off on the martinis."

Mari leaned out, caught the bartender's eyes, and signaled
with two fingers that they'd like more.

Lisa wasted no time. "Henning said to me that from the
dawn of the Church, its concern has been *evil*. From the very
beginning, the Church was focused on the absolute belief that
demons were real . . . and all that hell stuff too. So from the
time Peter became the rock of Christianity, the one true
Roman Church chased demons, recorded 'sightings,' noted
events. . . ."

"I know. I went to parochial school."

"Yeah. But the modern Church has moved past all that,
hmm? Or so it would like the world to believe. We know there
are no demons. I think people like Henning and the others know
there's no real hell, save for the one we make here on earth."

"Yet he was stalking demons?"

"Yes and no. He—" She stopped as the bartender arrived
with a pot of tea with two new cups.

"Brought you a pot this time," he said. "It will keep it
warmer."

Mari saw Lisa look up at him and smile. The scientist was
undoubtedly attractive, though clearly she didn't take too
much care with things like makeup and hair. The bartender
smiled back.

In a different world, maybe he'd be chatting them both up.

Now—Lisa returned to her strange story.

"Demons. Depends on what you call a demon, I guess.
Creatures who lived for pure evil? Lot of those walking the
planet today. And Henning explained that there came a point
where even Holy Mother Church became aware that there
were no demons—not the demons we knew from legend, from
all those tales throughout history."

Mari poured the tea.

"At least, no demons like that."

DAVID stepped out, the sun gone, and he could see a glow from a few blocks away, the neon of the surfside Coney. The season close to an end, the evening chill pointing the way to the winds that would soon start roaring off the Atlantic.

Though it was colder out here, and with just his brown sport coat on he was clearly underdressed, it felt good to be outside.

Out of that precinct house.

Where fingerprints meant nothing.

He stayed on the top step, looking around, wondering if someone could be watching him.

The owner of that print.

Hiding, watching.

That's what this felt like. That prickly feeling you got when you felt someone's eyes lingering on you.

But the street was deserted.

His cell rang.

"Hello?"

"David. I've been trying you. Have your phone off?"

"Yeah. I was with someone. An interrogation of sorts."

"We sold the place."

For a moment he had to think. Sold the place? What place?

Then he imagined their cottage on Block Island, on a day like this when the deep blue sky faded into an even richer indigo, the white of the waves catching the light of the stars, the moon.

A good place to retreat from all this.

Now—

Sold.

"I thought that the agent was going to wait."

"Right! Amazing, hmm? But a buyer showed up, saw it— and met the price."

"Great. That's great."

Not feeling at all like it was great.

"The paperwork will be mailed to us, so no need to go back there again. Least not together. We close in about six weeks."

"Gotcha."

"You don't sound very happy?"

"I am. Just been a crazy day. I'm in Coney Island."

"Coney Island? I won't even ask what for."

"Good. Don't. So—what do I have to do?"

"For now—nothing. I mean, the place is still ours for another six weeks at least. If you want to get away for a weekend or something. I'm all socked in. So I probably saw it for the last time."

Breakups—even when they were civil—still had a certain sting.

"Okay then, cool. The cottage is taken care of. That's good—and thanks for taking care of things."

"Yeah."

Then nothing, as now they both were on the same page.

The end of things. A finalization. Never good.

"I'll let you know if I go there. In case there's anything special you want me to bring back."

"Thanks."

"Bye."

The call ended.

It was fully night.

And time to go back to what people in this part of the world called . . . the City.

"I'M leaving a lot out here. But the Church has watched things for thousands of years. Looking for evil. The signs of Satan, demons, until they knew that, sure, evil existed. But they might have it all wrong."

"How's that?"

"Over the centuries—so many stories of killings, appearances, violence, ritual. It didn't take much for them to see in their ancient records that there were similarities. Some line that ran from Anno Domini one till now. Someone, something that killed in certain ways, that could always escape, leaving a trail of unexplained murders, killings, butcheries. Centuries of them . . ."

Lisa looked up right at Mari, her face set, grim.

Nothing funny or theoretical about this now.

"Until they knew whatever it was . . . whoever it was . . . was in fact toying with them. Playing with them."

Mari rubbed her arms.

Was the AC too high? It didn't seem that way when she walked in.

"Playing with them? You mean, the Church?"

"Initially, among others. But definitely a game. Like hunting. Some sick bloody game—"

Mari reached out and touched Lisa.

"But wait. You said . . . over centuries. That's—"

Now a trace of a smile.

"Impossible? Of course it is. Damn, I wish you still could smoke in New York. Might as well toss my cigarettes in the garbage. So yes—of course it is impossible. And—at the same time . . . of course it isn't."

"You're losing me."

"See, once the pattern was discovered, a pattern they kept secret, they started looking further, deeper."

"Deeper?"

"Into the past. Even though we know so little about early history, the first civilizations. But someone within this secret Vatican cell—for that's what it was—became convinced that the pattern was far more ancient than just the past few thousand years."

Mari reached down and clicked off the recorder.

"God, I think I need that drink now."

"Me too. Because, well . . . let's say I haven't gotten to the good part yet."

Mari turned and looked at the bartender, who, it seemed, had his eyes on them. He probably didn't have many customers coming down to the subterranean lounge drinking hot tea.

"Two green tea martinis," Mari said.

"Got it."

Then Mari turned back. "Before I turn this on again. I mean . . . I will have to play this for other people. I just need to ask you about what you said." She looked right at Lisa. Then: "This has something to do with me?"

Lisa took a breath.

"I don't have all the answers. But—I'm afraid so."

Mari nodded. Then—

"Let's go on."

And Lisa continued.

36

THE Los Angeles of 1947 . . .

So different.

The air, not yet tinted a permanent brown from the exhaust of the endless cars. Not yet bound by the freeways that would gird, enclose, and finally entrap the city and its surrounding areas . . . still in the planning stages.

This glittering city—still the preserve of those who could afford a certain lifestyle, filled with elegant Studebakers and Cadillacs, dinners at the Brown Derby and Musso & Frank.

It was a Los Angeles of dreams, and yet—for brief decades—it was real.

It was a Los Angeles that would lure and destroy, and continue to do so on a mammoth scale until it became a sea of strip malls, drive-throughs, and an exploding population that had dreamed of palm trees and riches but now lived with high gas prices, five-lane expressways, and air that could choke even the richest dream.

But then—for some—it gleamed with all the allure and promise and magic of Oz.

But even Oz had its dark secrets . . .

* * *

BETH walked out of the Biltmore Hotel.

The doorman, in top hat and tails, looked ready to burst into song. A Fred Astaire number perhaps, a little soft-shoe while he spun the door open and went to flag a waiting cab.

When the driver no doubt would jump out and join in the chorus.

It's what she loved about this city.

The electric feeling that it was all a backdrop; the trees, the cars, the beautiful women, the powerful men . . . a setting for her to have success.

But the words of Norma Jean were still fresh in her ear.

The voice, Beth would have to admit, of reality.

Compromises had to be made. You might have to do things you don't want to, to get ahead.

To get that shot.

That opportunity.

She imagined they all did it . . . Lana, Rita, any beautiful and sultry screen siren whose name ended in an "ah."

A cab pulled up.

A deeply tanned man in a sport coat and with sparkling teeth hopped out. He stood a moment, looking at Beth.

She was used to this.

Stopping men like this in their tracks was no big deal.

"Hello—don't tell me you're leaving, gorgeous?"

She smiled. You never knew who you would meet, and where you would meet them again.

"I'm afraid so. Early call," she lied.

"My loss," he said. One more flash of his teeth, his tan the look of lustrous leather, perfectly smooth, so evenly colored. He continued into the hotel.

The doorman, his eyes on Beth, probably—she imagined—wondering.

Starlet, hooker—? And was there any difference?

"Cab, miss?"

Beth shook her head.

"It's a nice night."

Which it was. Absolutely beautiful in fact.

"I think I'll walk."

The doorman nodded, tip lost—and slammed the door shut.

The yellow cab pulled away.

Beth turned right, and started to walk down to Sixth Street. Maybe she would stop somewhere for a nightcap.

Or maybe she'd head straight home.

Tonight, Los Angeles was beautiful and she was going to enjoy every moment.

37

DAVID sat in the cab, barely moving as it tried to snake into the Brooklyn Battery Tunnel. It was a good hour past rush hour—so this had to be something else.

An accident maybe, one lane shut down.

Nothing he could do about it now.

He picked up the earpiece for his phone and hit speed dial 4.

Funny, all the years he had a cell phone he'd never had a reason to use speed dial. Even with Johanna . . . it just wasn't something he thought about. How hard was it to enter a number?

But with Mari—it was different. He liked having her on speed dial.

That had to mean something, he thought.

He heard the trilling sound, then Mari's voice.

Immediately he detected that she sounded strained, rushed—there was the sound of music in the background.

"Hi. It's me."

"David. Where are you?"

"Stuck in a cab at the tunnel entrance, not moving."

"You should have listened to the traffic."

He laughed. "Lots of things I should do. So—want to come over? Did you eat yet?"

"I can't. I mean, I'm with someone right now. It's work."

"When do you think you'll be done? I want to see you. I need to talk to you."

"Me too. Look, I can't talk now. But when I'm done, I'll come over. Unless it's too late."

"Never too late, Mari."

A pause, and David marveled that even he could manage to say the right thing on occasion.

"Great. Okay. I have a key, so I'll get there when I get there."

Then, almost an afterthought . . . and so sloppy for a detective.

"Where are you now?"

"Double Happiness. That place on Mott."

"Right. And you're with—?"

"I'll tell you later, okay?"

Secrecy, David thought. For some reason Mari was being secretive. *She's scared,* he thought. And for a moment he had that terrible feeling in the pit of his stomach when he remembered how he'd almost lost her in that warehouse, a place where the dreams hid a gruesome reality—and his own bullet had almost killed her.

"I'll wait up for you."

Another pause. Then:

"Okay."

"Bye."

The phone went quiet and—on cue—the traffic began slowly inching forward.

LISA looked around the room. She had no way of gauging whether her words made any sense to Mari, whether there was even a shred of believability.

Was she even sure how much of it *she* believed?

If Henning had been right, if all the signs were correct, then Mari—sitting inches away—was most decidedly in danger.

But there was also this opportunity, a slim chance to end this for now, maybe forever.

Risks would have to be taken, crazy chances, and there was no guarantee they would succeed.

Lisa reached out and grabbed Mari's hand.

"Imagine—two thousand years, generation to generation, a small group of believers, then real scholars and researchers, all detecting that, yes, there was evil, something that seemed to pop up here and there, this century and that century. A blood trail, if you will. Once they knew what to look for—the unexplained deaths, the disappearances, the similarities that stretched across millennia. And then—"

Lisa laughed.

"What . . ." Mari said.

Lisa could see that the other woman was nervous, frightened. Good. That's exactly what she wanted to happen.

"They found *images*, you see. The same image of a killer, a madman . . . in illuminated documents, carved into urns, in the corner of tapestries swirling with faces. A face. The priest showed me some of those images."

"I—I don't understand. Maybe the deaths, the similarities, were just a coincidence."

"No."

Lisa surprised herself with how strong her voice was. A reflection of how important it was to convince this woman of the truth of her words.

"No. The description, the images—from the Dark Ages in paintings, and even the descriptions in obscure texts gathered by the priests—all the same. Until they knew—the truth."

"The truth. That can be kind of illusory, no?"

"Sometimes. Not this time. Nothing illusory about this at all." She leaned close again. "They knew it was the same person. No demon. No Satan spawn . . . the same *person*."

Mari nodded.

"And you believed this. You—a scientist—accepted all this?"

Lisa leaned back.

She took a big sip of the green tea martini.

"Oh, it didn't take that much to convince me, Mari. You

see, when I watched Henning get killed, cut down in that alley-way, I saw the man's face."

She shook her head.

"And guess what? It was the same face. The same face. The same man. And thanks to Henning—I knew where he was coming next."

The bartender came over. "More drinks?"

Lisa shook her head and waited until he was gone, then:

"Henning said that the killer couldn't—wouldn't—resist coming here, Mari. And believe it or not, he was coming for you."

38

IT was past midnight when they both left Double Happiness.

They waited until they could flag two cabs together.

Lisa had wanted to go with Mari, but Mari said that the cab could take her straight to David's, right up to the front of the doorman building.

And Mari worried about Lisa.

But she said she could be dropped right in the front of the Soho Grand.

"Nothing will happen there," Lisa had said.

They made plans.

To talk again tomorrow.

Lisa got promises from Mari that she would be careful, that she wouldn't be alone.

They made plans.

Which was, of course, exactly as it was supposed to be. . . .

THE doorman at David's building let her in with a warm smile. Mari checked behind her, her heart racing, even though she didn't know how much of what she had heard she believed—could believe.

Talking to David would help.

But there was something—right now—that she needed more than talking.

She pressed the button for the elevator, turning to see that the doorman was still at his post, looking over at her, checking on her.

She smiled back.

The elevator door opened.

But Mari didn't just step in.

She first looked up at the curved mirror in the corner confirming that the elevator was empty.

Empty . . .

Did that really make a difference?

The elevator doors shut.

Yes, did the fact that this cubicle was empty now make any difference at all?

She looked at the floors as it went up . . . 3 . . . 4 . . . 5.

And it stopped.

She instinctively stepped back, to the rear wall of the elevator.

The door opened. She walked to the opening slowly, then looked down the brightly lit hallway to the left and right.

She could see David's doorway, three doors down.

She already had the key in her hand, and she walked quickly to the third door.

Mari heard the elevator close behind her, leaving her stranded.

David, and safety, and warmth—were all on the other side.

The hallway seemed almost too empty.

Late on this Tuesday night, now Wednesday morning.

The key went in, but Mari knew from experience that it sometimes needed to be jiggled, a copied key that needed to be coaxed to work.

The tumblers turned; she twisted the handle.

She had just taken an elevator up to David's apartment, something she had done countless times before.

But this time—it seemed like the scariest thing she had ever done in her life.

* * *

LISA locked the hotel room door behind her. She felt like another drink, maybe a bunch—but best she stay here, and the minibar would have to suffice.

Goldfish swam around in a small bowl; standard issue for the Soho. You get your own pet for your stay.

She slid the chain over its latch.

The door was now triply locked.

And she thought, *I don't feel any safer.*

She walked to the minibar and opened it. She scanned some of the most expensive little bottles of alcohol in the city.

She took out a green Gordon's gin, a perfect replica of a full-size bottle. Then a small tonic. The "bar" electronically recorded her removal of said overpriced items, an event that couldn't be changed by merely replacing them.

She shut the door. . . .

That's not so much different, she thought, from what most people think time is. An event occurs. That's it. It has happened, and there isn't a thing you can do about it.

"A" occurs, then "B"—and no going back.

But like a lot of things people thought, it just wasn't true.

She popped open the can of tonic, and poured it into a tumbler on the table next to the goldfish. She lit a cigarette and sucked in the smoke.

"Quite a life you got, buddy."

Then the gin.

She could have used people now, noise, the distraction.

Instead—all she could think about was what Mari might do. And think too about her meeting at the Morgan tomorrow.

She walked to the window overlooking the city, the glittering buildings, the bridges stretching across the river with lights strung like Christmas trees.

And she wondered:

Where are you?

Where the hell out there . . . are you *now*?

* * *

THERE was no way she could know, of course.

But he wasn't there at all.

DAVID turned to Mari, quickly hitting the mute button on the television.

He had stayed awake.

She stood there, looking at him, the flickering image of Letterman on the television, the drawn curtains.

Her face looked drained. Her dark eyes, always looking so deep-set, thoughtful sometimes, sparkling and flirty at other times, now looked somber.

He stood up and walked over to her.

"You okay?"

She managed a half smile. "Not too sure."

He put his hands on her shoulders. A gentle squeeze. A little caress.

"Want to talk?"

Her eyes rose to meet his now. She shook her head. Then: "No."

And she fell into him.

THEY made love there, and David felt a new ferocity. She pulled at her own clothes, and his—while all the while her lips seemed to attack his mouth, kissing, pressing.

It was as if they were in some kind of race, and Mari had started way ahead of him. In moments she had her clothes off, and tugged at his pants.

And though the moment was intense, animal-like—he felt himself respond . . . so quickly.

As if what she was doing was so primal, it went to the heart of what made a man desire someone.

Then he was with her, kissing, tasting. His mouth trailing down, kissing, nibbling—which brought even louder moans from her—further, until she could lie back and enjoy the hunger she had aroused, a hunger David fed by tasting her everywhere.

The lights were on. The TV. There was nothing romantic about the setting.

Bur Mari's passion had turned this into an arena.

One moment she had curled around to grab at him, to caress and kiss, careless about what her grazing teeth might do, careless that with this lust there was some pain for him.

Her leg banged into his knee, and that almost prompted him to say something . . . to ask her to be careful.

Pain was, after all, pain.

But the moment passed, and she climbed on top of him, her eyes alive now, her skin flush with color, and whatever darkness she arrived in the apartment with now gone.

And she let herself use him. That's what it felt like. Using him, much to his pleasure to be sure, but whatever world she was in was miles above his.

It ended.

Had to end, to be sure.

And when it did, she fell into him, and as her breathing returned to normal, it changed, shifting into a gentle sobbing.

He held her tight—and waited.

Then—just as quickly—she slid off him, picked up her clothes. Moved to the couch. He was tempted to make a joke—the transition seemed so fast, almost brutally so.

He knew that he shouldn't.

Score one for some instinct, he thought.

"So," he said, "we talk now?"

Mari had put on just her blouse . . . buttoning only a few buttons.

She dug into her purse and pulled out something small.

"No. Don't think so. I know it's late, but—"

She handed the object to him, a small microrecorder.

"Listen to this first. You can probably fast-forward some sections. But listen, then we talk?"

He took the recorder, and nodded.

She curled up on the couch.

"And I'll wait here, okay?"

"Okay."

He watched her shut her eyes.

In only seconds he saw her chest begin a slow rise and fall as she drifted off to sleep.

David looked at the recorder. He had headphones around here he could use. Sit at the kitchen table. Listen. Then talk to Mari in the morning.

Things could wait until the morning, he thought.

That's what he thought then, before he started listening. . . .

39

1947

THE night had taken on a slight chill. A Pacific breeze blew off the hill as Beth walked down Sixth Street.

She thought of her friend Norma Jean.

Did either of them have a chance at success, at becoming actresses rather than just two more beauties in Los Angeles?

What made one person have success—and the other not? Was there any plan that could affect chances? Were there decisions that could make your chances better than someone else's?

A chance meeting?

A chance conversation?

Tiny little things that could affect your fate?

She thought—on this night—that she should go straight home. It was getting late, and she did have an audition in the morning, another gaggle of young beauties showing up on the Paramount lot to be examined and scrutinized.

But the night felt good. The air cleansing after the smoky lounge of the Biltmore.

So she kept walking, turning down this street, then another.

Letting her path be determined by whatever whim moved her to turn this way or that.

She felt no one watching her.

The very idea would have seemed absurd.

If you had stopped her that night, stopped her right there on the corner of South Alameda Street, and told her to be careful . . .

Think it would make a difference?

Can any of us hear about possibilities, the chances we take with our lives, the risk and opportunities?

Even when something as simple as common sense is passed along, do any of us really listen to it, act on it?

Clearly, no.

We do what we do.

And all the words and advice given make little or no difference.

So—if you stopped her, saw her on that corner, dark beauty, the flowing hair, her coltlike legs sheathed in seamed stockings—such a vision . . . and told her, would she listen?

Imagine: hearing how she would end up blocks away, so far away from the houses and the closed shops here. In an empty field. Surrounded by warehouses.

How it would take some time to find her.

And then would begin the horrible reconstruction of what had happened.

Step by step, while all the while there was still hope in her heart that it might all turn out okay, that somehow she could return to her life, as troubled and confusing as it was.

Until, like the tumblers of some dreadful lock clicking into place, Beth would realize.

There was no hope.

No hope, and she was about to experience a horror beyond imagination.

If you told her this, would she listen? Could she hear?

Or would she run away from such crazy, mad talk, perhaps yelling for help?

Wanting the messenger dead, when the message was so grim and dire.

And finally—

If you told her what she would look like in the end. How even strong, battle-hardened police would retch looking at her.

Seeing her in two pieces.

So perfectly separated.

The grainy photos today—still hard to look at.

There would be, in fact, no way to tell her, no way to warn her.

Just as now, there was no way she could tell that it had already started. That she was being watched, studied.

In moments it would begin.

But then—what really is a moment?

40

DAVID clicked off the recorder.

Amazing—after hearing what was on the recording—that Mari could sleep so peacefully on the couch, curled up, a small blanket covering her.

He stood up with a slight kick in the kneecap rewarding the effort, and walked over to her.

For a few seconds David just stood there and looked down at her, the steady rise and fall as she breathed in and out. He debated letting her sleep. He could talk to her in the morning, when the sunlight would fill this room and make everything he'd just heard utterly impossible.

And as if sensing he stood there, she opened her eyes.

Looked at him for just a second.

And this was no sleepy coming awake halfway.

She was once again alert, and ready to talk.

"What time is it?" Mari said.

David looked at the numbers on his cable box.

"2:35."

She nodded and sat up, turning around on the couch.

"You could go back to sleep."

She smiled. "Yeah. I'm amazed I fell asleep."

"Happens to me all the time. After a long interrogation. Something to do with the intensity. Leaves you drained."

"Drained . . . that what it is?"

David sat down on the couch beside Mari.

"You listened, hmm?"

He nodded.

"Crazy stuff, right? Nuts."

"That's for sure. I skipped ahead on some sections. Lot of history she laid out there."

"History I never knew."

David smiled. "History no one ever knew."

She turned and looked right at him. "But it all makes sense somehow. The reason this guy is never caught. Not now, not sixty years ago, not a hundred—"

"Not a *thousand*."

She repeated his words slowly. "Right. Not a thousand. But—but what evidence is there? I know tomorrow I'm going to check on—"

David reached down and took her hand.

"I think I have to tell you something. I mean, I've been good about telling you nothing. But that clearly won't work anymore."

"About the murders . . . here . . . now?"

David nodded. "Though"—he held up the recorder—"based on what's on this recording, I'm not too sure what 'here and now' means anymore."

"Me either. If you believe it. I still—"

She stopped. And David felt her eyes on him, suddenly aware that he was going to tell her something really important.

"What is it?"

"It's a—I spoke to somebody who saw him."

Mari licked her lips. "What? But there are only victims, and the woman in the hospital. I wasn't even sure it was the same attacker."

"It was."

"So . . . how did you speak to someone who—Christ—saw him?"

"Not for publication, okay? Though I doubt very much you could publish any of this. Not with your editor."

Mari smiled. "Gully usually likes some facts in the piece."

"Yeah. So there's this homeless guy. Eddie. Probably the reason we didn't find Elaina Suro cut up into pieces, dissected, or whatever the hell this maniac intended—"

"He interrupted the attack?"

"Yes. Pushed open the door. Saw Elaina, the knife, the hallway. And the guy, the attacker. Funny, he must not even think about getting caught. Must be the furthest fucking thing from his mind."

David surprised himself. Getting angry like that, as if this killer's existence itself was an insult.

An insult that had to be stopped, caught, killed . . .

"Gave Elaina Suro—lucky girl—a chance to escape," he said.

"Very lucky."

"Out to the street. Hit by a car. Coma. But alive. And Eddie—"

"Saw the guy? You got a description, a sketch?"

"No. They're going to try. But I doubt it will be much use. Not going to find this guy wandering the streets of Brooklyn."

"Not if what Dr. Griffino said is true."

David took a breath.

He nodded. Then:

"It is."

THE kettle whistled, an early morning shriek that seemed out of place in the dark.

Mari poured the scalding water into two cups, the teabags and dollops of honey already in place.

"Disappeared?"

"That's what Eddie said, and I have no reason to doubt him."

Mari picked up the cups and brought them back to the small coffee table by the couch.

"That would explain things." Then a small laugh. "Or rather, not explain them. How do you catch a killer who can 'disappear'?"

David took his cup and inhaled the flavorful cloud.

"Not too damn easy."

"But if Griffino is right, I mean, if that priest is right, then there is a way."

"Yeah—unfortunately it puts us right in the middle of it."

"If she's right."

David took a sip. Much too hot to drink. But by blowing he could take the tiniest of sips.

The taste so good.

"I have no reason to doubt any of it," David said. "Not anymore."

"I do. And facts would be good; I want to research some of the things Lisa told me. She herself is going to The Morgan tomorrow—"

"I heard."

"We're going to meet again. Then maybe—"

David stood up.

"No. The man who butchered those women, who attacked Elaina Suro—he's here for a reason. And apparently the priest thinks that reason is you. Drawn by what happened to you."

"Weren't you listening? Us, David. Drawn to *us*. And it was only a theory."

"Us. Maybe, right. But I think you should get away."

Mari laughed.

"Get away? What do you mean?"

"Leave the city. Now. As soon as you can."

She shook her head.

"And what if they're wrong? I have nothing to do with this. You either."

"We can err on the side of caution."

Mari shook her head.

"No. I—I don't know enough about this yet."

David walked to the window.

The sky was still black, but soon the first hint of purple would bloom in the east.

What was the weather supposed to be today?

Cloudy, rainy, with all that humidity to make his repaired leg ache?

Or dry, sunny, a late summer's day, the type that only New York could serve up?

Mari was going to be hard to convince to leave.

No. Not hard.

Impossible.

He'd get nowhere by insisting.

"Okay. How about this? You do your research, meet Griffino again, then we talk. But if it looks like what she says is true—"

"We'll talk then."

"Good."

He wondered whether they should try to get some sleep before morning really arrived.

And Mari made the decision for him. She stood up, walked over, and took his hand.

"Come on. It's a nice couch but I could use a real bed."

And she led David into his own bedroom.

FOR a long time, neither slept.

They lay spooned, their two mismatched bodies curled into each other. Holding each other close, lying perfectly still, holding each other tight, David's arms encircling her.

In talking to her, he hadn't let her know how scared he was for her.

And—if he had thought about it for a moment—scared for himself.

But for now, all seemed safe.

Then—their breathing changed into that slow, steady rhythm . . . as they both fell asleep.

                         * * *

DAVID'S cell phone rang.

The curtains in the bedroom were drawn tight, but he could see that line of brilliant yellow-white that ran around the perimeter of the curtains.

Morning. And sunny for now.

He listened to the next trill and located his phone on the end table.

"Yeah."

He listened.

"Okay. Thanks. I'll be there. I'll pick up my partner. Right. Bye."

He turned to Mari.

"What was that?" she said sleepily.

"Elaina Suro. She's conscious. I can talk to her."

"That's good," Mari said.

David nodded.

Wondering . . . well, was it really?

41

"YOU can drop me here," Lisa said, leaning forward.

The morning had started off with brilliant sun, but now the cloud cover had socked in and Lisa wished she had brought an umbrella.

She handed the driver a ten-dollar bill.

"Keep the change."

And she got out at Madison and Thirty-sixth. The Pierpont Morgan Library was across the street. She didn't know much about it—only that it was a library and a museum, and funded by one of the great turn-of-the-century money barons.

Pierpont Morgan.

In all her trips to the city she had never picked it as a place to visit. What lay inside would be all new for her.

She walked up to what looked like the main entrance, a modern glass structure that sat oddly between what looked like a library building in the grand tradition and a manor house constructed out of heavy stone, both buildings proclaiming a solidity no matter what the ravages of time.

She walked up to the guard.

"Good morning. I have an appointment with Dr. Mathews?"

The guard pointed to a desk to the left, facing the still-closed ticket booth. "Yes, please check in there."

"Thanks."

Lisa walked over. A rail-thin woman with bobbed brown hair, all askew, looked up.

"Could I see some ID, please?"

The woman had a slight lisp, her "s" producing way too much of a hissing sound.

She took Lisa's passport, looked up.

Then:

"Dr. Mathews"—again the "s"—"is expecting you. His office is in the main library building. Go through here, and the guard will show you the private entrance."

Lisa picked up her passport and the woman handed her a small card.

"And show this pass to the guard."

"Thanks a lot."

The woman with mousy hair nodded, and returned to whatever important work in front of her demanded the speedy return of her full attention.

Lisa turned, and walked into the building.

THE door was open.

"Dr. Mathews? Lisa Griffino."

"Oh, yes—" He immediately stood up. "Come in, Dr. Griffino."

Lisa took a step inside, and a look of concern quickly passed over Mathews's face.

"Perhaps—shut the door?"

Lisa nodded, and shut the heavy wood door behind her.

"And please, take a seat."

"Thank you."

Lisa scanned the room, rich with wood, massive bookshelves, a window that looked out over a rear garden. It might just be the most elegant and imposing office she had ever seen.

Dr. Mathews, the curator of the Morgan collection, looked anything but imposing. Frosty white hair, with strands sticking

up. Untrendy wire-framed glasses, and an easy smile that
spoke more of nervousness than warmth.

"Thank you for seeing me," she said.

"No. Not at all. I've been corresponding with Brian—
Father Henning—for over a decade. Trying to help him. By
the way—"

Mathews got up and went to one of the shelves. He pulled
out a book, and Lisa saw her name, then her black-and-white
publicity photo on the back.

"I've even read it. Father Henning recommended it months
ago. Said it might help me understand." He looked at the
book. "It may have—a little."

"A lot of my peers understand only a little too," she said.
"None of us really have anything close to the big picture.
Quantum physics and string theory change everything, but we
don't yet have a clue how big that 'everything' is."

Mathews sat down again—his chair a worn leather office
chair, oversized, with beige patches where the leather had been
worn to a creamy burnish.

I want this office, Lisa thought.

"Yes. I think I got that. Still—I read this book of yours, and
I think I knew what had Mother Church so interested. I'm not
Catholic, you know. Not really anything. But there is all this
history, isn't there? This amazing amount of time they have
been looking at things, recording things. And your ideas on
time, well, it must have intrigued them." He pushed his glasses
back up the bridge of his nose. "They've come a long way, I
guess. From the days of Galileo."

"You mean Galileo's recanting?"

"Yes. Their rigid doxology . . . orthodoxy. All so important
to that organization. So when they came to me, when Father
Henning came to me—"

"You were shocked?"

"Absolutely. Our collection here ranges from Egyptian art
to Renaissance paintings to Chinese porcelains. For his library, Mr. Morgan acquired illuminated, literary, and histori-
cal manuscripts, early printed books, and old-master drawings

and prints. We have three of the original Gutenberg Bibles, Dr. Griffino. But what interested Father Henning went beyond this. A smaller part of the core collection."

"Objects that don't fit into the above categories?"

Mathews shook his head. "At some rather late point, Mr. Morgan began collecting items with the earliest evidence of writing."

"Such as?"

"Ancient seals, tablets, and papyrus fragments from the Near East. Amazing items, to be sure, all selected by Mr. Morgan personally."

"They must be something to see."

"Oh, yes—you really must. Amazing pieces. And to see our ciboriums from the ninth century, and reliquaries with pieces of the True Cross."

"The True Cross?"

"Or so it was claimed. Still—such incredible artifacts that they humble me."

Lisa leaned close.

"But those artifacts—they're not what the Vatican was interested in, what Henning was interested in?"

"No. Beautiful as they are. Important as they are. No. Mr. Morgan also collected other things, ancient things. And Father Henning and I traded much correspondence over these pieces, their meaning, their—"

Mathews seemed to have trouble with the next word. . . .

"—provenance."

"He told me that you had some items that I should see. That might help me figure out things. Explain things."

Mathews rubbed his chin.

"Yes. I believe that was the idea. But now, with him dead . . . I mean, what will the Church do?"

"I don't know, Dr. Mathews. I just know that he came to me. Thought I might help. Might understand."

Now Mathews's eyes narrowed. "You mean stop it. I don't profess to understand what they were watching and following. But stopping it—that was the goal, wasn't it?"

"*Is* the goal."

He nodded.

The curator turned and looked out at his garden. Just a glance, but Lisa wondered if he always grabbed a look like that whenever he left his office.

MARI stood in the bowels of the *Daily News* building, in a hallway that led to the warren of chambers devoted to the research rooms.

She stood alone, and the lighting—so bright and garish on the floors above—here turned a suitably dusky yellow from a row of single lightbulbs barely illuminating the hallway.

A man with a beard and thick glasses pulled down to his nose came out of one room.

"Help you?"

Reporters rarely came down here, to the mammoth hardcopy rooms. Their computers above would give access to the digitized record of the newspaper—as well as all the major newspapers of the world. They could still do that down here, but there was also the advantage of getting a real copy, looking at the actual photographs, the maps, the newspaper.

"Jed, right?"

"Yup."

Mari walked up to him and stuck out her hand. "Mari Kinsella. I need to do a little research."

He laughed. "Down here? Not enough Lexus-Nexus stuff upstairs for you? Don't see reporters down here much, unless they're looking for—"

He stopped himself, his grin revealing a crooked assembly of teeth going every which way.

"Just don't see many down here."

"Don't know why," Mari said. "It's so inviting."

Jed nodded for a second, not getting the joke.

"Right. So what can I do you for?"

"Two things to start. I need to see coverage of a murder, 1947."

"Got the exact date?"

"Yes."

"That's a good start. And—"

"You have access to other newspaper archives down here?"

"Yeah—well, you could do that upstairs too. If anyone bothered to learn how to use the research programs. They don't."

"That's why I'm here. In case I need help."

"Right. So—you want stuff from before the *News* started publishing?"

"Yes. About thirty years before. 1888. I'd like to search the archive of the *Times* of London."

Jed's eyes widened.

"More murders?"

She nodded.

Then he laughed. "Jack the Ripper?"

Mari smiled—but then felt immediately a little creeped out that old Jed was so familiar with the year of the killings.

"Yes. But not just the original reports. The investigation reports after the killings ended."

"Yeah—after he was gone."

Gone . . .

What a funny way to put it.

Gone.

The Ripper gone.

"I'll set you up. Give me your 1947 dates, and I'll meanwhile get you hooked up to the *Times* of London archive."

He turned and started to walk away.

"Hope you got a lot of time, Mari Kinsella. Because"—he turned and looked back at her—"trust me . . . there's a lot of stuff to look at."

And she followed him into one of the research rooms.

42

1947

HER full name was Elizabeth Short.

It was a name that she knew would have to be changed. For stardom, for Hollywood, for all the legions of fans that would flock to see her dark sultry beauty on the big screen.

"Liz" might, of course, be fine. But "Short"?

Never would work. Not for an actress, not for someone who would compete for the same roles as the stunning Ava Gardner.

Sometimes, like on this balmy evening, she played with different names . . . letting them roll off her tongue. Liz Aaron. Liz Blaine. Liz Richards.

Testing each name out.

Was it sexy enough? Did it sound like a famous actress. What did it—in her mind's eye—look like when the letters were a foot tall, dominating a marquee, towering over all the other players, towering even over the title of the film?

And as she played this game, she never had any doubt that this was her fate, her destiny.

It would happen.

It was only a question of how soon.

She let the reverie continue, walking down one street, not hurrying back to her apartment, a place that stood for reality, a place that seemed disconnected from her great destiny, her great future.

The dark night surrounded her—and that felt good.

Then—

A slight breeze.

The wind blew her hair back a bit, rearranging the carefully constructed waves.

A sudden breeze that was rare in Los Angeles this time of year, the last remnant of a breeze that fought its way onshore from the Pacific.

She stopped, and took note of her surroundings. The houses with a light on here and there, and others completely dark. A few streets ahead, the occasional car streaming by, hurrying back to a hotel, returning from some secret assignation, each car—she imagined—a story.

But with that breeze—something else.

She looked around.

Awareness.

An awareness that she was alone. Alone, on this dark and quiet street.

She hesitated. Suddenly surprised that this specific awareness took so long to emerge.

As if it had been pushed away, kept from her mind, as she followed the bread-crumb trail of her thoughts and fantasies.

But now quite clearly—the awareness there.

She looked around, and getting back to her small apartment had suddenly turned into a matter of importance, a matter of urgency.

CAN we feel things before they happen?

Can we feel the ripple of things to come?

For centuries such feelings were called *premonitions*.

That odd sense that something was about to happen, something good, something bad, something exciting, something surprising . . .

Something tragic.

Something—deadly.

Premonition . . . a word given to something to make it understandable. As if naming it could make us comprehend what the feeling is.

When quite clearly we can't comprehend; we can only feel the potential in events.

That where we are now inevitably leads to something else..

We can all feel that.

Quite clearly.

We can all sense the time, what lies ahead of us.

Just as Beth does now.

With that breeze, with the darkness, with the quiet—

WHAT'S the quickest way? she wonders.

Could turn down Hill Street, walk straight, a few more turns. That would be the fastest.

But that would also keep her on some quiet, secluded blocks. Take her past places where there were abandoned lots, empty lots with tall dry grass and desiccated bushes growing.

Or she could hurry back a few streets, to a place with more lights, more traffic, more people.

She did some quick calculations.

She felt the aloneness growing; she felt the dark around her.

And—oh, yes—she had a premonition. Undefined, but building slowly.

The basic message—not good to be here.

Then, as her mind in those fatal seconds still calculated— she had another thought.

Realizing that there was no reason for her to believe that.

None at all.

But the feeling so rock solid that it almost made her whimper.

(A whimper you might have heard. A whimper that, if you were close enough, you could have heard and felt in all its pure animal fear.)

The other thought:

I'm being watched.

Someone is watching me.

She spun around, seeing no one.

The thought receded just a little.

And in that glimmer of what may have seemed sanity, that slight recovery from an irrational fear, Beth chose to walk as directly as possible, staying on her course, but hurrying now.

She had seen no one watching her.

So—no one must be watching her.

And she hurried on, as we all do, to her destiny.

43

DR. Mathews, a good foot shorter than Lisa, walked ahead of her into the main library of The Morgan.

Crossing the threshold, Lisa stopped.

The library, a square box of a room, was girded by three massive belts of books, all locked behind glass doors. From a first look, the upper levels didn't look accessible.

"God—it's gorgeous."

Mathews turned and looked at her. "Isn't it? One of the finest jewels in this great city. Pity more people don't know about it. They hear library . . . and miss our collection . . ."

Lisa walked over to one locked glass-covered shelf, the thick glass guarding heavy leather-bound editions, a series of numbered volumes labeled *Shakespeare's Plays*.

Mathews came up beside her. "Very rare. And in this state? Unheard of. But then, you will find wonders here that can be found nowhere else. Some of the earliest illuminated Bibles, first editions from Dante, Renaissance books of psalms with a chip of a saint's bone embedded in the pure gold cover."

"Amazing."

"Truly." Mathews nodded. "It's the only word I can apply. But—perhaps that's for another time. Another visit—we also have a wonderful café here."

"Yes. That would be good."

But Mathews turned. "I took the liberty of having some things that would interest you brought out. Items I discussed with Father Henning. Some here, and others up on the second level."

Mathews walked to a massive wooden table that Lisa guessed must itself date back to medieval castles. Easy to picture it with tankards of ale and knights pulling at pieces of roasted pig.

Now, a single object sat on the table.

"First," Mathews said, "take a look."

Lisa leaned close. The object was rectangular, about sixteen inches by eight inches, crafted out of a dark grayish metal with an uneven pitted surface. It had a lid that looked like it came off, but no hinges. Four small clawlike feet raised the object about a half inch off the table.

But the intriguing thing about it was the handle.

The handle was some kind of creature, leaning backward like an acrobat. The creature's feet and hands were wrapped around—

Lisa came even closer—

People. Small people, each tightly clutched in the creature's hand.

She also noticed that what she assumed was a monster had a human face.

Mathews came closer to her, almost startling Lisa by suddenly being at her elbow.

"Go on. Look closer. Really *look* at the face."

And Lisa did so, coming so close her breath hit the gray metal.

So close that she could smell that metal, the scent exotic, ancient . . .

The face . . . a human face.

The hands and feet turned into those of a creature.

One word popped into her mind.

Disturbing.

The small humans all had their mouths open in some

exaggerated grimace, a pathetic howl. Or perhaps not so exaggerated.

Completely and totally disturbing.

Lisa finally pulled away.

"What is it? And how old?"

Mathews nodded.

"What is it? We're not too sure. Perhaps some kind of reliquary, designed to hold organs after someone died. Definitely designed to hold something important. But—"

Mathews rested his hand on the main figure, the arched handle in the shape of a body. Then he let his fingers run along the side.

"There are other images along the side here, tableaux. Some kind of ceremony. A mass funeral perhaps. This creature here, standing above people." He turned and looked right at her. "All conforming to no known mythology in the world. Nothing. It's unheard of."

"And the date?"

"As far as we can figure out—pre-Egyptian. Five hundred . . . maybe a thousand years. Found in what's now Iraq. So much lost there now, hmm?"

Mathews lowered his voice.

"We should move on. But one last thing—"

Lisa turned to him.

"Yes?"

"Take one more look. At the face. Please."

And Lisa did so.

THE nurse stood at the ICU door, all five feet of her announcing that she has guarded this unit from concerned friends and relatives successfully for a long time.

"A brief talk, Detective. She's still very weak and Dr. Phillips personally ordered me to keep this very, very short."

David turned to his partner, then to the nurse. "We will. Just a few questions and then we are out of here."

The nurse held the door open. "Over there. I told her you were coming."

David nodded, and Kunokine followed him to the bed.

Elaina Suro looked like a patient from a TV show, tubes and cables snaking around her, some leading to the tower of devices behind the bed recording every vital sign, others going under the bed. One side of her face had turned a puffy, dark purple.

Kunokine leaned close, to whisper, "You best take this one, David. I don't do too well in hospitals."

"Sure."

He had planned on that anyway.

He came closer to Elaina's bed. Her eyes were shut, her breathing steady.

"Elaina . . ."

Elaina didn't turn, but David saw her eyes slowly open as if even that took great effort.

"I'm Detective Rodriguez and this is Detective Kunokine. We'd like to ask you a few questions."

Elaina attempted a head nod, but could just bring her chin down a bit.

The slightest sign of assent.

"The night you were attacked—did you see the man before he came at you?"

Elaina's tongue snaked out. It looked cracked and dry, feebly trying to wet her lips.

A faint croak.

"No."

Kunokine leaned close. "Think she needs water. Ice chips or something."

David saw a plastic container with a straw.

"Like some water?"

Another croak. "Yes."

He reached for the container and brought the flexi-straw close to those dry lips. One suck. Then another. Then she pushed the straw away.

"Enough?"

The same tiny nod. David put the water down.

"So you didn't see him at all, until he attacked?"

"Yes. It—"

She struggled as she attempted to expand her sentence.

"—it was like he appeared."

David nodded.

Appeared . . .

"Then he pushed you into that doorway?"

"Yes. He must have . . . known it was there. Knew I'd pass . . . right there."

David could see that the words were a struggle. He couldn't do too much more of this. He turned and looked past Kunokine. The nurse stood by the station, pencil in hand, doing paperwork. But she immediately turned and looked back, catching David's glance.

The clock was ticking.

Time for maybe another question or two.

"Did you know the man?"

Her head turned slightly to the left. Then, to be sure . . . "No."

"Never saw him?"

Her head turned slightly left, then right.

"Was there anything strange you noticed, besides the suddenness, I mean, anything else?"

Her eyes looked away from David.

Away, thinking—and David knew from that look that, yes . . . indeed . . . there was something strange.

And she was about to tell him.

MARI had stumbled upon the report printed by the *Times* of London for the centennial of the Jack the Ripper killings.

"God," she said in the quiet research room. Her voice a whisper, but reassuring to have sound, some sound, *any* sound here.

The newspaper story analyzed all the explanations for the

inability for anyone to ever see or capture the Ripper, all broken down by the theories and the percentages of authorities who subscribed to them.

Gooseflesh sprouted on her arm, even though the room felt stuffy, the AC struggling to get some air into this basement hole.

Ten percent of the criminologists interviewed thought that the Ripper changed his garments to escape, swapping a dark coat for a light one. Fifteen percent said he acted with such precision that the work was done quickly, never getting a drop of blood on his clothes . . . hence the perfect getaway. Five percent thought he dressed as a butcher to cover any bloodstain. Another ten percent thought he varied his methods from crime to crime.

And then the odder theories: He dressed as a woman. He had some kind of special hiding place where he could quickly retreat, unseen. Or . . . he was simply lucky.

Lucky . . .

And then the largest group of all, thirty percent, said that even with that long list of theories and ideas, the methods used by this "Jack" were something else, something still unknown.

That everything Jack the Ripper did he did in a way that remained, even with all those theories, totally unexplained.

That, and the reason why he did it.

A word popped into her head then.

Game.

What if it was a game to him? The killings, the hunt, the methods used. That *that* was the real excitement. Beyond the blood and the screams and the death.

She turned to the large folder filled with yellowed editions of the *Los Angeles Times.*

She slid out the first paper, dated July 15, 1947. The front-page story reported on the brutal killing of Elizabeth Short, the glamorous would-be movie star.

Instead of stardom, her fate that night was to be sliced in half.

Sliced in half . . .

Was she still alive when it began? Mari wondered. Was there awareness when the—

(work)

—began?

Alive, screaming, surprised.

And then—the killer gone. A manhunt that ended up *nowhere*. Just more theories, more ideas.

There was one thing. . . .

She turned back to the monitor. The many "fan" websites had copies of the autopsy photos.

So far Mari hadn't looked at them.

I need to sleep at night, she thought. *Somehow get to sleep despite all this. And seeing those pictures—*

They would make sleep that much harder.

But even a quick scan of the websites told Mari that they knew something now that the L.A. police had never figured out over half a century ago.

That Short's killing fit into a pattern of other killings, each with their own strange "handprint." In some cases, the mutilated bodies weren't found for months after. In others, important people intervened to keep the scandalous murders out of the papers.

But in hindsight, using the simple facts, it was all clear. For a period of time, someone killed in a certain way, attacking certain women. Beautiful, ambitious—their futures wide-open to them.

Now—that stuck too.

Another word somehow resonating instinctively for Mari.

Future.

The killings had that theme—the beauties, the hope, the mutilations. The fact that such bright futures were cut so horribly short.

Could that have been the real idea? The real prize?

She thought of Lisa, the scientist, author, respected, brilliant—at The Morgan Library talking with the director about artifacts from the past.

For now, Mari knew she had to call and tell her these thoughts, these instincts.

She took out her phone.

No signal.

She headed for the stairs.

44

1947

IT was the same time; it was a different time. It was before; it was after. Things would happen while other things would not happen. And the strange thing, the most obvious thing to any onlooker—if there had been any onlooker—was that there was absolutely nothing that could be done now to change things, to stop it.

Nothing that could be done *then* . . . at all.

BETH turned again and looked at the HOLLYWOODLAND sign, so bright on the hills, as she struggled to be reassured by that brightness, the size of the letters.

But at the same time she felt even more how stupid—how really *stupid*—she had been to come this way. Now so deserted, with the dark houses all around, maybe empty houses.

And now, just to her left, a road ending in a hill that would be dotted only with dry grasses and fine yellow-brown sandy dirt.

Though alone, she reminded herself, she had seen no one. Nobody was following her; there was no one around at all.

She turned and looked over her shoulder to again reassure herself.

And there he was.

Standing yards away; a dark figure, backlit by the streetlight, the light distant, faint, as if it was operating at less than full power.

Someone watching her.

She turned around, ready to bolt, ready to run down the next street as fast as she could.

But the man suddenly stood ahead of her.

Hadn't she seen him just behind her? Standing there. Or— or was she confused?

She spun left. Down the street that led to a hill; a house with a porch light on. Someone here. A place she might easily reach.

She started running.

And almost the same second she did so, she stopped.

No, not just stopped. Froze.

Froze.

Like ice. Immobile. Rigid.

He was in front of her again, his face catching the light. An odd angle to the nose; eyes dark but wide, so very wide, savoring everything.

Beth attempted to say something, not even sure what she was going to say.

But the words—whatever they were—emerged as only a whimper. A pressing of the lips together, a slight "hmm" sound that was so sad, so pitiful, so resigned.

And then, to make things worse, he spoke.

"I am a legend and so will you be."

The sound of the words . . . sounding nearly foreign, but indefinable.

"That is what you wanted, no? To be a legend? You will have fans, people who will memorize *every* part of your story, at least the parts they know. And to think—"

Here he laughed. A cackle sound that made Beth's stomach wrench. She hadn't eaten, but she felt as if she could double up, throw up right there while the man spoke to her.

"—none of that has happened yet."

He took a step closer.

Beth knew she should move. But she was frozen, rigid. A block of ice.

He looked at her face—then slowly raised a finger, pointing at her mouth, her lips.

The finger made a slight curve, an oversized grin.

"And I think . . . I will start there."

The words . . . electric, the threat sickening, and now Beth spun around again and started running back, knowing, feeling, believing that such running was hopeless.

As it surely was . . .

45

LISA leaned close to the artifact, her eyes only inches from the twisted body that made a handle atop this artifact designed for holding who knows what.

She saw it. . . .

She didn't have to say anything.

But she turned and looked up at Dr. Mathews.

"Yes. You can see it. The face. Now—follow me . . ."

Mathews turned and, with surprising speed, he hurried to one shelf of books that girded the first floor. But this glass-covered shelf had a small keyhole. He stuck in a key, and the bookshelves—the false shelves—opened up.

Mathews wasted no time entering, climbing up a metal spiral staircase, and Lisa followed.

But after a few steps, he turned to her.

"Oh—please pull the opening closed behind you? These upper shelves aren't open to the public."

Lisa reached back and, grabbing a curved handle, pulled the door shut, and it locked shut with a clear *click*.

Then on up the stairs.

On the second level, Dr. Mathews walked to a small wooden table. Lisa saw that some books had been put on the table and opened.

Mathews turned to her. "I only arranged for three samples. I think that's all you'll need to see. But there are more. More here"—he gestured to the towering shelves of books all around—"and in collections around the world. But it's enough. You see, there was a time when he was seen."

He was seen. . . .

Like the face Lisa had just seen on the artifact.

The face of the man who killed Father Henning in an alley in Singapore.

Being seen wasn't such a damning thing.

Not if you couldn't get caught.

The curator stood by the table.

"First, take a look."

She came close, not sure she really wanted to see the images.

"This first," Mathews said, pointing, "dates well after the artifact I just showed you. A manuscript, very primitive, from the sixth century. But the illuminations, they're amazingly well done. Amazingly clear. You see that creature there—the Latin reads . . . *The Taker of Souls.*"

The "creature" Mathews referred to stood on a pedestal. It sported goat legs, and the hands ended in claws, but the *face* . . .

Perfectly normal.

The same face.

"The image of the legs, goat feet . . . the claws—all typical for the time. All to represent anything evil, anything connected with the devil."

Mathews looked at Lisa's face. "Is this too much for you?"

"No. I'm okay. Let's go on."

"Here are others. You'll see the resemblance, even in the roughest one. But it's this small one I want you to see. It's made from a marble tube, finely etched. Used to seal documents. This one, about 1500 BC, the Eighteenth Dynasty. The reign of Pharaoh Thutmose III. I had a print made—then enlarged it. This was used by some religious figure, I imagine. A ward against evil perhaps."

The print was amazing in its fine detail. Blown up, the fine etching made the face, even one crafted so small, clearly visible.

Lisa leaned back.

She nodded. There was nothing else to say.

"Y-you spoke to Henning?" she asked.

"Well, yes. It's why I told him to see someone like you. You see, all this seemed so clear to me. Of course, I didn't know that things would change, that he might—what does one call this man, this creature?—that he was coming here . . . that something new had been begun."

"Changed . . . how?"

"Not to frighten you. I don't want to frighten you. But it suddenly seemed clear to me. What had been happening over the millennia. Perhaps even *how* it had been happening. But now with Henning killed, and you here, the murders here, the detectives working so very hard—I'm afraid, you see—"

Mathews looked down at the empty library below. . . .

"It was what he wanted. Like a game, you know."

A game.

"Maybe even my talking to you now. And we—well, we are clearly outmatched. You see, he can be a man who is nowhere. And yet so deadly, all through history."

"You *are* frightening me, Dr. Mathews."

But the curator held up a hand. "One more thought. That if this game was new, if it was what I thought it was—that he was doing something new. Then maybe there was what, for lack of a better word, I will call a 'chance.' "

He took a deep breath.

"Which is why talking to you—right now—is so important."

Then Mathews explained exactly what he meant.

DAVID had to lean close to the woman; Elaina's voice was a croak, a raspy whisper.

"Yes?" he said.

Her eyes moved slowly to look at David. He could see that

she had been a beautiful woman. That she would be beautiful again.

"I—I was not just an accident." She took a breath. Her tongue snaked out over dry lips. David quickly turned to his partner, who handed him the water cup again. A sip. One, two—then:

"He knew me. *Knew* who I was. Said there were secrets to my work."

David knew that Elaina Suro did research with the Aquarium's whales and dolphins.

"He want—wanted to kill me . . . because of them." Her eyes moved away from David. "Some . . . thing . . . buried in their brains. Old. Secret."

Kunokine had come close to hear the faint words.

"What secret, Elaina?" David said quietly.

The woman kept her eyes looking straight ahead as if she was picturing it. David spotted a tear in the corner of one eye, building, growing, then beginning this slow trickle down her cheek.

Then another—

"The dolphins. Somewhere inside them. A secret. About them, about us, about life. It was all so new. My work with them. That—and—"

More tears.

"Elaina—anything else? That we should look for?"

Another tiny nod.

"He had . . . these two bracelets. On h-his wrists. Matching. They were . . . strange. Catching the light—"

She coughed.

And then the nurse was there. David felt a hand on his elbow. A gentle pull.

He expected a barked command. But the nurse whispered gently.

"You have to go now."

David nodded.

Instinctively, he reached out and rested his hand on top of Elaina's. The gentlest of squeezes.

He stood up, looking at Elaina.

"Thank you, Elaina. Rest up. Get better."

In answer, she closed her eyes, the tear tracks on her cheeks still wet.

He turned and walked beside Kunokine.

"**WHAT** do you think?" his partner asked when they were outside the ICU.

David rubbed his forehead. He didn't have a headache, but felt this intense pressure, as if rubbing might make it feel better.

"I am . . . *lost*. Lost. I mean"—he turned to Kunokine—"what are we doing? What the hell—"

A nurse down the hallway looked up, and David realized he had raised his voice.

He lowered his tone.

"What are we doing here? What's *happening* here?"

Kunokine smiled—a nervous smile. "I was hoping you could tell me."

"Yeah. Right. Me too. Me . . . too . . ."

They started for the elevators.

MATHEWS stopped talking.

"It is possible, yes?"

Lisa looked away. "In theory. I mean, that's what my book was about. Theories of reality, of time, of space. What the evidence shows, what we can guess at. But we live in *this* world. One thing follows another. We depend on time. We live in one universe, and—"

Mathews interrupted.

"Do we?"

Lisa took a breath. The main library room was deserted. A quiet midweek morning.

"You have to talk to the others, you know. The reporter, the detective. They could be in danger. In case these ideas . . . of ours . . . yours, mine . . . are correct. You know that?"

"Yes. I will."

Her phone rang.

Mathews smiled. "We ask people to shut their phones off in here."

She nodded. "Guess you can make an exception this time."

She dug out her BlackBerry. It was Mari.

And did she ever have things to tell her.

"Hello, Mari."

Mathews tapped Lisa's shoulder and pointed to the alcove with the stairway.

He whispered: "Maybe in there?"

Lisa moved into the alcove, just around the corner from Mathews and the table with the books.

It was dark.

Quiet *now*. . . . quiet *here*.

And no one heard any tumblers click.

No gears meshing together.

No sliding bolts falling neatly into place, blocking off this way, pushing them this way, as options and opportunity became—for all of them at least—severely limited.

46

MARI stopped outside, in front of the Duane Reade just around the corner from the main entrance to the *Daily News* building. A lone smoker stood a few yards away, but well out of hearing distance.

"Lisa, I wanted to call you. I've been looking at the paper's records for the Whitechapel murders, and—"

"Mari—hold on." The voice was dark, solemn.

"Yes?"

"Mari, you have to listen to me here. You have to talk to your friend, the detective."

Mari looked over at the smoker, who nodded, held the gaze for a moment, as if curious why she hadn't whipped out a Marlboro.

"Why? You found out something? At The Morgan?"

"Yes. A lot."

The scientist proceeded to describe what she had seen, and why they even came to her to begin with. She described the face, the artifacts and manuscripts stretching back a thousand years.

"Forget the killings from a hundred years ago," Lisa said. "That's nothing."

And then the two most important things.

"I know I warned you that this hasn't been an accident. Getting you two involved. Maybe getting me here. My guess is it's all part of his plan."

"I don't understand."

A pause.

"When you've been doing something as long as he has, you look for new ways to make it interesting."

"The killings? The slaughter?"

"Whatever the hell it is he does. He's playing with you, Mari. Playing with *us*."

The day was still September warm.

But Mari felt so cold. She looked up and down the street, still bright from the sun, which was now beginning to slip down toward the Hudson and New Jersey.

"Christ. You're freaking me out," Mari said.

"But listen—there's also a reason Henning came to me." A small, hollow laugh. "Lucky me. There's a chance here, Mari. In this game. A chance."

Mari thought of the word, such a slim word. *Chance*. Nothing more than the possibility that he could be stopped.

And she recognized what they were both talking about, the madness that they now both accepted.

There was a killer here in New York. Nothing terribly revelatory about that. Been killers here before, and there would be killers here again.

But they believed—no, now *knew*—this killer had come from across time, that his work filled the pages of history and legend, imagined as a monster, someone never to be captured, never to be found, someone from—

Who knows what time in the past.

And Lisa told Mari—he must come from the past.

She believed that. They had to believe that.

Because only with that thought, that possible fact, did they have this *chance*.

"Who-what do we have to do?" Mari asked.

And she listened to the words Lisa spoke, slow, reasoned words that on paper would seem absolutely mad.

* * *

LISA hit the button on her BlackBerry and the call ended.

She looked at her hands.

God, she thought, *I'm shaking.*

And for a moment she stood in the shadows just letting the idea wash over her . . .

That all her theories attempting to explain the great contradictions of Time and Space might just be true.

Not that she knew how it all worked.

And at this point, she wasn't even sure she wanted to know how it all worked.

Enough that she understood what little she did. Enough that maybe there was something that could be done.

Something to end it.

Because that was the goal, wasn't it? To end it. To stop it.

To stop *him.*

Did she believe it was possible?

Did she have the option of *not* believing?

She turned around and opened the door that led out of the dark alcove staircase, back to Dr. Mathews.

She took three steps.

"I'm sorry, but I had to—"

She froze.

At first, she didn't see the man. Had he gone around to the other side of the great row of shelves that marked the perimeter of the second floor of the library?

But as she stopped, she looked down.

Mathews lay on the ground. His right hand was wrapped around the middle of one of the slim iron poles of the railing. One leg looked buckled in a strange way. His head lay against part of a bookshelf.

Eyes open.

A thin red slit—a curved smile in his throat—pumping blood steadily.

The open eyes stared at the beautiful painted ceiling. Not seeing it. Not aware.

When you play a game, Lisa thought, *you have to think ahead. Not just match each move, but stay ahead.*

With a sickening twist, she knew she wasn't anywhere near ahead.

She heard the man's voice behind her.

47

BEHIND her.

Though there couldn't be anyone behind her. Not with the door leading up here locked, not with the stairwell *empty.* How could someone be here when she'd just walked out of the darkened stairwell?

But there he was.

The words sarcastic, mocking.

"Such a mess, isn't it?"

Mathew's throat seeped blood, now a pool on the polished wood floor, and a thin stream beginning to drip down—

Splat . . . splat . . . splat.

Hitting the floor like the lightest of rain.

Lisa's heart began to beat. Her mind searching for a solution, an option, a way out.

She turned so slowly, feeling as if she should see a hideous monster, a creature of demon proportions, a creature of pure evil.

When all that stood there was a man.

Not many people would think he looked so unusual. Though people would easily see that he wasn't from around here.

Wherever "around here" might be.

The shape of the skull, the eyes, the lips—all with a look from another place.

Except—Lisa knew it was a look from another time, another place—glimpsed so quickly in Singapore.

She took a step backward, her mind still trying to consider options, weigh moves, look for an opportunity.

She heard a voice from below.

Someone in the main hall of The Morgan.

Moving this way!

Could that do anything? Someone coming here. Seeing the red rain.

Splat . . . splat . . . splat.

"You played your part so well."

A grin, the mouth opening, even the smile having an odd look about it. A facial grimace from such a long time ago.

"What . . . part?"

She barely got the words out, croaking.

And even as she spoke, she came up with her only option.

Scream. Then turn and run. People would come. And if enough guards came quickly, if they hurried here in time, he'd go.

Because that's what he does.

He just . . . *goes*.

"Starting in Singapore, of course. I knew you saw me." Another smile, a breath in—and a small congratulatory laugh. And Lisa knew that to hear this man really laugh would be hideous.

"Making all this so interesting."

Lisa opened her mouth.

"Sorry—" he said.

The knife in his hand seemed to appear from nowhere. But then he'd had so much practice with it. Almost unable to follow its movements, Lisa watched it fly in front of her eyes.

No scream came.

She felt a stinging at her throat.

Her mouth opened. A salty taste.

Then a terrible, crashing sadness. To know that it was over.

"I do wish I could have taken more time with you. You really do deserve it, you know? But at least I do have something to look forward to."

She fell to her knees, her hands up at her gurgling throat now. Her eyes locked on his.

She shook her head ever so slightly.

Feeling that to do a more violent shake could send her head flying off from the severed throat.

No . . . she mouthed.

"Ah—you know what I'm talking about. A last act. For now."

The smile again.

"Oh, that is funny, isn't it? A last act for now."

And Lisa, who knew exactly what he was talking about, fell forward, unable to even remain kneeling, her head careening toward the man's shoes.

But by the time her head smacked against the hard wood floor—

There were no shoes there at all.

48

DAVID and Kunokine stood outside the hospital.

"What now?" his partner asked.

For a moment, David didn't answer.

"Okay. We get back to the city. I—I don't know—we got to write this up. We should talk to that scientist I told you about."

Kunokine nodded. "You know, they told me working with you would be interesting."

"Is that what they said? Interesting?"

"Yeah—and strange too, some of them said."

"Guess I have found my niche in the department."

"But this is beyond 'strange,' David. This is weird. And I'll be honest—" Kunokine looked away. "It has me scared. And I don't usually scare easily."

"Me too. This—"

David's phone rang. One Police Plaza calling, Biondi's number.

"The boss," David said to Kunokine.

He answered the call—and heard the news.

MARI looked at the screen, a public page set up by VICAP.

She had to wonder . . . did VICAP—the FBI's Violent

Criminal Apprehension Program—have a way of monitoring who visited their site?

Drop a little computer cookie so they can see if any homicidal nuts are stopping by and checking out their current ranking, scoping out the competition?

Are they watching me, she wondered, *while I watch it?*

The page she was on, though, certainly qualified as old news.

A general survey of the behavior of serial killers. A lot of concepts she knew. Words like *pattern* and *ritual*, but also new ones like *rehearsal* and *expansion*.

Expansion.

A few lines described exactly what the term meant . . .

The longtime serial killer will, in time, often feel the need to increase the excitement and satisfaction level and seek "expansion"; that is, expanding the scope and focus of his activities.

Makes them sound so benign.

Essentially, they will change their behavior, their modus operandi—and mutate their killing into something different.

Like this, she thought.

Like what's happening here.

Let's play in New York. Let's play with the nice detective. Oh, and that reporter.

Let's make their worst dreams, already so real, even worse.

She heard a creak.

A chair. Someone leaning back.

I'm kind of all alone down here, she thought. Sure the building had great security—all the big New York buildings had great security.

Still . . .

She turned and looked at the door. Jed, the guy in charge of the archives, was down here. She wasn't all alone.

Still . . .

She looked back at the screen. And thought:

Enough.

Time to get out of here. Get back to where there are people. A lot of people.

She closed all the programs on the computer, stood up, and walked out to the hallway.

Mari's phone beeped as soon as the elevator opened on the lobby floor.

A message.

Another beep, insistent that it be answered. Followed by a different sound. A missed call. The name on the screen . . . *David.*

She thought of calling him, but first she might as well see what message he'd left, then call Lisa, and maybe the three of them could think and plan.

The lobby was full of people.

But that didn't stop her from looking around as she pressed the key for voice mail—and waited.

David's voice. Low, somber, and so alarming in his effort not to scare Mari.

"Mari. David here. I want you to stay in your building. Stay right there. Then call me just as soon as you get this. Okay?"

Then again, as if she didn't hear too well.

"Don't go *anywhere*."

People moved around her, hurrying, moving, creating a precious sense of safety.

The message ended.

Standing there as though she had gotten off the wrong elevator, in the wrong building, and didn't know where the hell she was, she quickly called David.

DAVID was about to drive into the Brooklyn Battery Tunnel when his phone gave out a shrill ring.

"Mari. Where are you?"

"I'm in the building. Like you said. Look, David—"

"Hold on—"

David turned around, checked the other lanes, and gunned the car to get it away from the booths.

His partner looked at him like he was crazy.

He stopped the car on a ramp to the side.

"Okay. I was about to go into the tunnel. But I have to—"

Mari cut him off again. "I spoke to Lisa. David—this killer. This maniac who just appears from nowhere—he's not from . . . God, this sounds so—"

"Mari, I know." A beat. "He's not from now."

"He's from the past, David. That's why he's never caught. All scientific, according to Lisa. Exactly what physics tells us is the way reality really works—"

"Mari. Listen."

He took a breath.

"I got a call . . . Dr. Griffino is dead. She was killed at The Morgan."

Then—for a long time . . . nothing.

MARI turned to an alcove in the lobby. A place away from the stream of people gliding in and out of the lobby, picking up a coffee from the Coffee Republic kiosk, or heading straight to the rows of elevators.

"No," was all she said.

"I'm sorry," David said to her. "But now you know—you have to know—"

She knew what he was going to say.

But she said anyway, "What?"

"You have to get out of here."

"And you too." Mari was suddenly aware that she had said those words too loudly. A cleaning woman, wiping down the brass molding that ran waist-high along the black marble wall, turned and looked at her.

Whenever anyone did something strange in New York, everyone stopped . . . and looked.

Mari lowered her voice.

"You *too*, David. If he . . . it . . . whatever the hell it is . . . is here for us, because of us, because of—

Expansion . . . the need to increase the excitement and satisfaction level, seek expansion; that is, expanding the scope and focus of his activities.

"—us. Playing with us. Then you need to get out of here too."

He didn't say anything for a minute.

She heard him take a breath.

"I'm a detective, Mari. I have a job to do. Even if in this case it might be impossible."

"No, David, I spoke to Lisa—it had to be only a minute before she was killed and—"

"Mari. Listen. Stop. Will you listen to what I tell you? Then tell me—promise me—you'll do it."

The cleaning lady came closer, budding, polishing, looking—

"When you leave the building, take a cab to your car. Only a cab. If you walk at any time, make sure you are surrounded. You hear me? Surrounded by people. Then get in the car. And don't stop . . . don't stop driving until—"

"Excuse me, miss . . . but—"

The cleaning lady stood right next to her, indicating that she had to clean the part of the wall just behind Mari.

Mari moved, and listened to David's plan.

49

MARI nodded, stupidly, absently, before remembering that she was on a phone.

David's voice sounded so close, so near.

"Yes. Okay. I will do that. But David. There's something else. Something Lisa said just before she was killed. I mean, it sounded crazy."

"As if everything else happening here isn't crazy enough. We should be getting used to crazy."

"But there's something different about this time. Maybe more dangerous, but she had an idea—"

She heard David take in a deep breath. "The *idea* is to get you out of danger. Away from danger."

"Is that even possible? If we do nothing . . . nothing but run, hide, is it even possible?"

She waited—and David said nothing.

And she had this thought: *We're trapped. Trapped, because we don't know what we're doing, what we're facing.*

Like Lisa said, it's a fucking game.

"Okay. Tell me what she said," David said. "Then tell me you will go."

The cleaning woman had moved on. Still, people filed in

and out of the lobby. Life went on. One thing happened, then another, then another.

That's what existence was.

This endless flow of things happening.

"Okay. I will. Lisa said she couldn't be sure. But it made sense to her. She said it all fit."

Mari pictured David sitting in his car, while traffic streamed in and out of the tunnel, the afternoon beginning to slip into a crisp evening.

And Mari told him exactly what Lisa Griffino, brilliant scientist, had said . . . .

About this opportunity she felt they had.

An opportunity now, here.

They had what she called . . . *a chance.*

And when Mari was done, David had some questions. Questions, then additional instructions.

At one point, she told him to slow down. Telling her to watch this, to go this way, to call from a pay phone to make the arrangements, instruction after instruction.

His detective-machine mind ticking away, struggling to protect her from what might happen.

To protect her—and maybe do something else.

Until he said:

"Okay. You gotta go. You still have enough hours of light. You must make use of it. Want me to go through everything again?"

Mari turned away from the dark marble wall, the brass molding, to look at the street outside, still light, still looking so safe.

"No. I got it."

"Okay, Mari. Then only one more thing."

"Yes?"

"I love you."

Sometimes, she thought, unexpected words can be almost overwhelming. And all she could do was answer:

"And I love you too, David."

The words coming through a tiny speaker in the phone.

And Mari wondering when she would hear his voice in person.

When.

Then the harder thought—

Not *when* . . . but—

If . . .

BOOK FOUR

The
Chance

50

MARI watched the bald real-estate agent stick the key into the lock and begin wiggling it around. Headlights from his pint-sized BMW shined right at the door of the small cottage.

The agent turned to her and smiled.

"It's the right key. I'm sure of it. Just these old locks, you know. They get sticky. I think the new owner's going to have to replace them."

"Guess so," Mari said.

The man went back to fiddling with the lock. How long can it take to open a goddamn door? She turned to look at the land around the cottage, but there wasn't much to see.

She had hoped to get to the island when it was still light. And though standard time hadn't yet struck its fatal blow to evening sunlight, it still got dark by seven.

She had been able to look back at the coast from the ferry leaving Westerly and watch the sun slowly vanish.

The ferry crew seemed more than confused as to why she was going to the island in the middle of the week post-season.

One of the crew had even said to her: "Not much happening now."

Then, maybe thinking he had a shot—

"You staying at the hotel?"

Mari answered in a flat monotone.

"No. Staying with friends."

And she remained outside, watching the sky darken, her car with only a few others inside the ferry. There was only one more back-and-forth ferry run ahead.

A click.

"Ah, there we go. I was getting worried maybe I had the wrong key."

The man turned the handle, and opened the door. He reached in, looking for a light switch. More fumbling, but then he found it.

Two lights came on inside the cottage. A pole lamp, and another small lamp on a mantel. Both a pale yellow, neither doing much to chase the shadows from the corners.

The agent stood to the side and let Mari walk in.

A damp musty smell filled the room.

"There you go. The heater is over there, by the kitchen."

Mari looked up. "Yes. I see it."

She walked into the center of the room.

"And if you need anything else, you have my cell."

She shook her head. "No, I'm fine. I'll be okay."

The agent sniffed. "Kinda musty in here. You may want to open some windows. Just, maybe close them before you go to sleep? They say there's a storm blowing in. The island had a rough season last year, you know. Real rough. People are getting ready for another hard time."

"I will. And thanks."

She waited. It was time for the man to go.

Even though she felt like she wanted him to stay exactly where he was.

"Okay then." He smiled. "Gotta go see if the wife saved me some dinner."

A smile.

"You take care now?"

"Thanks. I will."

She walked to the door as the man nodded, turned around, and walked out of the cottage. She watched him get into his undersized Beemer, start the car, and slowly begin backing away from the cottage.

He did a three-point turn, then a final wave at Mari and he pulled away.

And as he pulled away, as the car lights disappeared from the doorway, she could see with the faint glow where she was.

Features began emerging as she stood in the darkness.

She saw the glow of the town, with the dock, the fishing boats, the general store, the hotel.

The slope leading down to the main road, a fairly steep incline that had to be a lot of fun in winter.

And then, to the right, a rocky incline, not much of a hill, dotted with scraggly bushes but leading quite clearly to a cliff edge, just as David described it.

Nothing much to look at now. Nothing to look at in the darkness.

But in the morning—

She stopped herself.

In the morning . . .

The words chilled her. Or maybe it was the gathering clouds, the wind beginning to whip off the sea.

She rubbed her arms.

She turned and went back inside, shutting the door behind her.

It was time to get ready.

AS the agent had predicted, it wasn't long before the cold salt-tinged air seemed determined to overwhelm the cottage's heater.

Mari went around shutting the windows. Each one fighting being shut, then—as if yielding in a fight—slamming down with a great wooden reluctance.

With the last window shut, she looked outside, at the dark, but also at the clouds that now made it impossible to see any stars at all.

She walked back to the chair in this cottage. She thought of

what it must have been like when David stayed here with his
ex-wife, the plans they must have made, the coziness—

And the intimacy too.

The moments in the bed, in the other room.

When the future ahead seemed gleaming and bright, all
ahead of them.

Because that's what the future is.

What lies ahead.

And as their breakup and a million other things that occur
in a couple's life together show, the future is anything but pre-
dictable.

She sat down in the chair.

She had poured a glass of wine an hour ago.

It was still there.

Untouched, on the end table.

She would have liked to sip it.

But she didn't.

Her cell phone was also on the table beside her, though it
showed no bars, no service. Totally useless.

She opened her book, *Love Is Nothing,* the biography of
the luminous Ava Gardner.

She continued reading, fighting the heaviness in her eyes,
fighting to stay awake.

But after this day—this amazing day—it was only moments until she was asleep.

TINY sounds.

Entering the consciousness like imagined events from
dreams.

Wondering, perhaps: Are the sounds in this dream?

But then something that says that they are real.

These sounds are *real.*

Perhaps even an idea what they are.

Rain. Spattering against the window. Then, a new sound.
Something rattling. Window rattling. Wind, rain.

Feeling the chair.

Mari feeling the chair where she feel asleep.

And now opening her eyes.

Still in the chair. The storm now raging outside, the rain hitting the window like pebbles, the windows shaking. The two lights on.

Something on . . . her mouth. Tape on her mouth.

(*God no . . . God no . . . God no . . .*)

Then she looked down to her arms, taped to the arms of the chair.

She tried to move each one, but she seemed perfectly mummified, perfectly trapped.

She kept listening.

For any other sounds. Anything but the storm.

But then something.

A creak. The shuffle of something being moved on the floor.

She writhed against the tape some more. Pointlessly. Tears. Why tears, she wondered, why tears now?

Her tongue could barely slip past her taped-tight lips, and taste the adhesive.

Then . . . *dragging.*

Seeing the chair, the old wooden chair, and the man, holding a candle.

She made a small moan against the tape, the tiniest of sounds. A small, pitiful sound. He put the candle on the table near her and—at the same time—he shut off the pole lamp, so now there was just the candle and the faint light on the mantel.

He sat down facing her.

And what was once the future—unknown, unknowable, unpredictable—had suddenly turned into the present.

She looked at him. The man's hair—now short, sand-colored, with a few stray strands curving over a forehead. That prominent forehead, the hair receding.

And the look of his face, staring at Mari, somehow odd, somehow more than foreign.

Not a face that one sees.

Not today.

He smiled and stared back at her, saying nothing. In one eye, a tear made her vision go blurry.

But there was no way Mari could wipe away that tear.

His eyes, though . . .

An eerily brilliant blue, catching every bit of the candle-light.

He was ready to begin and, as he would explain, this was indeed something so very different for him.

Someone to talk to, to explain, to stun and amaze.

Before he did what simply must be done.

51

THE man had talked for what seemed like hours.

But it may have been minutes. Time had lost all its bearings, all its stability.

Mari sat and listened; some of it incomprehensible, other parts making perfect sense.

In this new world.

The man spoke quietly, now with the blade he had retrieved sitting on his knees. He turned to the windows.

"The storm will be here soon. I think—that might be a good time to start. And don't worry . . . I will give you time to ask a few questions. It would only be fair. I mean—"

And here he brought the chair close—

"You understand so much. How I am here, now . . . but could be anywhere. Any time—but I was drawn to you. You and your friend—such a terrible thing that happened to you. And don't worry, I haven't forgotten him—the two of you, looking at secrets, looking at nonsense. All of it lies. All of it true. All at the same time."

The man grinned.

He reached out and laid a hand on Mari's knee. She squirmed. The man's hand sickeningly gentle.

"You see, you and poor Dr. Griffino—didn't quite see the

bigger picture. Do you know who"—he laughed—"I am? Do you have any idea? Listen to this—*sed-emef ceved mer-eief, k-lier, sedem.* Do you know what I just said . . . what you just heard?"

Mari shook her head. The sounds rolled off the man's tongue with such ease.

"No one alive has ever heard those words. No one for more than two thousand years." Another smile. "Middle Egyptian. A totally lost language. Save for me. And you know what?"

Another hand on Mari's other knee. Her eyes went to the blade as if it might slide off the man's knees to the floor. And for some reason that prospect seemed a terrible thing.

"I learned that language so many years later. My own language was so much older. So much. So maybe you begin to understand now?"

With his hands on her knees, she could see two matching bracelets, one on each wrist. The metal a dull gray that somehow, in the candlelight, still managed to send out iridescent flickers of color.

The rumble of thunder.

"Ah—it's getting close. Not a lot of time left. So let me allow you to ask a few questions. You are a reporter after all; you should have so many questions."

He picked up the blade.

"Open your mouth as much as you can."

Mari didn't do anything.

"I can do this without making you bleed—but if you insist. Open your mouth *now*."

Mari could only get her lips just a bit apart.

"Good. Now—"

He took the point of the blade and stuck just the tip in. Then he began gently sliding it left and right, opening a mouth hole. Though her jaw was locked, she could now open her mouth a bit, and speak . . .

"There. So, your questions?"

"H-how do you do this?"

The man pulled back, suddenly aware of his extended arms, the bracelets.

"Let's say it was a gift from a long time ago. As to where the gift came from, use your imagination."

"Someone gave you this—ability?"

Mari's eyes went down to the bracelets and the man immediately caught it.

"*Gave* may not be the right word. I had an opportunity, a chance. And once I had it—well, how could anyone ever find me, catch me? As your dear departed friend Dr. Griffino could tell you, Time and Space are such a big thing."

The blade was back on his knees. But now the rumbles came even more quickly.

"Who are you?"

The man grinned.

"Like in that book? Quite an appropriate book in these circumstances, I imagine. *Who are you?* It was a caterpillar who asked Alice the question, correct? I've been so many things. Hundreds of *whos*. As to what I started out as, why, I don't even want to think about it. Let's just say I won't be going back to that . . . *then* . . . and that *who* . . . and—"

He stood up.

The knife in hand.

And then he was gone.

MARI looked around the room, thinking he might be anywhere.

But then he stood right in front of her.

The blade in his hands had a thin sheen of blood.

"Thought you deserved to see it up close. Here—"

He slowly wiped the blade on Mari's skirt.

"Have something famous."

Mari made an audible sob, her lips barely free from the tape. Where had he been? she wondered. 1888? 1947? Maybe even today at The Morgan Library?

"No more questions?"

The rain kept up its fluctuating blasts against the window, like waves from the ocean, heavy spatters, then light, then more rattling, the booming thunder growing.

"Why?"

"Good. The big one. I would have been disappointed if you had not asked that one. To paraphrase someone, with great power comes great boredom. Wealth? Too easy. Possessions? No challenge there. But this, this hunting, the escaping, the prey. Well, even after hundreds—"

Hundreds . . .

"—it never loses its ability to thrill. I'm not a religious man." Another sick grin. "But still, when *life* is in the throes of trying to protect itself, to escape death—and I am the person controlling it, feeling that power . . . well, it's so good, it should be illegal."

He laughed.

Mari turned away. To see that face *laugh*.

"Oh, guess it is illegal. Everywhere and every time."

He looked down to the blade.

"And I think we are about out of time now. This has been interesting. As I said—something new. Pleasure calls. And I want to take special care with you. But first—"

He stood up suddenly, kicking the chair against a far wall. Sending it sprawling.

And at that moment—

Entering the room at what should have been just in time—

David.

52

DAVID entered—as discussed, as planned—and immediately Mari knew that it had gone all wrong.

He had his gun out, ready.

But the man—despite all those plans—knew it, and he moved in a split second.

Leaving David rushing toward nothing, seeing Mari bound to the chair.

The attacker moved quickly, his blade slicing out and catching, then stabbing David's side. Mari watched the shirt separate, skin open, blood begin to soak it.

David reeled back. He still held the gun, but the wound was deep.

The attacker ignored Mari, and moved quickly to David.

She would have only seconds.

Seconds in an eternity of time that might represent the only chance to stop this killer and save their lives.

Mari's fingers felt under the arm of the chair.

Searching, then finding what she'd planted there.

The sharp blade, one of many hidden here, in the room, under chairs, by the bed, all over.

She grabbed this one and started slicing through the tape on one hand.

She looked back toward the door to the cottage. The man was focused on David. He came close, kicking the gun out of David's hand, ready to drive his knife deep.

Free, Mari leapt to her feet, the blade still in her hands.

It was three steps to the man.

Just three—but based on what she had seen, she doubted she would ever complete those steps.

One.

The man's bloody blade was diving for David's midsection even as David tried to ignore his wound and stand up.

Two.

The man within reach.

But now, God . . . now—

He turned. The man *turned* and could see that besides David getting to his feet, he had a freed Mari coming for him.

The look on his face.

In a night of firsts for this man, yet another.

A surprise.

Just as Lisa had said . . . just as she had guessed.

What was the expression?

This time—he didn't see it coming.

Mari grabbed the single-edged blade tight, sharp end facing out.

Three.

She leapt on that last step. The pressure incredible. What happens when you do something for the first time, some movement that absolutely needs to be precise?

And everything hinges on doing it perfectly.

Mari grunted with her effort.

She aimed for the back of the man's neck, inches below his left ear.

She struck, and then with another animal grunt she continued moving her arm, swinging the blade sharply to the right until it slid off into space and—slick with blood—flew out of her hand.

She reeled back.

It took only a second to see the effects of her action.

* * *

DAVID looked up.

He didn't see how Mari got out of her chair. But he knew they had planned as best they could with knives and blades hidden, taped out of sight in the cottage.

It was the best trap they could lay.

But he also knew that the killer knew that he was coming, clearly expected him.

Now he looked at the man.

Had Mari done something?

The knife that had been ready to jab deep into David seemed suspended in the air. The man's eyes narrowed, staring down at David.

Then, the man reached behind his head—to feel the blood.

And he screamed.

MARI reeled back, thinking the man would turn to her now, attack her.

Instead, she saw him bring a bloodied hand around to his front, stare down, and then almost drunkenly stagger out of the cottage.

"David," she said way too quietly. Then again: "David, we can't let him leave."

David had already started to get to his feet, pulling himself up.

The man took a staggering step outside the door, then another. She hoped David knew what she meant.

Can't let him leave . . .

She didn't mean from this room, from the cottage.

Leave *here*. Leave *now*. To nurse his wound. To start it all over again.

If Lisa's theory was right, all this was new for the man. A surprise. Because in his search for new thrills . . .

For someone who could move through time like a phantom, there was only one last twisted thrill left.

To go right to the edge.

Where time was *new*.

To that moment that had not yet turned into the past.

Somehow, this moment was fresh. The billions of causes and effects all new, rippling backward, creating alternate times, alternate worlds, even alternate universes.

But for now—there was only this *one* moment.

Still being enacted.

Still being written.

David stood up.

"His wrists," Mari said. "Something to do with the bracelets."

David's eyes looked filmy, but he spun quickly and followed the man outside.

THE killer still grabbed at the back of his neck. David could see him stumbling, moving closer to the cliff edge.

The man stopped.

David hadn't picked up his gun, kicked away to a corner of the room. That would have cost a precious few seconds.

The man turned to him and even while fighting his agony, he managed a sick grimace of victory.

David watched him raise his wrists in front of him.

A quick thought: Was this a ritual? Some ancient ceremony, a secret lost in time, lost to a civilization long gone?

Or was what was about to happen merely some incomprehensible science?

And if so . . . where did it come from? *Who* did it come from? And where did this massive murderer—

(a murderer that dwarfed all others)

—get it from?

The man moved slowly, as if somehow the muscles in each arm were connected directly to his sliced neck.

David moved fast now, fighting back his own pain.

* * *

MARI came out of the cottage. The rain fell in torrents, a near-constant stream of water that felt as if a giant tap was over her head, nearly making it impossible to breathe.

Behind the two men, just past the cliff edge, repeated flashes of lightning highlighted the dark clouds. And thunder, so close now, barreling, booming, cracking.

David had one hand to his side, tight on his wound.

And the man who would have cut her to pieces jerked his arms together.

He's trying to touch the bracelets together. Something about those goddamn bracelets—

But the movement was jerky, off.

And then—

David was there.

DAVID smashed his fist down hard on one of the man's arms. He heard a crack that wasn't thunder.

The man howled, a moan that cut through the noise of the storm.

Had this monster ever felt pain? Never caught, never trapped?

David wasted no time doing a quick sidearm smash to the other arm, and he knew that both blows connected to the wound Mari had delivered to the man's neck, muscles pulling . . .

David tried not to think about success.

That they might be able to do this.

That it could possibly end here.

He reminded himself, as much as he could in the cacophony of the storm, with his own constant bleeding: Be careful.

Don't fuck up. Christ, don't fuck up.

Now, David launched a blow that would surely send insane spikes of pain into the man.

He threw his fist at the man's head, putting all his body weight into it, ignoring the pulling and stretching of his own wound, telling his goddamn brain to just *ignore* it.

And his fist struck the man just below his nose, a perfect hit. The nose smashed back, teeth jammed up into his jaw.

Excruciating.

But worse—the quick snap back of the man's head had to tear open even further the wound on the man's neck.

The man rocked back, collapsing right at the cliff edge.

His body landed hard first, then his head smacked back, obviously hitting the stone of the cliff.

But the man's eyes were still open.

He still held the blade, and now, flat on his back, he swung his free arm out to grab David's ankle.

The next move so clear: driving the knife into David's left leg, perhaps slicing a gouge out of his calf that would make David collapse to his knees, close enough for another blow, a fatal blow.

Then—

Mari was there, beside them both.

SHE looked down at the man, at his maneuver to save himself, now just like the countless hundreds he had stalked and slaughtered, littering history with his corpses and terror.

Mari quickly reached down to the ground. Fingers closing on jagged stone, feeling so heavy.

"No fucking way," she said.

Did he hear her over the blasts of thunder?

No matter—a lightning bolt made Mari glow.

So he could easily see what she held in her hand.

He could easily see it being raised over her head, and then lowered with a force that even someone from millennia ago could appreciate in all its primal fury.

A new cracking sound.

And the stone had found its mark.

"For all of them," Mari whispered. "Past and to come. All of them . . ."

The man's hand released David's ankle.

And for seconds, neither of them moved.

53

BETH Short crawled on the ground, moaning, crying, seconds away from this horror that came out of nowhere.

Her knees dug in the sand, moving like a toddler's.

She kept muttering to herself, over and over, "No . . . no . . . no."

But then, she allowed herself one look over her shoulder, to where her attacker had been standing, ready to make good on his threat.

But there was no one there.

She waited.

He could appear anywhere, out of nowhere.

She knew that now.

As if by magic . . .

She pulled herself up to a sitting position.

The air cool. The Los Angeles night sky so clear; the stars bright pinpoints.

She waited.

Her breathing slowly returning to normal.

And when she felt as if she had waited long enough—she stood up.

With unsteady steps, she began her walk back to the road,

to the quiet, sleepy street that had offered her no help, no salvation.

Where the houses were to be just the dumb and silent witnesses to her slaughter.

A slaughter now turned into a fantasy.

A dream, an illusion.

She kept walking until, on one step, she burst into tears, crying, sobbing so loudly, not giving a damn.

Elizabeth Short was alive.

And suddenly—she had a future.

Destiny.

The past shapes it. Events that have occurred triggering a multiplicity of things that will occur.

Or, things that might occur.

All those possibilities hinging on what went before.

And in a way that only a physicist might understand, if even slightly, dependent on the things that might occur after.

All Beth Short knew, walking, her tears slowly ebbing, was that she couldn't really tell anyone what had happened.

(After all, who would believe it?)

And somehow . . . something that was destined to happen . . . didn't.

A life was saved.

And on a lesser note, as her hordes of fans would testify to, movie history was inexorably changed.

DAVID looked at Mari.

"Turn away," he yelled over the storm. A flash of lightning caught her face.

"No need for that now, David."

He nodded, then reached down and removed the stone from the man's imploded skull. At first he could see nothing, then a flash, and David could see the crater that was once his face.

The bits of white bone, the blood coating the bone,

almost able to see the jagged shape of the stone in the man's face.

David pulled the dead killer's arm out and looked at one of the bracelets. Another flash, and David could see that the metal, for all its dull grayness, also reflected a prismatic flash of rainbowlike color.

He touched the metal with his fingers, thinking, maybe even tempted.

"David, what are you going to do? Keep it?" Mari asked.

David held the rock in his hand.

"Whatever for?" He shook his head. "I don't think so."

He smashed the rock down on the metal. At first he thought that the bracelet had somehow amazingly resisted the blow. But then it broke into pieces.

David picked up a small chip.

Mari looked at him.

"And now?"

"Give me a hand."

He began pushing the body to the edge.

"One more little push," he said.

Another flash—and if anyone had been there looking, they would have seen the bizarre sight: the two of them rolling a body to the edge of the cliff.

The last push, and it went tumbling over.

Mari leaned over to watch the body careen downward, hit the sides of the cliff, and then somehow bounce out before crashing into the sea.

David pulled her to her feet.

"With luck, the sea will chew the body into bits. I think— the less anyone knows about this the better."

He winced.

A sick look came on his face.

"And maybe you better get me some help."

He threw an arm over her, his weight nearly dragging her down, and they stumbled back to her car, leaving the cliff, the storm, the cottage that would, they knew, hide one of the great secrets of all time.

Mari helped David slide into the passenger side, smearing blood on the seat.

"Just don't tell the new owners." He smiled. "It might screw up the sale."

And Mari hurried to drive him to the small island's clinic.

EPILOGUE

THERE were tons of questions. David had no problem proving that Mari had been attacked, and that they had killed the "unknown man"—which is what the department was calling the attacker—in self-defense.

But Biondi knew there was more to it.

"You're not telling me everything."

"The guy followed us. He tried to kill Mari. I killed him. End of story."

As if . . . David thought.

"And the scientist. What was her deal?" Biondi asked.

"Not too sure, Captain. She had some theory about serial killers. About patterns and stuff."

"Which is why she was killed?"

"Guess so. Maybe."

Biondi shook his head.

"You're a crazy prick. I spoke to Kunokine, you know?"

David looked out the window of Biondi's office. His partner sat there, waiting for the grilling to be over.

"She didn't have much to say. The paint chip revealed nothing. She said that Elaina Suro said some odd things, but she might have been delusional."

"Yeah, that's it. She was pretty out of it. Shock, you know."

"I bet."

Biondi shook his head. "The blood from Block Island—Christ, why did he follow you there?—anyway, that blood matches the paint chip. So he's the guy. Probably did the other killings too."

David nodded. "That would be my guess."

"You're not going to give me anything, are you?"

David looked out at the office then leaned close. "Frank, what if I told you that I don't have anything else to tell?"

"I'd say you were full of shit."

A nod.

"Then, what if I told you that you, the department . . . was better off knowing just what you do now. It's all you need."

Biondi seemed to think about this. Then:

"Maybe so. Maybe it is. I guess it wouldn't do any good bringing Mari in, huh?"

"Doubt it."

Biondi turned to look at the Brooklyn Bridge in the background. "Okay. That's it then." He turned back to David. "But some day, before I leave One Police Plaza, maybe you can tell me, hmm?"

"Maybe. When we're both out of here."

"How's your wound?"

"Better than my leg."

Biondi laughed. "You're a regular Six Million Dollar Man. Okay, get out of here. Take your time. Get some rest. But I will want what's left of your ass back here."

David stood up.

"I wouldn't want it any other way, Captain."

And he walked out of the office.

ELAINA Suro stopped at the administration entrance to the Aquarium. Thick blue-beveled glass hid what was on the other side.

My life, she thought. Or what used to be my life . . . and might be my life again.

Only things were different now—and not just because of the shock of what had happened to her. She'd never forget the attack and the strange secret that seemed to be part of it, a secret she might never understand.

Her walking . . . had changed.

She favored one leg, and every step brought a little spike of pain. She used to jog, and work out on the elliptical machine. Physical therapy might help, but her work with the animals was so physical.

Was she still up to it?

The answer to that—and so many more questions—lay on the other side of the door.

She pushed it open.

Inside, the subdued lighting that filled much of the main exhibition rooms continued here, leading to the offices.

Least I still have an office, she thought.

She let the door shut behind her.

And the overhead lights, so rarely used, suddenly flashed on.

And everyone was there, clapping and cheering. Julio, her friend who watched over the place in the night, whistled and then grinned. The other Aquarium workers, the curators, the cleaners, the secretaries, everyone was there.

She wished she hadn't started crying.

But that was impossible.

Dr. Derrick Kemp, the director, walked over to her. For a moment it looked as if he might put an arm around her—and that would only have triggered more damned tears.

Instead, he stuck out his hand. A professional shake, with a big smile on his face.

"Welcome back, Elaina. We've missed you more than you'll ever know."

She nodded, smiling, and Kemp's response, so warm but low-key, helped her hold it together.

"Thanks," Elaina said. Then louder to everyone, "Thank

you all." She looked around at all the smiling faces. "I couldn't wait to get back."

More claps and cheers, and the welcoming party began to disperse.

Dr. Kemp stood there a moment.

"Tell me . . . how is Susie?" Elaina asked about her dolphin, last seen looking so ill.

Kemp nodded. "She is doing amazingly well. For her age. But—"

The director hesitated.

"But *what*? Something wrong?"

Kemp shook his head. "No. Not really. Well—I think there's something you need to see. Now that you're back. Unless you want to just settle in first, in which case—"

"No. If there's something to see, I'll see it now."

"Okay. It's in your office."

And she followed him, trying hard to walk as strong and steady as before, but each step reminding her . . . that *that* was impossible.

ELAINA sat down at her desk, marveling how everything looked the same. All her papers, Post-its, files scattered on the nearby table were exactly as she had left them.

Except for one thing.

A new file folder positioned next to her keyboard.

The name on the tab at the edge: *Susie.*

"You said she's okay?"

Dr. Kemp stood beside her. "She is. You can look in the file. It shows everything. But I also have all the readouts up on your screen. Might be easier that way to see—"

For some reason Elaina felt her hand shake as she reached for the mouse. She was much more comfortable looking at material on her computer, keeping a dozen screens open at once while switching back and forth between rows of data, testing ideas, comparing figures.

The monitor came to life with the touch of the mouse.

Elaina took a second to see what the information showed. Then: clarity.

Susie had an incident. While Elaina was away. Susie's brain function stopped, all vital signs seemed threatened, and—

Elaina froze.

The dolphin, already sick with age and who knows what invading bacteria and parasites, went into a *coma*. Susie had fallen into a coma.

"I—I felt you should see this before you got back to work. You'd see it anyway. You're too good to miss it."

Elaina nodded. But she wondered: What was Kemp talking about. . . . Miss what? Discovering that Susie went into a coma, and recovered? Unusual, maybe even unheard of— she'd have to research it. But to be this dramatic, why would—

She stopped.

She looked at the onset date of the coma.

Then, she looked at the date the dolphin came *out* of the coma.

The hour. The minute.

Probably the goddamn second . . .

She turned to Kemp.

He took a breath. "I missed it at first. But I knew you wouldn't. And I know with your work into the dolphin's 'dark matter,' well maybe there was a connection."

The "dark matter" Kemp referred to wasn't the mysterious stuff found at the edges of the known universe. In this case, the "dark matter" was the hidden part of the dolphin brain, a vast unknown devoted to . . . who knew what.

Elaina turned and looked Kemp right in the eyes.

"Susie went into a coma the exact moment I was attacked. And she came out—"

"At precisely the moment you did." Kemp smiled. "Guess she is really connected to you."

Connected? Was that the word? What really happened? Could the dolphin really know what had happened to Elaina . . . could that really have triggered the coma?

Then this amazing thought—

Did Susie *know* it was coming? Was that why she was so sick, acting so strangely?

"God," she said.

"His handiwork?" Kemp said with a smile. "Could be."

Elaina had chills. Gooseflesh on her arms. If there was any doubt about her wanting to return to her work, it vanished like that.

Then this: She remembered what her attacker, her would-be killer had said, leaning so close to her:

The dolphin knew secrets.

Did all this have something to do with those secrets? Elaina supposed that this somehow should scare her.

But it didn't.

"I imagine you'll want to see her."

Elaina nodded. "Yes. Soon. But this—there's so much to figure out here, test—"

"Yes. So much." Kemp put a hand on her shoulder. "And I'm just glad we have the best person in the world to do it. So"—a gentle laugh—"get to it."

Elaina grinned back, and turned back to her screen.

As she fell back into her work, now more deeply than ever, she barely heard Kemp leave her small office.

DAVID used his key and opened the door to Mari's apartment. He smelled fresh basil.

On the couch, he saw Lisa's book, *The Reality Revolution*, open. They were both reading it, carefully.

Mari hurried to the door, dressed in a skirt but wearing a white apron with flowers.

"How domestic," he said.

"It's fun to play house."

She came close and kissed him, and his arm went around her and pulled her tight.

A quick shot of pain from the clutch, but he didn't care. Her lips felt so good, warm, inviting.

She pulled away.

"Glad to see you too, sailor. But dinner is soon. Then, we can get back to *this*."

"Smells good."

"Mama's recipe, and fresh basil from the fire escape. Last batch I'm afraid. Some vino?"

"Please. Many glasses."

Mari laughed and headed back to her small kitchen.

David followed her, marveling once again how the worst madness can recede, and that life in all its simple routine and pleasure can pick up exactly where it left off.

During dinner, they raised their glasses and Mari made the solemn toast.

"To Lisa Griffino."

David nodded, and added:

"To them all."

And they clinked glasses.

MARI sat at her desk, researching the history of the abandoned Second Avenue subway.

She was supposed to be working on a feature reviewing how New York almost got that additional subway line, and how the lack of funds stopped it.

But she was finding all sorts of peculiar things connected with the tunnel.

Maybe, she thought, *this story wasn't so boring after all. . . .*

Outlook Express flashed in the corner of her screen, giving her a tease of the contents of the e-mail.

The lab results are in for your test sample, and below you will—

She opened the mail.

"BIT chilly to meet here," David said.

They sat side by side on a bench in Madison Square Park.

"I wanted to come here." She shivered. "I met Lisa here. Seemed only right."

She watched David look. The leaves were flying off the trees now. People were still in the park, old people already in winter coats, a few dog walkers.

In a month more, the park would be empty until the return of spring.

She turned to David. "I got to get back to work. Maybe you too. But wanted to tell you right away." She nodded. "And tell you here."

David rubbed his arms.

"Good. As long as it's fast."

"You know—you asked me to send that piece that you chipped out of the killer's bracelet for analysis."

"I didn't want to run it through the department people. Too many questions already."

"I know—so the forensics place we use, they do it all. DNA matching, material survey, carbon dating."

David's eyes widened.

"You got the results back?"

Another nod. Then:

"Are you ready?"

"I'm pretty sure there's nothing in that report more weird than what happened to us last month. So shoot."

"Don't bet on it."

She handed him the paper and he read it.

Then he looked up, thinking.

"Something, hmm?"

"Oh yeah. It's something."

" 'No known material.' What the hell does that mean?" she said.

"Means what it says, I imagine."

"Right. So where did it come from?"

"Beats me."

"And the date. Did you see the date?"

"If it's accurate."

"That thing—whatever it was—is old."

David read from the next line: " 'Fabricated ten thousand

years ago, give or take a few centuries.' I'm a little shaky with my ancient history, but what was going on around then?"

"Before Egypt, before Sumer, before Ur—I checked. Only one thing we know that matches that time."

"And what is that?"

"The Sphinx. And you know what? No archeologist has a real idea of where the hell it came from. It was millennia before the earliest Egyptian dynasties. Who made it? How did it get there?"

David took a breath.

"Interesting."

She noticed him shift a bit. She could read him so closely now.

"And the sample?"

"On its way back to me."

"Good. I think—we want to put that away somewhere."

"I agree." Then a small nervous laugh. "Keep it at your place, though—not mine."

David laughed then too.

"Agreed. Now"— he pulled her close, and kissed her, the warmth so good in the chilly park—"back to work."

Mari stood up.

"See you tonight," David said. "El Quixote for paella?"

"Wouldn't miss it," she said.

David turned, walked away, and Mari took a second to think how good those simple words sounded, and how she hoped she'd always hear them. . . .

See you tonight.

ELLIOT Ahlgren looked at the piece of the artifact. Just a small chunk.

But what an amazing report! Of course, he was ethically bound to not reveal any of those results.

And he wouldn't.

No, he was good at keeping secrets.

He knew lots of secrets here at the GenTech Lab.

Lots . . .

And now he was supposed to send the chunk back to the reporter who had ordered it tested.

But first—

He took out a diamond-knife, a tiny crystal blade that could cut through anything.

This material, as amazing as it was, could be cut, Elliot knew.

So, wearing his jeweler's loupe, the 15x eyepiece, he took the blade and sliced off the tiniest shard from the artifact.

There.

Invisible. No one would ever notice.

He used another tiny metal prod to put the tiny sliver on a flat blade; then he grabbed a minuscule plastic bag. He opened the bag and slid the tiny piece in.

Then he folded it shut, the ziplock tight.

He took the other piece and put it in a slightly larger bag to be boxed and expressed back to the reporter.

But now he had a small piece of this amazing material.

And for some reason, for Elliot, that felt incredibly good.